'You really ⟨...⟩
be worth th⟨...⟩

Okello no⟨...⟩
to do with it, ⟨...⟩
three other p⟨...⟩ ⟨...⟩ing at him, he turned
abruptly, pushed his mistress almost roughly towards the door and seconds later bundled her into
a taxi summoned by the commissionaire.

And Craig smiled, pleased with himself for selecting an adversary worthy of him. He knew that he
would enjoy swindling Samuel Okello, or rather his
government, out of ten million dollars.

Triple Take

JONATHAN KANE

SPHERE BOOKS LIMITED

A SPHERE Book

First published in Great Britain by Sphere Books Ltd 1990
Copyright © Jonathan Kane 1990

Printed and bound in Great Britain by
Cox and Wyman Ltd, Reading

ISBN 0 7221 9073 5

Sphere Books Ltd
A Division of
Macdonald & Co (Publishers) Ltd
Orbit House
1 New Fetter Lane
London EC4A 1AR
A member of Maxwell Macmillan Pergamon Publishing Corporation

Prologue

The lioness lay belly to the dust, tense, still, her colour merging with the scrub-covered earth, eyes fixed on the score or so Thomson's gazelle browsing fifty feet away.

The man who called himself Calvin Craig watched, enthralled, binoculars trained on the cat's heaving flanks. He moved his gaze through an arc to pick up the 'tommies'. The little herd moving slowly, lazily, across a wide clearing, cropping grass and low bushes. Dainty creatures with black and white striped sides, they looked relaxed. It was an illusion; one or other of the males always had his head up, eyes scanning the undergrowth, nose testing the air. Downwind, the lioness rose and advanced a pace, in a single flowing movement.

Inside the van the tourist guide tapped his client on the shoulder and held out the cine camera. Americans always wanted to catch everything on film. Craig frowned, angry at the disturbance.

'The sound'll scare 'em.'

His gaze did not waver from the unhurried cat as she crept closer to a gazelle on the edge of the herd. He felt at one with her. Sensed her enjoyment of the long, patient stalking; the watching and waiting, the flowing adrenaline, the tension in the muscles. Anyone who thought animals only hunted for food knew nothing of the pure, almost religious thrill of the chase. Craig knew all about that thrill. It was what he lived for.

'Lot 55, Child's Head, attributed to Van Dyck. Ladies

1

and gentlemen, the history of this fine painting cannot be traced back beyond the beginning of the last century but it is believed to be a study for a group portrait, now lost.' Every pair of eyes in the Great Room at Christie's focused on the small canvas held up by a green overall-clad attendant. Every pair of eyes except one.

Calvin Craig, tall, thin, bespectacled with thick, waved fair hair, stood in the doorway of the crowded gallery and watched carefully but unobtrusively the prey he had come to London to stalk. Samuel Okello now stood six feet away. Craig noted every detail of his dress and behaviour: the immaculate grey-pinstripe suit that flattered the black man's ample figure, the paisley patterned silk tie held with a pearl pin, the fresh rose on his lapel, the handmade shoes encasing his tiny feet, and the velvet-collared topcoat draped casually round his wide shoulders. He observed with particular interest the young white woman less than half Okello's age who was pressed deliciously close to him in the crush. Lively and vital, her 'animal' nature was accentuated by the red fox blouson and the Caron fragrance that overwhelmed the mingled odours of antiquity, dust, and humanity.

'Darling, it's exquisite.' She stood on tiptoe to look at the head and shoulders sketch of a brown-eyed, solemn-faced boy, about seven years of age, his intricate lace collar overlaying a costume of stunning pink velvet. 'Do let's buy it.'

The big Ugandan laid a finger to his lips. With his other hand he stroked the girl's hair. Secure, content, unaware of the stalking hunter.

The dun-coloured cat flashed into sudden motion. No transition from crouching to running: one instant she was at rest; the next, streaking towards her victim. The startled gazelles exploded into the landscape, arching in all directions over bushes, fallen trees, and termite mounds.

Fifty yards on they stopped and resumed their browsing, detached from the drama being played out nearby. One of their number had been marked for death. It leapt off all fours, at the same time twisting away from its pursuer. The lioness streaked across the ground, closing the gap to a few yards. The prey bounced over grass and bushes, his hunter gaining on him. The lioness put extra energy into a great leap. The gazelle swerved through ninety degrees and gained ten yards while the heavy cat made a skidding turn. In his panic the quarry collided with a boulder and stumbled momentarily. Again the lioness closed on him. Then, the small deer seemed to sense that all was up. He came to an abrupt halt, lowering his slender, black horns as a soldier might lower his standard to acknowledge defeat. Standing thus, he took the onward rush of the predator. In a blur of flailing limbs the two animals tumbled into a *donga* out of Craig's sight.

The slim New Englander lowered the binoculars with a sigh. The kill itself was an anticlimax. No need to see it. Enough to note that conspiracy between hunter and hunted which always marked death in the wild. At the last the prey always acquiesced in the outworking of a higher law. It was the same with human conflicts. That was why Craig was a wealthy man. There always came the point at which the victims participated, often eagerly, in their own destruction. It was their greed, their vanity, their ambition as much as his cunning which doomed them.

The putative Van Dyck was knocked down for £42,000 to a little man in a black overcoat and Okello's companion was clearly annoyed.

'Sam, you said it was worth much . . .'

Without a word the African took her arm and steered her firmly from the room and across the outer gallery towards the wide staircase. Seconds later Craig followed. He found the couple in the foyer where Okello was looking at the

3

catalogues of forthcoming sales and the girl was hovering impatiently. He paused on the staircase as if examining a large Kirman rug hanging down from the banister above and as he did so the man in the overcoat hurried past and walked straight up to the African.

Strolling to the catalogue sales desks, the pursuer was able to overhear the conversation.

'Bit of luck that, Mr . . .?' He raised an eyebrow but Okello ignored the implied question. 'I thought we should have to go at least another five thousand. We were up against Iver but he was holding his fire for the Ruysdael and a couple of Cornelius Janssens later in the sale.'

'Yes, Mr Prescott, you did well. You'll attend to the formalities?' Okello took a pen from his pocket and scribbled an address and telephone number on the back of his catalogue. 'See that the painting is delivered there and arrange the details with Miss Leggat. She will attend to your account.'

The other man stuffed the catalogue into his overcoat pocket. 'Do you think the painting is a genuine Van Dyck?'

Okello slipped a hand inside his jacket and withdrew an envelope. He took something from it and held it up for the man and the girl to see. 'That photograph was taken two weeks ago in a country house in Holland. The picture it shows has been in the family for generations.'

'That little boy; the one on the left!' Miss Leggat was wide-eyed. 'He's the same . . .'

'This is a well-authenticated Van Dyck group portrait?' The man was more prosaic, though clearly impressed.

Okello re-pocketed the photo. 'It has impeccable provenance.'

'You really are a lucky man, sir. That painting must be worth three or four times what you paid.'

Okello nodded, unsmiling. 'Luck has nothing to do with it,' he said. Then, aware that two or three other people were staring at him, he turned abruptly, pushed his mistress almost roughly towards the door and seconds later bundled

4

her into a taxi summoned by the commissionaire.

And Craig smiled, pleased with himself for selecting an adversary worthy of him. He knew that he would enjoy swindling Samuel Okello, or rather his government, out of ten million dollars.

'Drive around the park for a bit. We'll look at the zebra, the giraffe and the buffalo.' The lanky American stretched his long legs before him with an appreciative sigh and gazed out on the Kenyan landscape. The rapid equatorial dawn had given way to full daylight. Colours, shapes and shadows stood out hard and well-defined. The red murram of the potholed track twisted and turned over a saffron plain scattered with sparse-leaved trees and bushes. The sky was a slab of solid blue with tiny flecks of cloud painted on it.

'You staying Nairobi long, bwana?' The driver turned to grin at his wealthy client. The van left the track and hit a minor crater, grounding the suspension. Still smiling, Joshua yanked the wheel hard over.

Calvin watched as two maribou storks flapped their ungainly wings and climbed, complaining into the air. 'Just a few days. My business is almost completed.'

'Very satisfactorily completed,' he thought to himself. His discoveries in London and Nairobi had brought to an end the research phase of his current assignment (he always called his swindles 'assignments').

The man's passport named him as Calvin Craig and proclaimed his point of origin as Lewiston, Maine. It also described him as a 'financial and business consultant' – and that was not true either. People meeting for the first time the angular, stooping figure and the thin face with the receding, fair hair often took Calvin for a harmless, dull, fuddy-duddy academic, prematurely aged by too much poring over books. It was an image he deliberately cultivated.

He stretched himself and yawned. Already it seemed a long time since he had been woken with coffee and croissants in his room at the Norfolk Hotel. He felt the need of another and more substantial breakfast, before embarking on the round of calls that would complete his file on Samuel Okello. Already he was eager to embark on phase two – the recruiting of staff.

'Home, Joshua,' he ordered. 'And don't spare the horses.'

TAKE ONE

'The good old rule
Sufficeth them, the simple plan,
That they should take, who have the power,
And they should keep who can.'

Wordsworth

Chapter One

The apartment in a downtrodden quarter of Queens was like its tenant: small, neat and cheerful. Its psychedelic drapes and bright paintwork presented a brave face to the world.

Louise Sondemann sat on a deep cerise-coloured settee, her legs drawn up under her, and studied the contents of a thick dossier. On a chrome and glass coffee table at her elbow was a small pile of books. The discreet jacket on the top announced itself as Foss and Stratton's *Principles of Accounts*. Another spine bore the legend J. Hardwick, *International Money Markets*. Like their companions these two volumes bristled with little slips of paper marking passages to be read. She sipped Coke from a tall glass stacked with ice cubes and frowned with concentration. This was more difficult than anything she had had to learn before. Or perhaps she was just out of practice. It had been six years since she had had a major part.

Louise Sondemann wore purple jeans and a cotton shirt of the same colour. Round her waist she had tied a lime green scarf. By deliberately fostered habit she dressed carefully and enjoyed creating a striking effect. She knew that when an actress became careless of her appearance she had taken the first step on the downward slope of despair, leading to drink, drugs and overdose. She had seen others go that way when joblessness stretched from months into years and agents stopped returning their calls. Therefore, Louise looked after herself. She wore her chestnut hair long so that she could vary the style easily and cheaply with a few pins and a whiff of lacquer. Today it was drawn back and coiled into a tight pyramid to which she had fastened a purple ribbon. For today she was expecting a visitor.

She had tried to persuade Mr Craig to hold the interview somewhere else but he had insisted on calling on her at home. That meant that soon he would be driving in his smart car or in a cab through the sordid streets of Queens, stopping at the tenement with its peeling paint and graffiti-scrawled walls, and climbing the staircase to her third-floor apartment, holding his nose against the odours of garlic and stale beer. Perhaps he would change his mind and look for someone else.

She closed the file with the name 'Louise Traille' printed on its green cover and laid it tidily beside the pile of books. She stretched and looked at her watch. 2.10; her visitor was due in five minutes. She walked round the small room straightening and adjusting things she had straightened and adjusted half a dozen times already. She moved to the open window and felt the heat pulsating from the sidewalk and the buildings opposite. The only signs of life were old Mrs Haffner returning from her daily excursion to the liquor store, and a pathetic-looking black dog lying in a narrow strip of shade at the base of a wall.

God, what a place to live! What a place to bring up children. Only last week a seven-year-old girl had been sexually assaulted and strangled not two blocks away. And one of Simon's school friends had been caught sniffing cocaine. Nine years old and a junkie! What chance did her son have? What chance did she have to bring him up decently?

A yellow cab turned the corner and came slowly down the street, its driver leaning out to check the numbers on the doors. Louise stepped back from the window. She fingered the lucky charm bracelet she always wore for auditions. 'Dear God, let everything go all right. Let him not change his mind.'

The doorbell rang.

Minutes later Calvin Craig was seated on the cerise settee and drinking Louise's freshly-made coffee. 'Have you heard from young Simon since he's been at summer camp?'

'No, not yet. You know what children are like about letter writing. Thank you again for making it possible . . .'

Craig held up a hand. 'My dear Louise, not another word. I know what a lot it meant to you. I'm only glad you were able to arrange it at such short notice. I expect you miss him. Is it the first time he's been away from home?'

'Yes, it's almost six years now since Frank . . . went away. It's hard for a boy to be without a father. I guess I've tried to compensate by being with him as much as possible.'

'To the detriment of your career, I suspect.' He looked at her over the top of his glasses like a kindly uncle.

'Well, I have had to turn down one or two really great parts,' she lied.

'I can well believe it. Your record at the agency is most impressive.'

Now she knew he was lying. Why? Suddenly a new thought struck her: was he, perhaps, some kind of sex freak? She had had one or two odd propositions but that was before she passed that dreaded thirtieth anniversary milestone. She dismissed the idea immediately. It was impossible to imagine this quiet, short-sighted, gangling man with his old-world courtesy as a menace to society.

He smiled encouragingly. 'Well, I guess we'd better settle down to business. How are you getting on with the role I asked you to study?'

'Oh, fine . . .' She hesitated, awkward and embarrassed about the question she knew she had to ask but did not want to ask. 'Look, Mr Craig, there's just one thing . . .'

'You want to know what it's all about; why I'm asking you to act the part of a highly-successful business woman on a real life stage.'

'Well, yes.' She was relieved at not having to spell out her misgivings. 'I've never been asked to impersonate someone before; I wouldn't want to be involved in anything . . . underhand.' She could not bring herself to say 'illegal'; the thought of Mr Craig being mixed up in anything like that was rather comic.

'Louise, I'm sorry if I've given you the wrong impression.' She read real concern in his weak, grey eyes. 'There's no question of your being asked to *impersonate* anyone. I assure you that "Louise Traille" is an entirely fictitious character. But look, before I go into the details, perhaps we ought to tie up the financial end of things. After all, if my terms aren't acceptable, further discussion of the job would be academic.'

'Oh, I'm sure . . .'

'No, my dear Louise, we must be businesslike. Now, as I explained at the agency, I don't exactly know when I shall want the job done. All I can say right now is that it'll be some time next spring. If that makes it difficult for you to fit in other engagements I appreciate you may have to turn the offer down. However, to compensate for your possible loss of income I propose to retain you at $2000 a month, starting now and continuing for one year. We can regard the money for Simon's summer camp as a bonus. For the actual job I suggest a fee of $100,000.' His brow creased in a diffident frown. 'I do hope that sort of figure is acceptable . . . er . . . any expenses you incur would, of course, be dealt with separately. Throughout the term of the contract it would be vital for me to be able to reach you at short notice. I would have to ask you to get a phone installed – charged to my account, of course.' He hesitated. 'Unless you decided to move to another apartment . . . but, no, that's presumptuous of me.' He hurried on, as if embarrassed at having pried into her private affairs. 'Now, there would be a trip to Singapore early next year. Have you ever been to Singapore?'

Louise shook her head. Her mind was still wrestling with calculations involving thousands of dollars and how much more she could afford to pay in rent and where she and Simon might be able to live.

'You'd be fascinated by it – the waterfront crammed with sampans, the markets where you can buy silk and jewellery incredibly cheaply if you're prepared to bargain for them. From there I would need you to go to East Africa for a few days. Hopefully there would be time for you to visit one of the game parks or spend a few lazy days on the beach at Malindi. However, that would be after your meeting with a certain African gentleman in Kampala. At the meeting you would have to hand over some documents and explain them. You would of course be fully briefed beforehand.' Craig finished speaking abruptly and looked expectantly at his hostess.

'That's it?'

'That's it – if everything goes according to plan. It might be necessary for you to attend another meeting here in New York. But I would be present at that. The only situation you'd have to handle by yourself is the Kampala one.'

'But all this?' Louise waved a hand at the pile of books and the green file. 'It seems such a lot of work for one meeting.'

Craig shook his head firmly. 'Not at all, Louise. It is absolutely vital that you master the character; that you know all that she would know; that you can answer any question you may be asked. Please don't underestimate the difficulty of the job. If you are in any doubt about whether you can handle it please say so now.'

'Oh, no, . . . it's just . . .'

13

'Louise, that's great. I'm sure you'll do a fine job and enjoy it, too.' He stood up and looked at his watch. 'Would you mind looking out and seeing if my cab has returned?'

Louise went to the window. The taxi was standing outside. As she turned back into the room she saw that Craig had taken his wallet out.

'I'll call again at the same time in two weeks. I hope then that you'll be able to let me know what you have decided about the phone and the apartment. I shall be in Europe for most of August, so I guess I'd better give you two months' retainer now. You'd prefer cash, I'm sure.'

He counted out four thousand-dollar bills and placed them on the coffee table. 'Now, if you'll excuse me, I have another meeting.' He shook her hand with an abrupt jerky motion and strode across to the door.

Moments later, as Louise watched the yellow cab turn the corner and disappear, she realised that her strange visitor had not, in fact, explained what the elaborate and expensive masquerade was all about. She fingered the four crisp notes and knew that she would not ask again.

Sitting back in the taxi, Craig smiled. One of the little luxuries he enjoyed more as the years went by was the warm glow he always felt when he was able to help some deserving fellow human being.

As with everything else, Craig was meticulous in the selection of his accomplices. He used as few people as possible; he used the best people available; he never used the same people twice; he gave each member of the team no more information than he needed; he expected complete loyalty and he paid handsomely to secure it. It was only by rigidly adhering to these simple, self-imposed rules that he was able to go on his anonymous way, leaving behind no one who could set about tracing him.

In the first week of August Craig flew to Paris to recruit another team member for the Ugandan Assignment.

Aziz Hafid had a suite at the Bristol Hotel but it was not there that Craig decided to meet him. It would have been pointless: the young Omani slept most of the day. Hafid was a nocturnal creature and his haunts were the city's leading casinos. For Aziz Hafid was – or rather, he aspired to be – a professional gambler. That was why Craig found himself in a crowded salon at Ricci's at 4.30 a.m. a few days later.

The atmosphere was tense. Two score pairs of eyes – tired eyes, smoke-reddened eyes – were concentrated on an eighteen-inch square slab of inlaid wood and thirty black and white counters. Over the past eighteen hours all the other tables had been vacated and cleared away, one-by-one, as players lost their games and their money and withdrew from the competition. Now only Ahmad Hassan was left, as everyone had known he would be, challenged by Pierre Labecque, the newcomer everyone wanted to win.

Everyone, that is, except Aziz Hafid. He leaned against the ornate marble of the fireplace and resented the little Franco-Turk. The thought which expanded to fill his mind as he watched Labecque's every move critically was, 'I should be sitting there with a million francs riding on a single game.'

Suddenly there was two million riding: Hassan, looking as fresh as though he had not been playing since nine o'clock the previous night said calmly, 'Double'. Labecque nodded, accepting the raised stake.

'The Saudi's bluffing,' Hafid said to the tall American beside him. 'The game is well balanced. He's trying to scare Labecque off.' He watched as the Arab scooped the dice into the leather shaker, and cast them out on the strip of green baize beside the board.

15

Two fours!

'The man has the luck of the devil.' Craig perched himself on the arm of a Louis Quinze style gilt and velvet sofa.

'He can be beaten. That pathetic half-breed of an opponent plays backgammon like a two-year-old child. Three moves ago he could have forced the Saudi to take one of his pieces and leave a blot on his home board. Instead he played safe.'

'You sound like an expert. But I guess you must have lost out in one of the earlier rounds.'

'That's not true!' Hafid's resentment burst out in a torrent. 'Four rounds I played. Four rounds and I won all of them!'

'So, why did you drop out?'

'Because in this place they have a stupid rule. Every round they raise the stakes. It doesn't matter how well you are playing; if you don't have enough chips you are out.'

'I guess that's to prevent headstrong players getting in too deep.'

'Well that's not how we play in my country!'

The two men concentrated on the game in progress.

Labecque was sweating. His own pieces were still well scattered but his opponent's inner table was almost full. He faced not only defeat but the risk of a 'gammon' – seeing all his opponent's counters thrown off before he had begun to clear his own pieces from the board. Under Ricci's rules that would mean an automatic doubling of the stake – four million francs. The Arab, who seldom spoke while playing, raised an eyebrow and Labecque threw the dice.

Two and one. The audience groaned.

Ahmad Hassan threw a four and a six and began removing his pieces from the board. His face showed no emotion at the prospect of walking away from the table four million francs the richer and, perhaps, seven million richer than when he had taken his seat the night before.

16

Hafid gazed at the expressionless eyes with mingled loathing and admiration. 'One day, you Saudi bastard,' he muttered under his breath. 'One day . . . soon.'

Labechque just managed to avoid the gammon. He pushed his chair back from the table at last, stood up and extended his hand. The Arab rose, nodded slightly at his defeated foe, turned and walked away.

Craig stood up and stretched. 'Well, it's been quite a night. How did you make out?'

The bearded swarthily-good-looking young man in the white tuxedo pulled a bundle of notes from his pocket and counted them. '15,200 francs!' He almost spat the words out. 'It's pathetic, paltry!'

'Well that's better than my showing.' Craig fell into step beside the Omani and they made their way through the other, deserted, gaming rooms. 'I'm down by more than fifty thousand.'

On the boulevard Craig breathed in the crisp, dawn air appreciatively. 'All that concentration sure gives you an appetite. Why don't we go back to my apartment and fix some breakfast?'

Hafid shrugged by way of reply. Craig found a cab and gave the driver an address in the Boulevard des Capucines. Fifteen minutes later the two men were enjoying coffee and croissants in Craig's elegant drawing room. It took little more than a few words of sympathy and encouragement to get the indignant young Omani to pour out his life story. Craig knew most of it already but he listened carefully, all the same.

Aziz Hafid was the eldest son of a successful Muscat import-export agent. He had been educated in England and generally indulged by a parent who wanted him to develop cosmopolitan tastes and contacts which would enable him to extend the family business. The old man's hopes were fully realised but not in the way he had envisaged. Hafid became too much at home in the fleshpots of the western world. He spent his time and his father's money on parties, women and drugs, but particularly on gambling. He only returned to Muscat for his father's funeral. Displaying, perhaps, a belated twinge of remorse and filial affection, he settled to his family responsibilities. For seven months he pushed paper around on the top floor of a twenty storey glasshouse with an extensive view of several other office blocks and the mountains beyond. Then he took off again.

The family – specifically his uncle – retaliated. Hafid's bank account was frozen. He was assailed by a constant bombardment of letters, most of which he dodged by the simple expedient of moving frequently. There was even a bungled attempt to kidnap him. Such tactics only strengthened the young man's resolve never to return home.

Now, after eighteen months, he was at his wits' end. Most of his assets – his Ferrari, his two racehorses, most of his personal jewellery – had gone. If he had ever learned to economise, the proceeds of those sacrifices would have lasted much longer but 'making ends meet' had not been a part of his education. So he continued to stay at the best hotels, eat at the most expensive restaurants and patronise the most exclusive gaming clubs. Self-knowledge was not high on the list of Hafid's personal qualities but he was perceptive enough to realise that he had but one talent – backgammon. He had played the game, and played well, ever since he could remember. Now he saw it as his yellow brick road to wealth and real independence.

'All I have to do is accumulate enough money to get into the big game – to get a shot at Ahmad Hassan. Just one shot – that's all I need.'

Craig stood by the large penthouse window watching the first gleams of sunlight touching the trees in the Tuileries Gardens.

18

'How much stake money would you require?' he asked casually.

Craig sat in the cocktail bar of Frascatti's, not far from the Peabody Institute and waited, with some anxiety, for William Kemp to arrive. He did not like hiring dishonest men. Those who teetered on the brink between legitimate business and crime – and none knew this better than the man called Calvin Craig – were devious, suspicious and inquisitive. But he had no choice; the Uganda Assignment called for the kind of expertise that only a clever and none too scrupulous commercial lawyer possessed.

At seven minutes past one Craig saw his guest arrive and hesitate in the doorway. He watched as the head waiter exchanged a few words and pointed the newcomer to Craig's table. Kemp peered myopically in the indicated direction and came towards him across the crowded room.

The little lawyer with the crumpled suit, heavy spectacles and wrinkled forehead looked out of place as he steered a course through the throng of Baltimore's élite – bankers, corporation men, realtors and their chic wives fresh from the beauticians and exclusive dress shops. They gave him not so much as a glance. But Craig had more respect for William Kemp. He knew that that insignificant exterior concealed one of the most brilliant legal minds operating on the east coast. He knew, because he had made it his business to know, that Kemp had acquired his own city practice by the age of thirty and in the ten years since then had earned the gratitude – generously expressed – of hundreds of rich clients, reluctant to shoulder their share of the nation's financial burden. Tax-avoidance schemes, trust funds and international money transfers were Kemp's stock in trade. His tools were a pernickety attention to detail, a nose for loopholes in the law and a passion for hard work.

But Craig knew other things about William Kemp. He knew that the legal genius loved money. He knew that Mrs Kemp and the three little Kemps, loved it even more. However much their breadwinner gave them, they were never satisfied – a condominium apartment in Miami, European holidays, cars, home computers, parties, clothes – nothing seemed to still their clamour for new luxuries and fresh experiences. He knew that to satisfy this craving and his own avarice Kemp had crossed the narrow divide between the permissible and the possible. He had used clients' money for short term investment, had been known to associate with dubious characters and had been twice examined by the state bar association.

'Will, thank you very much for coming. What'll you have to drink?'

'Good to m-m-meet you, Calvin. T-t-t-tonic water, please. I have to be c-c-careful of my stomach.'

In fact Kemp hated eating out. Restaurant food disagreed with him. When a red-jacketed waiter appeared with the drinks and the menus, he surveyed the extensive bill of fare with the utmost suspicion.

'G-g-give me an omelette, an undressed green side salad and a g-g-glass of m-m-milk.'

'Certainly, sir. What kind of omelette?'

'Just a p-p-p-p . . . just a p-p-p-p . . .'

'Plain omelette, sir. Certainly, sir.' The waiter took Craig's order then moved away among the tables. Kemp knew he was grinning. He hated it when other people finished his sentences for him.

Watching him Craig thought, 'The next hour or so is going to be tough.'

He had not changed his opinion twenty minutes later when he and his guest were seated at their table and the food had been served. Watching Kemp prod his omelette with his fork and peer at it as though it were a laboratory culture of some particularly nasty virus almost put Craig off his own meal. Time to get down to business. Craig began cautiously.

'Will, I have a very important deal going down with an overseas client and I need some help with the complicated legal aspects.'

'What k-k-k-kind of deal?'

'My company is setting up the finances for a major building project.'

'What c-company?'

'Before we get down to the nitty-gritty, Will, I think I ought to go over the basic requirements of the deal so that we understand each other. Then you can let me know whether its the kind of thing you can handle.'

Kemp said nothing as he tentatively transfered a tiny fragment of omelette to his mouth. But he watched his companion carefully with his dark, deep-set eyes.

'There will be a four-way transaction. My own company is acting as agent between the borrower and the lending bank, and there will also be a loan guarantor organisation involved. The money will be routed through an offshore bank in Nassau, the Bahamas and accounts in Switzerland. Most of the business meetings will take place in London and they'll inevitably generate a great deal of paperwork.'

'What size l-l-loan are you negotiating, Calvin?' The lawyer's face was expressionless.

'I'm afraid I must regard that information as confidential until I know you are working for me.' Craig tried not to be aggravated as he watched Kemp excavate his salad for slices of cucumber and line them up around the rim of his plate.

'Calvin, I have a very busy p-p-practice. I don't know whether I can take on more work at present. That's why I have to know the sort of f-f-figures we're talking about.'

'Well let's just say that the fee I had in mind for the legal work is one million dollars, paid in cash wherever in the world you want it.'

The forkful of lettuce on the way to Kemp's mouth paused but only momentarily. 'Now, Calvin, you must realise I c-can't agree a f-f-fee in advance. My charges depend on the amount of work involved for me and my staff. Letters, ph-phone calls, t-t-travel – they all have to be n-n-n . . .'

'O.K., let's stop bullshitting around.' Craig changed his tactics. 'We both know the kind of deal we're talking about and the kind of risks and profits involved. One million, tax free, is a generous payment, for the degree of involvement I have in mind for you.'

Kemp laid his fork down and looked at Craig straight. 'If you're s-s-suggesting what I think you're s-s-s . . . s-s-s. Dammit! I think we'd better end this c-c-conversation right here!'

Craig sat back in his chair. 'Don't try the holier-than-thou routine, Will.' He took a leather-bound note pad from his pocket, tore off the top sheet and pushed it across the tablecloth. 'In the last six months these two prominent citizens both made payments into a Cayman Islands bank account on your instructions. The details of the account, as you will see, are also written down. I guess the last thing those guys would do is testify in a court of law but I sure as hell know the IRS would be interested in those transactions.'

Drops of perspiration appeared on the lawyer's brow. 'If you think you can get away with b-b-b-b . . .'

'Blackmail my ass! I just want us to be clear that we're both in the same line of business. Now if you accept that and relax, perhaps we can get down to details – and you can stop aggravating your ulcer.'

They got down to details. Craig went over the whole plan in outline. He had no alternative. The legalities of

22

the swindle had to be watertight. And Kemp listened, fascinated, and asked questions, hardly noticing when the waiter removed his half-consumed omelette. They talked till mid-afternoon over several cups of coffee and eventually parted company, agreeing to meet again in a week by which time Kemp was to have worked out a scheme for setting up an offshore banking operation in Nassau.

Chapter Two

On the third Saturday in July the great and the good of
Long Island paid two hundred and fifty dollars a head
to drink lapsang souchong, nibble little bits of toast and
puff pastry topped with Strasbourg paté, quails' eggs and
caviar and gulp down mouthfuls of *fraises du bois* with
crême Chantilly. Like many traditional fixtures on the social
calendar it was of recent origin and like all such fixtures
attendance was *de rigueur* for those who had 'arrived' and
those who wished to be considered 'en route'.

On the appointed afternoon in 1986 they were all
there, scattered in little clusters over Melton's terrace
and the lawns which sloped gently to the Sound and
the distant hazy prospect of the Connecticut shore –
bankers, professors, corporation men, politicians, and their
carefully-dressed wives.

But the annual Melton Charity Garden Party was not
just another gathering of the élite. All members of the
local Somerset Cove community were admitted free of
charge to this grand event. And in one of the nearer
meadows there was a small fairground and a special
tea tent where the children could stuff themselves with
soda pop, ice cream and chocolate fudge cake between
rides on the dodgems and the 'Inter-galactic Whirling
Shuttle'.

Colin Hartley – tall, distinguished and avuncular –
moved among his guests, leaning almost imperceptibly
on an ivory-topped ebony cane.

'Good afternoon, Mr Hartley. Lovely party.'

'Good afternoon, Trudy. I've just seen those two scamps of yours having a pony race down in the long paddock. They're going to be accomplished horsemen in a few years.' The host stooped slightly and doffed his fedora.

Trudy Oppenshaw reflected, not for the first time, that she did not know any other man these days who raised his hat to a lady. But then, there was much which, to her chagrin, she had to admit was unusual, enigmatic about Somerset Cove's wealthiest citizen. Trudy Oppenshaw was a woman who liked to know about her neighbours. She detested mysteries. And the man who had bought up this old Berkley estate a dozen years before was still a mystery.

'Nice to have you back again,' she said.

'Nice to be back. The more I see of the world the more I love Long Island. Hello Brett.' He waved his ebony cane at Trudy's husband elbowing through the crowd with two bowls of strawberries. 'Don't forget the committee meeting on Tuesday. Say, have you got time for a round first?'

'Sure. It would be an honour.' The stocky insurance man beamed his pleasure.

'Good, good. See you about six, then.'

He turned to move on to another group of guests.

'Staying home long this time, Mr Hartley?'

Trudy's conversational lasso missed its target. The reply was thrown back over Hartley's retreating shoulder.

'Ah, who knows? When our masters call . . .'

Brett Oppenshaw scowled at his wife. 'You never give up, do you? Why can't you just accept that C.H. does highly confidential work for the government?'

Trudy prodded at her wild strawberries, trying to detach the fruit from as much cream as possible. 'Do you know anyone below the level of senator who lives like this?' She waved a hand at the neo-colonial house. 'All those rooms stuffed with pictures and antiques – not to mention his

25

apartments in Santa Barbara, London, Paris and I don't know where else.'

'So, his old man left him well-heeled. What's it matter? He's a good neighbour. This community would be a lot poorer without his generosity.'

'Oh, I know he can do no wrong in Somerset Cove! Because he's president of the golf club and paid for the library extension and heads the annual charities appeal and throws swell parties people round here regard him as some sort of *king*. It's positively . . . feudal! Well, I don't care what you say. I think there's something funny about your precious *Lord* Hartley.' She pushed her unfinished dessert into his hands. 'I'm going to see what the boys are up to.'

Even Trudy Oppenshaw would have been dumbfounded at the truth about her host. Colin Hartley had many reasons for enjoying his garden party and his Christmas banquet and his intimate dinners and his theatre suppers and his musical soirées. But the greatest pleasure he gained from patronising the establishment was the unhurried, regular, delicious savouring of revenge. Though none of them recognised him, these men of finance, these denizens of Capitol Hill who paid so handsomely for his hospitality and drew him aside to share *sotto voce* confidences as he passed graciously among them were corporately and, in some cases, individually those who had presided over his character assassination a quarter of a century before. Now, like the Count of Monte-Cristo, he had returned in a different guise, though not to take savage vengeance, for, unlike Dumas' hero, his bitterness and hatred had long since mellowed. They had been very real once – real enough to set the man known as Hartley, Craig and a dozen other aliases on a criminal career.

As a young man in the early sixties he had been a brilliant student at Harvard – first in his class in Economics. He was offered a research degree and chose to write his thesis on the role of government in an industrialised society. In it he argued for the virtual abolition of state control and a vital reduction in government spending on welfare. The study was immediately recognised as a radical and brilliant contribution to the current politico-economic debate. It seemed a foregone conclusion that Craig would be offered a permanent teaching post.

Then there was the excitement of being taken up by the politicians. These were the Kennedy years – the years of a fair deal for the poor and massive overseas aid investment. Liberalism was riding high. Right-wingers and the once-powerful commercial lobby desperately needed a charismatic intellectual to put their case. In Craig they discovered a natural television performer who could think on his feet and tie seasoned Democrats in knots. The brilliant young economist was flavour of the month.

And that was about as long as it lasted. The Harvard greybeards were furious. In a university proud of its greatest son, criticism of the Kennedy dream was high treason. Former friends and colleagues were now as bitchy as only academics can be. Craig's vision of a fellowship went straight down the pan. But there were compensations. At least he had powerful backers – men who could offer other tempting careers in business and politics.

Then someone decided to assassinate the president. Suddenly the air was thick with suspicion. Now, no one wanted to be seen by shocked Americans as an open opponent of their martyred leader. Overnight, Craig, the public face of reaction, became a political liability, a social leper. 'Friends' and supporters cancelled dinner engagements, were unavailable when he phoned, never returned his calls. And that was only the beginning. Press and TV journalists were quick to sink their fangs into the unprotected scapegoat. They could not discover who was behind the death in Dallas. So they slashed with the claws of suspicion and innuendo at those they headlined as

'Kennedy's Enemies'. High on that list was the 'ambitious Harvard smart-ass' who had challenged the administration so publicly.

Craig had to go into hiding – from media jackals, obscene phone callers and the writers of anonymous death threats. For weeks he was in a state of shock. Paralysed by fear and uncontrollable fury. Then he began to plan his revenge – to plan with simple logic. When the establishment ruined a man's reputation and career it acted unjustly; it put itself outside the natural law. It was, therefore, within that man's rights to recover the life taken from him, even if it meant breaking the mere man-made laws with which the establishment protected itself. If such activities were criminal they were less so than the thefts, frauds and murders perpetrated daily in the name of business, democracy and national security.

Craig's first foray into grand larceny was a computer swindle on the federal social security system. It was easy. It went undetected. And it made him richer by almost a million dollars. After that Craig no longer bothered to justify himself.

Two decades later he had graduated to the first division of international fraud. He reached this eminence through a series of increasingly audacious swindles, every one meticulously researched, smoothly executed and successful. Except the Venezuelan oil scam, which ended with Craig heftily bribing his way out of an exceedingly uncomfortable Maracaibo jail.

Apart from that hitch, he had avoided detection by sheer originality. Craig's handiwork figured prominently in the unsolved cases of fraud squads and internal revenue departments around the world but no one had ever thought to link them together. That was because every assignment was different, thought out from scratch. There were no common elements, no behavioural fingerprints. How stunned Trudy Oppenshaw and all the other good folk of Somerset Cove would have been if they had known the truth about their leading citizen.

Not that Colin Hartley despised his neighbours. Far from it. He found Somerset Cove comfortable and comforting. He liked its solid, suburban self-confidence – its watered front lawns, its hardworking senior executives, their cute kids and fashion-conscious wives. He even liked Trudy Oppenshaw and her two loutish sons. He would not have admitted it but playing paterfamilias to this respectable community gave him a sense of being needed – loved even. As the years passed he found that he identified more and more with the avuncular 'C.H.' whom the folk of Somerset Cove had taken to their corporate heart. Solid citizen Colin Hartley had become the Dr Jekyll to his multi-faceted Mr Hyde.

As the last Cadillac crunched away down the drive, Hartley turned, mounted the short flight of steps and went back into the now quiet house. He laid his hat and cane on one of a pair of George II giltwood console tables, crossed the marbled coolness of the hall and let himself into his study with a key he took from his waistcoat pocket. With a profound sense of well-being he helped himself to a glass of whisky from a decanter on the table just inside the door. He carried the drink across to his large mahogany partner's desk. Then he froze.

The wide expanse of tooled green leather should have been empty, save for the neatly arranged lamp, telephone, blotter and silver ink stand. It wasn't. Staring up at him was an 8″ × 6″ black and white photograph. He snatched it up and turned it over. The reverse was blank. Again he looked at the picture. The shock was almost physical – like a punch in the stomach. He sat down in the leather swivel chair and downed the scotch at a gulp.

The photograph depicted a crowd of people in the foyer at Christies', London. In the foreground were Samuel

Okello and Alison Leggat. Behind them, full face and quite unmistakeable, was Calvin Craig.

'Like the calling card?'

Craig's gaze jerked towards the doorway. He saw a young man in jeans and an expensive leather jacket. Grinning.

'My boss wants to meet you.'

Craig made no move.

The visitor stopped grinning. 'Now,' he ordered.

Craig rose slowly and walked round the desk. He did not protest. He did not argue. You don't argue with a man who is pointing an automatic pistol at your stomach.

Chapter Three

The study in which Dr Samuel Okello, Finance Minister of the Republic of Uganda, sat, was very different from the tidy, expensively-furnished room from which Calvin Craig operated. But then he was a very different man in very different circumstances. He was facing the awesome task of rebuilding the economy of a country all but destroyed by fifteen years of civil war.

Okello's house, built for a colonial sahib, owned for decades by an Asian sugar baron till Amin sent him and his ilk packing, commandeered for 'the people' and lived in by several brief holders of government office (most of them now dead) throughout the troubles, was one of the few in the once-smart residential district of Kampala, that had not been looted and vandalised. Whether it was the present occupant who inspired this respect or the twelve-foot security fence, the arc lamps, the armed *askaris* and the guard dogs was not clear.

The minister's bulk, encased in lightweight well-pressed khaki bush jacket and trousers, was wedged between a desk overflowing with documents, magazines, reports, books and plans and a table in the bay window piled precariously with box files. Bookcases bulged with books, trophies and African carvings. The walls were lavish with photographs among which a large portrait of President Museveni took pride of place above the door.

The door opened and Grace Okello, an imposing, tall woman in a lustrous green, tribal costume and matching turban, came into the room.

31

'Susan Hayward is here, Sam. We're having tea in the garden.'

He nodded. 'Good. I'll join you shortly.'

He sat for several minutes thinking about Sue Hayward. She was vital to his plan, to the achievement of his vision. She was a formidable woman, of that there was no doubt; an enthusiastic, no-nonsense, British memsahib of the old school. Introducing her to a cross-section of African politicians would certainly be a calculated risk. She might get their backs up. Yet, all in all, he doubted it. She was so transparently good, so dedicated, and, unlike himself, so free from all taint of ambition and political scheming. If she believed in his idea she would be able to sell it to the sceptics.

He stood up, lumbering round his desk and across the room. Yes, there really could be no better advocate for his great brainchild. She would do the job well. It only remained to persuade her to co-operate.

Okello emerged onto the verandah, descended the four steps to the lawn and walked towards the two women sitting beneath a jacaranda tree.

'Sue, thank you so much for coming.'

He squeezed her hand enthusiastically and eased himself into a wicker armchair beside her.

'That's O.K., Sam,' the young white woman replied. 'I had a week's leave owing to me.'

'I'm so sorry I didn't have time to visit your father on my last trip to England. Is he keeping well?' Okello smiled at the slim woman with the untidy auburn hair and furrowed brow who looked more than her thirty-four years. He remembered the little tomboy who had given every promise of turning into a vivacious and beautiful turner of heads.

Dr Sue Hayward also had her memories. She recalled the thin, intense young man known as 'Sammy' whom she had found rather frightening when she was tiny. He always seemed to be arguing with her father about politics and religion. In fact, as she had later discovered, the two men had had great respect and affection for each other. Samuel Okello had been one of the brightest pupils John Hayward had ever taught and the old missionary had followed with interest and pride his protégé's subsequent career at the national university and then at colleges in Britain and America. When Samuel had returned in the late fifties and fallen foul of the colonial authorities as a political agitator it was the Haywards who had given him refuge and spoken up for him in court on several occasions. Now here he was, one of the leaders of his country, totally vindicating his old teacher's belief in him.

'According to his letters he's very fit. He seems to spend all his time lecturing to Women's Institutes and church meetings.' She stretched appreciatively. It was good to relax in this lovely old garden near the capital. The air was softer and the sunshine somehow less aggressive in this southern part of the country. She gazed up into the sparse branches of the jacaranda tree, then down at the purple carpet of discarded flowers beneath her feet.

'How long is it since you saw him?' Grace Okello poured tea for her husband. She sat erect in her chair, and as she spoke the faint scars of the geometrical incisions made on her cheeks at puberty caught the light.

'Just over two years. I haven't been home since Mother's funeral.'

'But that's terrible. Why that poor, lonely man!'

Sue laughed. 'He's not a bit lonely. He has lots of friends and he keeps very active.'

But the minister echoed his wife's anxiety. 'Even so, Sue, you should visit him more often. You only have to let me know and I can arrange a diplomatic flight to London for you at any time.'

'I don't think that would go down very well with my colleagues at the mission, Sam. It's sweet of you but I

33

couldn't ask you to use your influence and Dad wouldn't want it either. Still it is nice to come here and relax once in a while.'

'And how are things at the mission?' Okello perched on his chair rather than sat in it. Even here, in his own garden, he was an alert political animal. Relaxation he left for his trips abroad. Okello had seen too many public men destroyed, not because they lacked brains or cunning but because they allowed their guard to drop. That was why he had always yoked wariness with ambition in the driving harness of his career.

'You don't need to ask me, you know!' Susan spoke with a directness which those who did not understand her often took for rudeness. Okello did not make that mistake. He knew how deeply she cared about her work; how committed she was to the people in her care. Uganda's people. His people. 'Since you and old Nsibirwa, the Health Minister, ventured out to inspect us last July things have gone from bad to worse. The original hospital buildings are so ramshackle it's a wonder they haven't fallen down years ago. We need a new Land Rover for the long-distance clinic work. Our X-ray machine has packed up on us. Not that it matters much; we haven't any film. We need more dressings, more drugs, more staff. Every day we're turning away dozens of AIDS victims. No point cluttering the place up with incurables.' She glowered at her host. 'You do know, don't you, that one baby in ten is born with AIDS. We can do nothing for them. We can't even cope with routine medicine. We ought to be mounting a proper family planning advice centre and a hygiene education service. Most of our work would be unnecessary if people could be shown how to look after themselves and regulate the size of their families.' She sighed and shook her head. 'Just how are we expected to cope? Six doctors and a handful of auxiliaries among a population of three million. It's crazy!'

Okello only half listened to the eloquent tirade. He was reinforcing his conviction that it was vital to get Sue Hayward to bring her obvious passion and commitment to the Nairobi conference. There were some who would sneer at his cause being advocated by a white woman but surely they would soon see that here was no ordinary ex-patriate do-gooder. Anyone who came back to Africa immediately after qualifying, settled in a remote and arid region with no thought of career prospects or home or marriage, and had stuck at her post through the carnage of the Amin and Obote years had earned a respectful hearing.

'You're doing a wonderful job, Sue – all of you. The government is extremely grateful . . .'

Sue leaned forward in her chair, scornfully brushing aside the platitude, 'Sam, you can't set broken bones with gratitude. You can't cure river blindness with gratitude. You can't inject gratitude into a child dying of *kwashiorkor*! We need facilities, staff, supplies.'

She stared wearily at the man before her and saw only a calculating politician, a man who had judged carefully his moment to grasp for power, a man who had lost the Marxist fervour of his youth. That judgement was not altogether fair.

Samuel Okello had joined Milton Obote's Uganda People's Congress in the 1950s and in the elections of 1962 had been returned as the youngest member of parliament. Like most African politicians, he personally profited from office in the immediate post-independence years, apparently seeing no contradiction between the egalitarian principles he advocated in his speeches and the wealth he amassed through his growing commercial interests. But Okello was no mere cynical opportunist. In the national assembly he spoke frequently but in vain against the progressive economic suicide being committed by the administration.

Uganda in 1963 was a land of great promise. Its fertile southern region was rich in varied crops, and the country exported coffee, sugar, cotton and tea. Its game parks were second only to those of neighbouring Kenya, and tourism accounted for a third of the national revenue. It shared communications and other services with Tanzania and Kenya in the East African Community, an organisation modelled consciously on the EEC. All was set fair for a stable and prosperous future. Then they blew it. Obote led a political lurch to the left and the stream of holidaymakers from Britain, Germany and the USA slowed to a trickle. Then he embarked on a programme of wholesale nationalisation. Inexperienced Africans were appointed to the posts vacated by sacked ex-patriates. Once-flourishing plantations and businesses collapsed. Economic disorder merely paved the way for the military takeover by General Idi Amin in 1971.

Okello went into exile with the deposed president and over the next eight years the two men grew much closer together, but the ex-politician was not content to kick his heels in Dar es Salaam waiting for Amin to overreach himself. He travelled widely in Europe and America, addressing student rallies, encouraging groups of Ugandan refugees, appearing on television and in the press to denounce the military regime – and also to extend his commercial interests and investments. Large sums of his own money went towards the support of Obote and his entourage and towards keeping alive the hope of a return to civilian government. But they were small compared with the fortune in cash, securities, antiquities and works of art that he built up in his London base. Then, in April 1979, the psychopathic Amin was driven from power by Tanzanian troops.

The stage seemed set for Okello's return to public life. It was a mark of the man's political acumen that he refused the proffered cabinet post. After Amin's legalised lawlessness Uganda was ungovernable. Hundreds of thousands – perhaps a million – men, women and children had been slaughtered by the army, by the police, by the dictator's own secret agents, by gangs of private enterprise looters and killers. Now there was not a family or village in the whole of the country that did not have scores to settle. Now ill-disciplined troops would wander the land intent on vendetta and personal profit. Now every region from Buganda to Karamoja would be throwing up its own warrior-heroes hoping to carve tribal autonomy and personal power out of the chaos. Now the politicians would be in the hands of the generals who alone could keep them in power. They might talk about restoring stability, but the only offspring of violence is more violence. And a land in chaos was no place for a man of peace – and ambition.

Like Br'er Rabbit, Okello 'laid low and said nothin'' for another five years while the gun and the panga continued to wreak havoc in Uganda. They were wielded by different hands but they had the same effect. He continued his role of unofficial ambassador while keeping himself minutely informed about affairs in his own country. In mid-1985 he made his bid for power. He recognised in Yoweri Museveni, the latest military saviour to emerge, a man who could unite the country – for a while. Judicious provision of funds to the leader's National Resistance Army ensured him a welcome home and an offer of high office a few months later, when Museveni took control. That was the point at which Samuel Okello became Finance Minister of the Republic of Uganda.

Administering the economy of a bankrupt country was a daunting task but the new minister applied himself to it with enormous energy. The taxation yield was hopelessly inadequate in a land whose farms had been trampled by foraging troops, whose shops had been looted and many of whose business premises had been burned or ransacked as 'reprisals' for their owners' imaginary crimes. So Okello went on his travels again, becoming the tireless mendicant, seeking grants and loans around the commercial capitals of the world.

Samuel Okello, now 53, *did* care. He cared deeply about his country. He knew that Uganda needed to escape from the stranglehold of a multi-billion IMF debt and rebuild a secure economy. He planned to be the man to lead the way into that brighter future. The next president. Of course, if the uncertain world of politics snatched that prize from him, there was always London, Alison Leggat and a fortune in works of art and industrial shares.

But there was no need to contemplate failure at this moment, when his great vision was about to dazzle the whole of Africa – the whole of the Third World.

He smiled at Sue and steered the conversation in the direction he wanted. 'Young lady, you are even more stubborn than your father. He would never take "No" for an answer. Sometimes obstinacy pays off. As you know I, personally, consider your work extremely important . . .'

'But there isn't the money. I know.' Sue sagged back into her chair. 'The government must pamper the army and the police because it would collapse without them. Then there's the continued rebuilding – clearing up the mess left by Amin – and getting tourism back on its feet to bring in foreign currency, and education, and agriculture – and right at the bottom of the list comes the health of the people.' She signed. 'I just wish there was some way we could make you politicians understand that the future *depends* on a healthy population. If Uganda goes on carrying a growing burden of sickness, disease and malnutrition, national recovery will be only a pipe dream.'

Okello stood, suddenly. 'Sue, what I'm trying to tell you, if you'll let me, is that I may be able to make the dream become reality – if you help me. Come into the house, I've something to show you.' He took hold of her hand in the unselfconscious African manner and led her towards the large bungalow.

They entered a wide hallway whose wooden floor had a scattering of brightly-coloured rugs, collected by Okello from various parts of Africa. He ushered Sue through a door on the right which led into the chaos of his study.

'Over here,' Okello ordered, steering his bulk round the desk towards the window. 'Let me prove to you that my protestations of goodwill are not empty politician's words. Eighteen months ago I asked you and your colleagues to write a report on the medical situation in the North? You remember? It was an excellent report – very clear, very thorough. I expect you thought it had gone into some dusty pigeonhole in the basement at Parliament House.'

On a corner of the desk was a small pile of glossy brochures. He picked up the top copy.

'The nub of your proposals was a new, fully-equipped centre at Soroti and six permanent up-country clinics to be staffed with auxiliaries trained by you. I took your idea and I improved on it. This is the result.'

She looked at the plain white laminated cover with the legend in blue lettering 'THE OKELLO MEDICAL RESEARCH AND TRAINING CENTRE, SOROTI, UGANDA'.

She opened the prospectus and gazed at the architect's plans, the artist's impressions of gleaming white buildings, the graphs and the columns of figures.

Okello smiled expansively.

'A training hospital.' He announced. 'You see there was one element missing from your report. It assumed our continued long-term dependence on ex-patriate staff, or, at least, staff trained and qualified abroad. I want to see a centre so well equipped that both nurses and doctors can be taught there; a centre that will attract some of the world's finest specialists in tropical medicine to come on secondment to share their skills and knowledge.' Okello

39

was now pacing the room, waving his arms enthusiastically. 'A centre Uganda can be proud of, where medical students from all over the continent will gather, instead of going to London and New York. We could set up the world's leading centre for the study of vitamin deficiency and malnutrition-related diseases. We could prove that, though Africa's problems are great, she has the resources to tackle them herself.'

He stopped and stood facing her. 'You do like the idea don't you?'

'Sam, I think it's a magnificent *idea*, but how . . .'

'Ah, yes, "how" is the question. That's where I'm going to need your help. I have to persuade the statesmen of other African nations to part with money for a prestigious development to be built in Uganda. Some will say they can't afford it. Others will ask why shouldn't it be built in their country. The only way we can overcome such objections is to make them see how important the medical centre is; to set them on fire with the idea. You can do that. You must do it.'

'Me?'

Okello nodded emphatically. 'In January there's a big Organisation of African Unity meeting in Nairobi. That's when I shall unveil this project and you must be there to help me sell it.'

The Susan Hayward who arrived back at the Soroti hospital a week later was a different woman to the exhausted, dispirited missionary who had left for the Ugandan capital. By the time the old Land Rover had grumbled the hundred and eighty miles, turned off the highway and begun the last bumpy stretch of the journey she was sweaty and dusty. But as she wrestled with the temperamental engine her robust soprano soared above its throaty protestations – favourite hymns, old pop ballads, even music hall songs she had learned as a child from old

78 r.p.m. records. As always, there were small groups of people making their way along the track to the hospital – mainly the tall Teso women trailing clusters of small children in well-patched but spotlessly clean shirts and dresses. Sue stopped to pick up as many as she could and by the time the protesting vehicle lumbered to a halt before the group of single storey, mud-walled, thatched buildings it was overflowing with humanity.

Out of habit she waited for the swirl of murram dust to settle before jumping out of the cab. She grabbed her canvas bag from the passenger seat and, swinging it by her side, walked towards the hospital. She entered through the door with the large signboard saying MEDICAL STAFF ONLY in English, Swahili and Kiteso and called a cheery 'Hello, Mary' to the receptionist as she went through another door into the open verandah passageway leading to the staff quarters.

Sue was feeling happier than she had felt for a long time. Surviving the Amin holocaust had been, she firmly believed, a sheer miracle but that epoch of fear, and violence, had taken its toll. The Obote years had been no better. Now, with the gradual lessening of violence, the pressures on the mission staff had become in some ways even greater. The war zone had drifted to the northern border. The country people were able to move freely once more. And they besieged the hospital in thousands. They brought their diseases, their shattered limbs and their suppurating sores for treatment. And the medical staff simply could not cope, neither in the immediate aftermath of the Obote regime, nor now, when bands of tribesmen, armed with the discarded weapons of the defeated army ranged far and wide maintaining chaos and havoc. She had to fight hard to stave off helplessness and despair and to maintain her belief in the ultimate triumph of good. Now, at last, her faith might be vindicated. Now there was something to look forward to. Now there was

41

hope. As she crossed the courtyard to her room she started again on one of her favourite old hymns, 'And can it be that I should gain an interest in the Saviour's blood'.

'You sound cheerful.' Mike Summers, the longest serving doctor on the staff apart from herself, emerged from a doorway opposite from which issued a long queue of people who had come for the daily out-patient surgery.

'I've got some marvellous news. I can't wait to tell you about it.'

'OK, put the kettle on. I'll take a break in a few minutes and pop over.'

It was half an hour before Mike knocked at the door of Sue's tiny bedsit, strode in and dropped into the battered armchair. He was younger than her but they were on an equal footing and Sue valued his judgement. Now he smiled encouragingly at her from behind his thick beard.

'Tell all. What have you been up to in the big city?'

Sue poured boiling water from a kettle on the electric ring in the corner into a mug containing Nescafé and powdered milk. She handed it to her colleague. Then, perched on the edge of the bed, she narrated the story of her meeting with Okello.

Mike showed no reaction and sat silently sipping his coffee after Sue had finished.

She looked at him anxiously. 'Well, say something, Mike. What's the matter? Do you think I shouldn't have agreed to go to Nairobi? I know it puts more on everyone else's shoulders but it would have been churlish to refuse after all he's done.'

He shook his head. 'It isn't that, Sue. We can cope.' He paused awkwardly. He did not find it easy to express himself at the best of times. Now he was groping badly for words 'Look . . . I know this Okello is an old friend of yours, but . . . well . . . he's still only a politician. If I don't leap up and give three rousing cheers it's because I've heard it all before – we both have.'

'But, Mike, this time it's different. I mean, if you could have seen him you'd have known that. He's really enthusiastic. Look,' she fished in her bag and pulled out a copy of Okello's glossy brochure. 'Here's the prospectus he's had drawn up, and he's thought out ways of financing it in collaboration with other countries.'

He flicked through the pages of shiny art paper with their full-colour illustrations and shook his head. 'You know, Sue, this sort of thing makes me pretty angry. What we need is just a few simple things like drugs, surgical dressings and new engine parts for the vehicles. And what does the government wish on us? This damned great white elephant. Why? Because it's what the people need? No, because it has enormous prestige value.'

'I don't think that's altogether fair . . .'

'Oh, come on, Sue. How often have we asked for some modest financial assistance only to be told the country is too poor and that every cent is needed for national recovery? And what's this extravaganza going to cost?'

'About a hundred and twenty-five million dollars, I think.'

Mike laughed. 'A hundred and twenty-five million! I can't even envisage such a sum. A gift of a hundred and twenty-five would be an exciting event. We're supported by church people back home dropping their coins in the plate. It doesn't amount to much but at least it's given with love and understanding by folk who want to be involved. But this . . .' He tossed the brochure onto the bed with a gesture of contempt.

For some moments Sue sat deflated, lost for words. At last she said, 'Mike, I'm sure you're wrong. This could be just what we've hoped for and prayed for – a chance to be really effective.'

He shrugged. 'Well, I've said my piece. I suppose the truth is I'm a bit afraid. All this talk of astronomical sums of money and making speeches to groups of politicians. I'm out of my depth.' He paused again before adding, 'I think you are, too. I think you could get hurt.'

'But what do you expect me to do? Turn the whole thing down? Say "No thanks, Mr Okello, we don't need new equipment, new buildings, more drugs and more staff. We're quite happy to muddle along as we are, watching people die needlessly because the service we offer is criminally inadequate"?'

Mike stood up. He looked down at her and shrugged 'Well, perhaps I'm wrong. But do take care. We can manage without a new building. We can't . . . I can't manage without *you*.' He turned quickly and walked from the room.

Chapter Four

The drive lasted about an hour. Craig made the journey wedged on the car's back seat between the young man in the leather jacket and an older colleague who chain-smoked. Their destination was a back alley on Second Avenue not far from the UN Building. A door was propped open to release on the evening air the unmistakeable smell and noise of a busy restaurant kitchen. Craig was marched up a fire escape, along a first floor corridor and pushed into a small office, empty except for two large cardboard cartons.

His captor said, 'You wait there till the boss sends for you.' Then he made the order unnecessary by locking the door.

The light outside the panes of grimy, translucent glass faded as Craig awaited the 'boss's' pleasure. There was no bulb in the light socket.

It was fifty minutes and very dark before leather jacket came back. Craig was taken to the far end of the corridor. To a door guarded by a burly black man. Inside was a comfortable room, part office, part sitting room. The furnishings were expensive and tasteless. The man who sat in a deep, white leather armchair looked mournful, lugubrious. The effect was largely created by a long face, accentuated by a drooping moustache and an almost completely bald head. He was going through some papers with an older, bespectacled man. Apart from waving Craig to another armchair he gave him not so much as a glance for several minutes. Only when the documents had been put back in the little man's briefcase and he had been dismissed did the 'boss' turn to Craig.

'Drink?'

'Scotch, please.'

Leather jacket poured the spirit then he, too, was discharged.

Craig's host tossed a copy of the Christie's photograph onto the marble-topped table between them.

'What's your interest in this nigger?'

Craig's first instinct was to try incomprehension.

'My interest? I'm afraid you're mistaken . . . Who is this man?' He put as much nervous tremor into the voice as he could manage and hoped he sounded like a bewildered, upright citizen scared out of his wits.

'You've been following him around, checking up on him. That's you in the background.'

Craig picked up the photo and made a show of examining it. He tried a nervous laugh. 'Oh, I see now how this has happened. This fellow in the photo . . . yes, he does look a little bit like me, but . . .'

'Steve!' It was a raucous shout.

Leather jacket entered.

'Teach this guy not to waste my time.'

Out came the grin and the gun again. Steve grabbed Craig by the shoulder and yanked him to his feet.

Now Craig *was* scared. 'Look there's no need . . .'

The boss was not listening. 'Get out! We'll talk again when you're in a more co-operative frame of mind.'

Steve and the negro fell in behind Craig and marched him up two flights of stairs. He knew he was in for a beating. At least they were not going to kill him, not until they had got what they wanted from him. As he stumbled up the stone stairs grabbing at the metal banister for support, Craig forced himself to think clearly. As far as he could see there was only one item on the credit side of the ledger: these mobsters needed some information and they believed he had it. They would try to knock it out of him. He would have to stall. But how much pain could he take?

They stopped before a nondescript door in a nondescript passageway. The black man unlocked it and felt inside for the light switch.

The first thing that struck Craig as he was pushed inside was the stench – excrement and stale vomit. The second thing was the naked man. He was huddled, foetus-like on a blanket in one corner.

Craig stepped back stunned, nauseous. He felt the gun barrel against his spine. The 'thing' before him was almost like something from an old newsreel about the liberating of Belsen. The skin drawn tight over bone, the twitchy body, the glazed eyes half-seeing, half-pleading, the pallor, the sores. But the sores were different.

The dehumanised form pulled itself into a sitting position and held up an arm. The negro took the necessary equipment from his pocket, a cord to tie round the flabby biceps and the syringe. He held it up to the light. He squeezed the plunger till the heroin oozed out, found a tiny area of unbruised flesh, inserted the needle. With a sigh, the naked form curled up again. Eyes closed, rehearsing the oblivion that would soon be its reality.

'Get the message?' Steve asked as they retreated into the corridor.

Craig nodded. He got the message all right. Fail to 'co-operate' and Colin Hartley would mysteriously disappear. Then, a few weeks later another dead junkie would be added to the city's statistics.

He inhaled deeply the non-foetid air outside the room. It was not difficult to work out the appropriate tactics – 'Look scared and tell them whatever they want to hear'.

'OK, let's get down to business.' The man with the drooping moustache watched expressionless as Craig sagged into a chair and wiped a handkerchief across his forehead. 'What do you know about this man?' He pointed to the photograph.

Craig took a hurried gulp of whisky. 'His name's Okello

. . . Samuel Okello . . . He's a big shot in one of the African states . . . Uganda.'

The inquisitor leaned forward. 'What else?'

'Well . . . he's pretty smart. You have to be to survive in African politics. He makes out he's a man of the people. Gets plenty of publicity – laying foundation stones, handing over cheques. He likes to pose as some kind of financial saviour. He's ambitious. Keeps a high profile in pan-African and Third World affairs. Always going off to international conferences, making big speeches about western economic imperialism and how we're trying to keep the poorer nations poor by saddling them with massive debts. . . . But I guess you know all this.'

'Stop guessing and keep talking. Tell me about Mr Squeaky Clean's other life. Who's this woman?'

'That's Alison Leggat. She's an English antique dealer.'

'Okello's mistress?'

Craig nodded and swallowed the rest of the scotch. 'Mistress and business partner. The apartment she rents in Chelsea . . . overlooking the Thames . . . is paid for by a standing order drawn on Okello's account with the Union Suisse bank. Over the years he's used money from various international funds . . . charities, political and religious organisations . . . to buy and sell high class pictures and antiques. He's quite an expert. The woman's business is partly a front for building up a personal fortune in paintings, furniture, old master drawings, antiquities. Mr Okello certainly has a taste for the western culture he claims to despise.'

'A kind of insurance in case Uganda gets too hot for him?'

'Like I said, he's smart.'

'And now, Mr Hartley, we come to the $64,000 question.' He fixed Craig with an unblinking gaze. 'What's your interest in this character?'

It was the moment of truth. Or, more accurately, the moment of falsehood. Craig had to decide whether he could get away with a lie. That would depend on how much these people knew about him and his previous operations. And Craig did not know how much they knew. He had no intention of giving away the details of the Uganda Assignment if he could help it. But if his story failed to convince . . . He thought of the shadow-man upstairs and shivered. Then he reminded himself that lies, disguises and subterfuge were his stock in trade. He had talked himself out of desperate situations before – though none quite as desperate as this.

'Well . . .' He cleared his throat nervously. 'This Okello is a rich man with a guilty secret. I guess he'd pay pretty handsomely to keep it.' He stared back at his questioner.

The other man frowned, thinking over Craig's reply. 'Blackmail?'

Craig shrugged. 'He's a prime mark.'

'How much were you planning to take him for?'

'He must be good for a million at least.'

'You'd go to all that trouble and expense for a million lousy bucks?'

'Well . . . it's . . .'

'Steve!'

The door opened immediately in response to the shout. Craig felt fear in the pit of his stomach.

The other man stood up. 'Well, Mr Hartley, I don't know whether I believe you or not.'

'I assure you . . . If I'd known that you were interested in Okello, Mr . . .?'

'Names don't matter. And I'm not interested in the nigger. But some overseas associates of mine are and they don't like small-timers blundering around in their territory. So here's what you do: you forget everything you know about this Okello. If you don't, I'll have you picked up and brought back here. And you know what that'll mean. Goodbye, Mr Hartley. I hope for your sake we never meet again. Steve, show our guest out.'

Craig made a fresh brew of Kenya coffee. He carried it through to the study and transferred it to the Victorian chased silver pot with the long curved spout. He set the pot carefully on its stand and lit the small spirit burner. He poured the first of several cups and carried it to a low table. Then he stretched himself on the leather chesterfield – to think. He had been thinking all the way home in the cab but that had not been pure, rational thought – the only kind Craig valued. He had been too busy fighting back emotions – anger, indignation and fear – mostly fear. Now he had to take himself in hand, neutralise feelings. Feelings clouded judgement. And Craig needed to evaluate the events of the evening carefully. Calvin Craig never allowed himself to be panicked into action.

Not that he did not take the threat very seriously. Only a fool tangled with the Mafia. He cursed himself for whatever slip-up had enabled *cosa nostra* to make the connection between Calvin Craig and Colin Hartley. But had they made that connection? Throughout the interview he had been addressed as 'Mr Hartley'. What did they really know about him? Craig played over, again and again, the recent conversation. He recalled every word and gesture. They knew that he had been in London making enquiries about Okello. They could only have discovered that by grilling the English private detective he had employed.

The more Craig thought about the events of the previous evening the more they puzzled him. He had deliberately distanced himself from the world of organised crime. But he knew how it worked. Anyone muscling in on the families' operations was not treated to elaborate, theatrical warnings. He simply got a bullet in the head down some deserted alley. New York mafiosi executed contracts for their associates in South America, Europe, Asia without asking questions. So why had he simply been told to stop being a naughty boy? Everything pointed to the fact that the mobster with the

50

sawn-off mandarin moustache regarded Colin Hartley as a small-time crook of little consequence who could be easily scared.

Which left Craig with the question, 'What do I do now?'

He went across to the computer whose grey, mass-produced modernity jarred against its elegant surroundings. He accessed the Ugandan Assignment and surveyed the years of carefully assembled data, the months of planning, the tens of thousands of dollars that had gone into setting up this advanced fee fraud. It was beautiful. Beautiful and intricate, yet so . . . obvious. Like a Bach fugue or a classical scene by Poussin.

The first seeds had been sown in 1973. That was when, with a short-sightedness exceeded only by greed, the OPEC cartel had quadrupled the price of crude oil and plunged the world into hyper-inflation. Craig had been one of the few to see the criminal possibilities of that disaster. It was obvious that the poorer countries would be worst hit. The fragile economies of the Third World would be smashed to pieces. Most ex-colonial territories were still governed by men who had promised to lead their people from enslaved peasanthood to a new life flowing with consumer goods and free education. Encouraged by trade delegations from Washington, Moscow, London, Paris and Peking, they had set about diversifying their economies: building factories and establishing cash-crop farming. For capital investment they had turned to foreign banks and especially to the World Bank and the International Monetary Fund. The 1970s crisis hit them when they were too far along this road to turn back. To meet soaring import costs they borrowed more heavily and pegged the prices of home-produced goods.

It was a mistaken policy, as Craig the economist could have told them. Third World governments should have encouraged food crop farming by allowing producers to charge market prices. They should have closed their borders to expensive imports and made a bid for self-sufficiency. But that would have involved laying their heads on the political chopping block. Their support lay among the swollen urban populations of the new cities – men and women clamouring for white-collar jobs, transistor radios, bicycles, German motor cars and cheap food; men and women whose mass discontent could be fanned into action by rabble-rousers, shouting their mouths off about government corruption.

So they had gone on, plunging like self-deluded lemmings deeper into debt. Between 1977 and 1981 the IMF deficit run up by non oil-producing countries rose from thirty billion to a hundred and ten billion SDRs*

The details rolled up on the screen. Brazil, with an annual inflation rate of over 250 per cent, threatening to lead a Latin-American rebellion and simply refuse to repay international debt. President Reagan warning the world of 'an economic nightmare which could plague generations to come'. And the list of nations which had overrun their credit, together with the extent of their international debts. Nations whose leaders were desperate men, desperate to support their Monopoly-money currencies, desperate to perform economic miracles and so preserve their hold on power. Men who, if offered vast quantities of cheap capital, would grab at the opportunity without asking questions.

Craig polished his glasses and studied the short list of African politicians he had selected a couple of years ago. A short list which had eventually been whittled down to just one name. He checked over the calculations which showed just how much money could be diverted out of the Ugandan Treasury into his own pocket. Ten million dollars.

But it was not the money. He did not need it. It was not even the prospect of months of effort and calculation being thrown away. The truth was that he could not live without

* SDR = Special Drawing Rights, the IMF reserve currency, broadly equivalent to the U.S. dollar.

fraud. He was an addict. Whatever the cost, whatever the danger, whatever the voice of prudence might say, he had to have his regular fix.

When Craig retired to bed shortly before three in the morning he knew that, Mafia or no Mafia, he was not going to abandon the most perfect scam he had ever devised.

Chapter Five

For six months he kept a low profile. As far as any interested party could tell, Colin Hartley lived his conventional and very comfortable Somerset Cove life. Behind the facade Craig was very active and very thorough. He checked and double checked the members of his Ugandan team for any possible connections with major crime syndicates. Hafid, he knew, had twice bolstered his income by acting as a heroin courier. But on the second occasion he had come within a hair's breadth of being caught at Heathrow. The experience had so terrified him that he had broken his connections with the Geneva-based drug cartel that had employed him. As for Kemp, it was difficult to get tabs on all that man's less-than-kosher activities. But Kemp was not a fool and Craig could find no connections between him and the underworld. The lawyers who acted for leading crime bosses were well known. Kemp was not one of them. Any suggestion that he was employed on the wrong side of the tracks would immediately have lost him several wealthy clients for whom he carried out very sensitive deals and negotiations. On balance and after exhaustive investigation Craig decided that the lawyer could be trusted to do his job and keep his mouth shut. The thought of Louise Sondemann having Mafia links was, of course, ludicrous.

Craig was encouraged to discover that he was under surveillance. He soon recognised the three men who, by turns, kept a watch on his house and followed him around. He was encouraged because they provided an easy way of checking on the vigilance of his adversaries. After three weeks the surveillance was called off. But Craig did not drop his guard. Throughout autumn and the Christmas season he made no discernible move which could have indicated that he had not been scared into abandoning his interest in Samuel Okello.

With ten million dollars at stake he could afford to wait.

When, at last, Craig did move he covered his tracks very carefully. In mid-January 1987 he flew to Nairobi. But not directly. He travelled to Rio de Janeiro as Colin Hartley, booked from there to Lisbon on another passport, changed his identity yet again for a flight to Frankfurt and arrived as Calvin Craig in the Kenyan capital.

By then the foundations of the Uganda Assignment had been securely laid. Louise Sondemann was word perfect and, though the Omani had a marked aversion to taking orders, he, too, had mastered his less demanding role. Kemp had made a short visit to the Bahamas where, with the co-operation of an investment consultant he had frequently done business with before, he had set up a brass plate company bearing the impressive title the Arab Overseas Investment Bank.

Craig checked into the Norfolk Hotel, the antiquated establishment close by the university which he preferred to the brash modernity of the more fashionable Hilton or Pan Afric. He went to Nairobi because in ten days Okello would be there to attend a conference for finance ministers from member states of the Organisation of African Unity.

Politically the OAU is a pretty moribund association. Its ideals of black brotherhood have long since been upset by bloody conflicts and savage slanging matches. Even the united stand against the white-dominated south has been undermined by the economic realists of Malawi, Mozambique and Nigeria who put rands above racial indignation. But useful work is still done by non-political agencies which rarely hit the headlines. The finance ministers' gathering is an annual event where the continent's chronic problems are regularly discussed and solutions are occasionally suggested. This year, as Craig knew, Samuel Okello was billed to make a major speech, containing some radical proposals.

Over the next few days Craig studied carefully the timetable and list of delegates for the forthcoming conference, documents he had obtained by posing as a foreign journalist at the government press office. He put through telephone calls to Accra, Lagos and Kinshasa. He made certain detailed arrangements with the head waiter in the grill room at the Nairobi Hilton. On Friday he took a cab to the Muthaiga Country Club.

He sat on the terrace sipping a very dry, pre-lunch sherry and admiring the bougainvillea hedges. He looked beyond the wildly scattered clusters of orange, pink and mauve flowers to the neat lawns and rose beds beyond and thought how unmistakeably colonial it all was, this incredible survival from pre-independence days. Even its membership seemed to have been little affected by the 'wind of change'. Before 1963 this exclusive establishment had been decidedly 'whites only'. Looking around at the other members (Craig enjoyed temporary membership, thanks to a reciprocal arrangement with his own club, the Harvard, in Boston) he could only see three Africans, sitting at a table by themselves. The rest of the clientèle were European diplomats and businessmen, some with their wives, come to enjoy a game of tennis, squash or golf at the nearby course or bring their children for a dip in the pool before taking lunch in the long, panelled dining room.

Craig had chosen his seat carefully. From it he could see a section of the drive and the cars which came and went along it. At twelve minutes past one the black Cadillac with the CD plates made its stately appearance and moved with discreet ostentation towards the clubhouse. Unhurriedly, Craig finished his aperitif. He stood up and strolled through the french windows into the cool interior of the lounge. He was standing by the table in the corner where all the international papers are laid out when Harvey Patterson, the United States Ambassador, entered by the far door. Craig knew that the next few minutes would be vitally important. He felt his heart-beat move into top gear and took a deep breath to calm himself. Over a copy of the *Herald Tribune* he watched the tubby Californian settle his guest, a diminutive Kenyan with spectacles and hair greying at the temples, in an armchair, then move to the bar to order drinks. By the time Patterson had reached the counter, Craig was at his elbow. The ambassador ordered two double scotches.

'It's good to hear a voice from home,' Craig remarked conversationally.

Patterson turned towards the stranger and returned the pleasantry. Then he noticed Craig's tie, as Craig had intended he should.

'A Harvard man, I see.'

Craig nodded and smiled. 'That's right. Class of '52.'

'That's a coincidence, '52 was my year.'

The information was superfluous to Craig, who knew all the details of Patterson's career, during and after university. Craig, had in fact, gone up to Harvard five years after the man he was now drubbing up an acquaintance with.

'That's incredible,' he said. He stepped back a pace and scrutinised the other man. 'You know, I'm sure there's something familiar about you. Of course, time plays some nasty tricks on all of us.'

'Two scotches, Mr Patterson.' The bartender appeared almost as if on cue.

'Patterson! That's it, Harvey Patterson. Stroked the first eight! Majored in oriental languages! You were the brightest man in our year – and I was as jealous as hell! You wouldn't remember me, of course. You stayed on to do research. For me it was the Korean war.' That deft, patriotic touch came to him on the spur of the moment. He liked it. He pulled out a wallet and handed Patterson a card. It read:

> FOX FINANCIAL CONSULTANTS INC
> CALVIN C. CRAIG
> President
> Providence House   New York
> Broad Street   40350

This impressive-sounding address in the heart of the Wall Street area was, in fact, a dingy twentieth-floor transfer office.

'Glad to meet you – again – Mr Craig. What are you drinking? If you're in the money business you must come and meet my guest. He's the chairman of the Standard Bank.'

Craig held up a hand deprecatingly. 'Oh, I mustn't intrude . . .'

'Nonsense. To tell you the truth, yon Mr Gachanja is not the most scintillating of companions – and he plays a terrible round of golf.'

The little charade could not have gone better if Craig had scripted it himself. The old, well-tried logic was inescapable: 'Most successful men are vain. Vain men are easy to con. *Ergo* most successful men are easy to con'.

Matters moved even more satisfactorily over the next couple of hours. Craig kept up a witty flow of conversation into which he casually dropped some pretty important political and commercial names. Patterson, otherwise doomed to a tedious meal with the monosyllabic Gachanja, insisted that Craig join them for lunch. It was only during

58

the fish course (lake tillapia) that Craig 'discovered' the exalted rank of his host and amused the ambassador with his feigned embarrassment.

'Calvin, I'm sure your life is every bit as exciting. In my experience it's you financial wizards behind the scenes who are more important than us front guys, at the end of the day.'

'I have also found that to be true, Harvey.' The little banker turned to Calvin. 'What exactly is it that brings you to Nairobi, Mr Craig? Or is that a dark secret?'

'Not at all, Mr Gachanja. Many ancient societies, including I believe, some African ones, valued the services of someone, usually a woman, called a matchmaker. If you had a daughter you wanted to get off your hands you would consult the matchmaker. She'd find a suitable young man for a bridegroom and act as go-between with the two sets of parents. I look upon myself simply as a financial matchmaker. There are in the world certain substantial would-be investors – individuals, trusts, corporations and so on – looking for worthwhile as well as remunerative ways of employing their capital. There are also many excellent projects looking for funding. It's one of the tasks of my consultancy to arrange suitable marriages.'

Gachanja peered at him. 'You must be a very popular man, Mr Craig. More like Santa Claus than a marriage broker.'

Craig laughed. 'You could be right at that – but only a Santa Claus that gives toys to *good* children. The investors we represent obviously require the most stringent guarantees before lending to a government or corporation.'

The ambassador replenished their wine glasses. 'Would your visit to Nairobi have anything to do with next week's OAU finance ministers' conference?'

'You're very shrewd Harvey. The conference gives me an opportunity to meet several potential clients all in one place. There are so many excellent projects crying out for funding. Sadly there's always a bigger supply of good ideas than funds to finance them. But we do have some clients who have a commitment to Third World development which is more important to them than deriving large income from their investment.' He smiled a sudden, disarming smile. 'But I shouldn't be talking shop on an occasion like this. Harvey, this is a delicious steak. I'd forgotten how good Kenyan beef is.'

The conversation drifted into small talk and Craig was happy to relax and enjoy his meal. He knew that he had already said enough to give his companions plenty to think about. They moved back into the lounge for coffee and at 2.50 p.m. Craig stood up to take his leave.

'Thank you so much, Harvey. This has been really delightful. I do hope you'll give me an opportunity to repay your hospitality before I leave.'

'That's kind of you, Calvin, I'd really enjoy that. I'd certainly like to talk some more about your business activities . . . perhaps suggest one or two people you might contact.'

Craig took out his diary. 'Unfortunately I don't have much time left. Let me see . . . How about dinner on Thursday?'

Harvey shook his head. 'No, I have a reception that evening.'

Craig frowned. 'That's a pity . . . unless. Forgive me for asking, but is your reception the one the President is giving for the members of conference?'

'That's right.'

'Well, I'm going to that. I was going to suggest that we met first for an early dinner. Say . . . 6.30, at my hotel . . . Is that possible?'

Harvey Patterson looked genuinely pleased. He liked this urbane New Englander and if he really was in a position to bring private investment into Kenya he was certainly a man to be cultivated. 'That sounds OK. Of course, I'll have to get my secretary to confirm with you. How about a game of golf? You do play, don't you? I have a round booked every Friday at 11.00.'

Craig knew all about the ambassador's golfing activities. He had checked the bookings in the club register himself when he called three days before on the pretext of enquiring about temporary membership. He said, 'I'm afraid you'll think me a terrible heretic, Harvey, but I agree with Mark Twain: "Golf is the best way of spoiling a perfectly good walk".'

They all laughed. They shook hands. Craig strode from the room, head bent slightly forward, long arms flapping, looking like a genial, disoriented crane.

'Come in, Sue. Come in.' The Ugandan Minister of Finance opened the door in person. 'Are you here to wish me good luck?'

Susan Hayward gave him a little half frown as she passed him and entered the suite reserved for Okello and his staff. 'Not luck, Sam. Luck has nothing to do with it. I've come to let you know I shall be praying for you. Is the speech ready?'

'I hope so.' He sank heavily into one of the Hilton's cavernous armchairs and motioned Sue to another. 'I was up half the night – adjusting, polishing, honing.'

'Don't worry. Everything's going to be fine. I know it. We just have to have that hospital.'

'The hospital will come up later, at tomorrow's private meeting, as I explained. That's where you have to do your stuff. First I have to make an impression on the whole conference this morning,' he glanced at her over his reading glasses, 'With my UFO.'

She laughed 'UFO? Unidentified Flying Object?'

Okello was pleased with her spontaneous response. It was exactly the kind of reaction he wanted from the delegates – he had to make them sit up and take notice. 'Well, it's certainly going to have the impact of a flying saucer when some of the western governments get a sight of it. Actually the letters stand for United Funding Operation.'

'That sounds like something much too complicated for me to understand.'

Okello carried out minute adjustments to his spotted pocket handkerchief. 'It's really a very simple idea. It's based on the rule that in the world of international finance "big is beautiful". Look.' He stood up and began pacing to and fro. 'When Peru, or Sudan or any other poor country defaults on interest payments what happens? Leading banks simply withdraw support. Then, heaven help them. But when Brazil, with an annual interest bill of $15billion, or Mexico or Argentina threatens a moratorium on repayments, that's a different matter altogether. It scares the pants off international bankers. Conferences are convened, experts summoned and ways are found to aid the economic recovery of these major borrowers. Well, my UFO is simply a scheme for drawing African states together into a powerful consortium, one which can't be pushed around by the bully boys of international finance. It's about time the "have nots" began acting together to force the "haves" to support recovery programmes initiated *within* Africa and not imposed from without.'

'Bravo!' Sue clapped. 'If you sock it to them like that at the conference, they'll have to agree with you.'

'I wish it was as simple as that. These African statesmen are a bunch of little Englanders.'

Sue wanted to giggle at the odd picture that conjured up. But Okello was deadly serious and she stifled her response.

'No. This is a big test for me, Sue. It's going to take all my powers.' He smiled down at her suddenly. 'My powers and your prayers.' He glanced at his large gold wristwatch. 'It's time we were going. The car will be here.'

'Car!' Sue could not contain her laughter this time. 'It's only a hundred yards to the conference place. I'll walk over and see you afterwards.'

Minutes later she took her place in the public gallery and gazed down into the main hall of the Jomo Kenyatta Centre where the delegates were slowly gathering. She closed her eyes to pray. 'Lord, give Sam the right words. So much depends on him.'

Three rows behind her Calvin Craig sat with no less expectancy. But he was not praying.

'Members will be familiar with this special report recently drawn up for the World Bank.' Okello waved a slim pamphlet in a wide, exaggerated, theatrical gesture. 'I quote from it. "The external resource position of sub-Saharan Africa is likely to become disastrous in the next few years." The report points out that our countries need an *increase* in foreign aid of at least two billion dollars a year whereas capital inflow from private and IMF sources is actually estimated to *decline* from eleven billion to five billion by 1989.' He paused for the figures to sink in.

Okello was in full flood. He had risen to speak at 10.30 am. It was now 11.07. He had given his audience a tirade of black nationalism, larded with humour and packed with statistics. Now he was coming to his main point, his voice urgent with passion. It was vital to hold their interest now.

'Of course, the report is full of "suggestions" about how to reverse this trend. But when we look closely at these "suggestions" what do we find? We find that they're not suggestions at all; they are orders. "African governments *must* formulate national rehabilitation programmes. Such programmes *must* be closely monitored by the donor countries. Governments *must* abandon new projects and

63

concentrate on strengthening their existing infrastructures." Mr Chairman, I do not approve of these "musts". I do not enjoy being treated like a schoolboy and told that if I behave myself I may be given some sweets.'

Okello took a long drink of water and gazed once more around the chamber to satisfy himself that he had the attention of his audience.

'Members are, as I say, familiar with this document and its insulting demands. What members may not know is that even now a secret meeting of the Group of Ten is taking place in Paris. This rather sinister cabal of the leading western industrial nations has been called to consider ways of disciplining IMF debtor nations. You see, the schoolmaster not only holds sweets in one hand, he wields a cane in the other. And we are the naughty schoolboys who are threatened with six of the best if we disobey our betters.

'Well, Mr Chairman, the time has come for a classroom revolt. We have to make it clear to the rich, industrial nations that we will not dance to their tune any longer. We have done so for too long and we have found it a discordant, uneven measure which simply lurches from one crisis to another. Mr Chairman, these "big brothers" of international finance do *not* know what is best for Africa. It is the delegates seated in this chamber who know that. And if we take common action – *action*, Mr Chairman, not words but action – we can attract investment to this continent on *our* terms. African problems, Mr Chairman, have *African* solutions. That is why I suggest that we launch into the deep space of international finance our own UFO.'

Okello gazed around at rows of amused, puzzled faces. He had the audience in his hand and he pressed home his advantage. Swiftly, he outlined the main points of his United Funding Operation. With all the rhetoric at his command, he commended its urgent acceptance. He asked for the setting up of a committee with himself as chairman which would explore the UFO in detail and select some projects for immediate support.

He sat down to enthusiastic applause. Then came the debate. Various speakers endorsed his general thesis. But gradually the voices of caution began to make themselves heard. Urgent as the financial situation undoubtedly was, they argued, the Ugandan delegate's proposals raised issues of national sovereignty which could not be hastily resolved. A Malawi representative got a laugh when he cynically observed that after Mr Okello had solved his own country's one hundred per cent inflation his views on African economics might carry more weight. When it came to the vote the conference narrowly passed an amendment calling for the referral back of the UFO scheme to member governments.

From the gallery Craig watched, smiling, as Okello strode angrily from the chamber.

'Does that mean they'll discuss the project again at next year's conference?' Sue Hayward was not enjoying her lunch. Okello was silent with anger.

'It means,' the minister gulped down his second scotch, 'that the project has been blocked by fools who see no further than the end of their nose.'

They sat in silence while a red-jacketed waiter fussed around serving food from a trolley. Sue looked around the grill room at the throng of African politicians and businessmen attacking their expense-account steaks and imported wine with obvious relish. She thought of the children with distended stomachs and the walking skeletons which confronted her every time she drove into the remote regions to conduct a local clinic.

'But the hospital idea doesn't have to be abandoned, does it?'

Okello shrugged. 'Tomorrow's meeting is still on. Seven or eight delegates have promised to come. But without any organisation to arrange the funding . . .'

65

'Perhaps you ought to put up a less expensive proposal.'
She had thought a great deal about Mike Summers'
comments. 'We don't need such a prestigious scheme.
We could do a lot with a fraction of the money a big
hospital would cost.'

'You're wrong, Sue!' He kept his voice low but the way
he glared at her and struck the table with the flat of
his hand showed the intensity of his feelings. 'All you
missionaries understand is quiet, humble, steady labour
for the glory of God. It doesn't matter if what you do
goes unnoticed. Politics is very different. The good I
do must be seen – by the people of Uganda, by other
African statesmen, by foreign bankers, businessmen and
governments. We *do* need a prestigious scheme. Rich
nations and individuals will not channel investment where
it's most needed unless we catch their imagination. To do
that we need big ideas and we need to shout them from the
rooftops.'

'So, if the OAU won't sponsor some grandiose hospital
project the only alternative is nothing?' Sue's temper
fought against the tight rein she tried to keep it on. 'I
may be only a simple missionary but that really doesn't
seem to make much sense. If tomorrow's meeting is going
to be just so much hot air then the sooner I start back to
Soroti and get on with my quiet, humble labour for the
glory of God, the better.'

Okello stared across the table with an expression Sue
had never seen before. 'I have made the arrangements for
the meeting and you will be there to play your part, as we
agreed. If you fail to do so it will not be Soroti you return
to. You will be declared an undesirable alien and will find
yourself on the first London flight out of Kampala.'

From a nearby table in the Hilton's grill room Craig
watched, fascinated, as Okello's companion rose from her
seat and walked away with brisk, agitated movements.
Who was this woman? He had noticed her three or four

66

times in the minister's company over the last couple of days. Unlikely that she was a mistress. Not if Alison Leggat was Okello's kind of woman. Yet there was obviously some kind of bond between them. Craig made a note that she might be useful. His Nigerian guest said something and Craig came out of his reverie with a smiled apology.

He had booked this central table in the Hilton's circular restaurant because he wanted to be seen. Seen lunching or dining with important delegates. Today it was the Nigerian Finance Minister. Last night it had been two senior officials of the Bank of Zaire. This evening it would be the Deputy Prime Minister of Ghana. It had been easy to set up these informal meetings over the previous months. No prominent African politician turned down an invitation which emanated from Fox Financial Consultants, an obviously important international credit company operating out of the very commercial heart of New York. At these little parties Craig discoursed knowledgeably on the needs of sub-Saharan Africa. He alluded to the vast private funds at his disposal.

He was not touting for business. His sole object was to be noticed by Samuel Okello. It was vitally important that the Ugandan should come to him. Should actually ask to take the bait. So far Craig had failed.

It was the third day of the conference. A dozen or so delegates had introduced themselves to Craig and Craig had noted their addresses in his diary, promising to call on them during his 'next African tour.' But Okello seemed oblivious to his existence and Craig was beginning to worry. It was time for Plan B.

Chapter Six

Plan B was to have himself introduced to Okello at the President's reception. That was why Craig had told Patterson he would be there. The only snag was, he had no invitation.

He sat in his hotel room, looking out at the angular, functional buildings of the university and brooded over the problem.

He unfolded his legs and emerged from the deep armchair like a hermit crab sidling out of its borrowed shell. From a file on the dressing table he extracted the notes he had made during his earlier visit to Nairobi on the security arrangements for the reception:

1. President Moi has three secretaries.
2. Invitations to state functions issued by third secretary, Mrs Mkuthe.
3. Invitations printed by government printer. Standard format used.
4. Invitations unlikely to be checked at main gate of State House.
5. Invitations checked against list in main hall.

Clearly there was no way in without the appropriate piece of embossed card. That was a small matter for a man of Craig's resourcefulness.

He crossed to the bedside cabinet, picked up the telephone directory, found the number he wanted and dialled it straight away.

To the switchboard operator at the President's Office he

said 'Put me through to Mrs Mkuthe, please.'

The line gave a few clicks.

'Secretarial office, Mary Mkuthe speaking.'

'Mary, hi! Sam Freeman, US Embassy. How you doing? Listen, Mary, I've run into a little problem here. The President's reception on Wednesday? Well, I look after the ambassador's social engagements and, well, the truth is I went and mislaid the invitation. I'm going to get my ass kicked if I don't come up with another one.'

'Would you like me to send you another, Mr Freeman?'

'Well, I sure hate to put you to all that trouble but it would certainly save my hide.'

'Very well, Mr Freeman. I'll see to it right away.'

'Well, I sure do appreciate that. Look, to save you bother why don't I come by and collect it?'

'All right, Mr Freeman, I'll send it down to the front desk.'

'Why, thank you, Mary. You've got me out of a real mess.'

'Not at all, Mr Freeman. Goodbye.'

There was a click and the line went dead.

Okello's meeting to float the hospital project was a disaster. By 4.30 pm three people had cried off and two others simply failed to turn up. The rough ride given to the United Funding Operation resolution in open assembly had convinced them that it would be politically inexpedient to associate themselves too closely with the Ugandan representative. Okello and Dr Hayward found themselves presenting their great dream to a senior delegate from Kenya (he was there out of politeness as part of the 'home' team) another from Tanzania and a Ghanaian who kept looking at his watch. There were few questions and the meeting broke up at 5.55 pm ostensibly because everyone was anxious to prepare for the President's reception. Okello returned to the hotel in angry, embarrassed, brooding silence – and stayed there.

Craig had booked a private room for his early dinner with the US ambassador rather than entertain him in the Norfolk's near-deserted, large dining saloon. During the meal Patterson talked enthusiastically about a number of projects the Kenya government had in hand for which they were actively seeking finance. Craig made several notes on his pocket pad.

'I can't follow these up this trip, Harvey. I really do have to go back to the States tomorrow. But I'll surely look very carefully at anything that has the endorsement of your recommendation. Have the ministers concerned send me the details in New York and I'll see how FFC can help.'

After dinner the two men were driven to State House in the black Cadillac with the stars and stripes fluttering from its offside front wing. They were accompanied by a burly young man called Svenson who was an aide or bodyguard or, perhaps both. The car turned in at the open gateway of the presidential residence and was waved on by a policeman who saw the pennant and did not trouble to check the licence plate.

Craig fingered the invitation in his inside coat pocket and tried not to show his nervousness as he kept up the flow of conversation with his companion.

The Cadillac came to rest before the floodlit front of the mock-Georgian building, beneath an impressive *porte cochère*. The door was opened by an attendant in national dress – a long white robe bisected by a sash in the Kenyan colours of red, green and black. Craig followed Patterson up the broad flight of carpeted steps into the vestibule.

Here they joined a short queue of guests making their way past a table where two security staff were checking invitations against a list. Harvey was still chattering away and it was not until they were about fourth in line that Craig realised, with a sudden shock, what the guards were doing. They were passing the backs of the invitations under an ultra violet beam. Each card obviously had an otherwise invisible number which was supposed to tally with a number on the master list.

Before Craig could take in the implications of this Svenson had proferred Patterson's invitation.

'The Ambassador of the United States of America,' he said portentously.

One security man found Harvey's name on the list. The other scrutinised the card and read off the number. His colleague looked up, puzzled.

'Say that again.'

The other man repeated the number.

'It doesn't check.'

'Whadya mean, it doesn't check?' Svenson glowered at the man behind the desk. 'This is the Ambassador of the United States. Don't you recognise him?'

Craig knew what had happened. As a result of his call to Mary Mkuthe the ambassador's original number had been cancelled. The secret code on the guard's list was the one on the card that Craig now held in his hand.

The security man winced his embarrassment. 'I'm sorry, sir. Please lower your voice. I'll have to ask about this.'

'Ask nothing!' The young man showed all the belligerence of an American footballer. 'Do you wanna create an international incident?'

At this point a State House official, attracted by the small crowd of distinguished guests now gathered round the desk, hurried up for a quick consultation with his minions. He took the invitation and handed it back to Svenson. He smiled ingratiatingly at Patterson.

'Your Excellency, please accept my apologies. There appears to have been some silly mix-up . . .'

To the security men he said, 'Hurry up. You're keeping guests waiting.'

Craig grabbed his chance. He waved his invitation and muttered his name. One guard took it, put it through the machine and quickly called the number. The other ran his finger down the list. He could not find the name 'Craig' but there was no way he was going to admit it and risk another public dressing down. 'OK' he said. Craig calmly took the card back and followed Patterson up the staircase to the presentation area. Only when he reached the half-landing did he allow himself to dab his brow with his pocket handkerchief.

As they shook hands with President Moi, Patterson gave Craig an elaborate build-up as a 'leading US financier' and a 'great friend of Africa'. Then he led Calvin into the throng and introduced him to some of the other guests.

Craig mingled. All the time he kept a lookout for Okello but the evening wore on and there was no sign of the big Ugandan.

He did hear the minister's name mentioned once. It was while he was at the buffet table.

'I was glad to see that Okello fellow taken down a peg or two this morning.' The speaker was a tall West African in tribal costume.

'Yes,' his companion agreed. 'I think he rather fancies himself as some kind of pan-African statesman, a re-incarnated Nkrumah.'

The two men piled their plates and merged back into the crowd.

Craig swore under his breath. If Okello had suffered some kind of public humiliation during the conference that could well explain his absence from the party. If he was keeping a low profile he would probably not be in the mood for planning a large scheme. Damn the man! Why did he have to choose this moment to blot his copybook?

Craig left the reception early. He returned to his hotel, had several drinks in the bar and went to bed. So much for Plan B.

Before breakfast Craig was in the foyer of the Hilton Hotel. He had one chance left. The conference was due to end at noon. Already piles of baggage indicated that some delegates were leaving early. He went up to a bored reception clerk, waiting to go off duty. Money changed hands. Craig left with the information he wanted.

Later that morning Sue Hayward hurried down the steps of the hotel. She had some important shopping to do before she left Nairobi.

She walked purposefully although the heat of the equatorial sun, trapped and intensified by buildings and pavements, was stifling. A couple of blocks brought her to the Keswick Christian Bookshop and she went straight in. She was browsing through some of the latest religious paperbacks when she heard her name spoken diffidently in a soft American accent.

'Dr Hayward? It *is* Dr Hayward, isn't it?'

She looked up and saw a tall, bespectacled man looking at her across the bookstock.

'That's right. Have we met? I don't seem . . .'

'Oh, do excuse me. There's absolutely no reason why you should remember me. I was in Uganda a couple of years ago with a small delegation visiting with some of our American mission stations. We called in briefly at Soroti and saw something of the marvellous work you're doing there. I do hope you don't think it presumptuous of me to accost you like this.'

Sue smiled. There was something comic and rather sweet about this gangling American with his air of old world courtesy. 'Not at all. I presume you are involved with the Baptist Mission. They're good friends of ours. Who was it who brought you over to see us?'

There was a sudden clatter of falling books on the other side of the stack.

'Oh, how clumsy of me. I'm afraid I'm so short sighted . . .' The man bent down and disappeared from sight.

Sue went round and helped him pick up the books. The man was profuse in his thanks.

'Say, I don't suppose you'd be free for half an hour or so would you. I'd count it a great honour if you would let me buy you a cup of coffee. Our church members back home would just love to hear more about your work.'

Sue looked at her watch. 'Well . . . Oh yes, why not. I'd love a coffee. Thank you.'

A few minutes later they were sitting at a shaded table in the Thorn Tree, the New Stanley Hotel's pavement café, Nairobi's most famous meeting place.

When the pot and cups had been brought Craig said, 'Will you be mother? I think that's what you English say, isn't it?'

Sue laughed. 'Yes, that's right, Mr Craig.'

'Oh please call me Calvin. It's rather a presumptious name but it is the one I was christened with.'

'Oh, but I thought Baptists weren't christened as babies.'

Craig thought hard. 'Just a little cream please, and no sugar. Well, Sue, it didn't take you long to sniff out my guilty secret. You see I was brought up a good Episcopalian but I guess I backslid. I became a Baptist when I was about twenty.'

'I see, and you work for the missionary society?'

'Oh gracious, no. I'm just a humble businessman. Allow me.' He took out one of his FFC cards and handed it to her. He had earlier scrawled the words 'Norfolk Hotel' on the back.

'Fox Financial Consultants – how very impressive.'

'We have a lot of interests in Africa, finding backing for development projects, that sort of thing, and we make certain charitable donations. Our founder, Nathaniel Fox – long since gone to his glory.' Craig noticed the sudden

74

smile on his companion's lips and wondered whether he had gone slightly over the top. He hurried on. 'He was one of the founders of the American Baptist Mission and we administer certain bequests he made to the society.'

'And that's what brings you here now, I suppose?'

'Not principally. There's been a conference of African finance ministers meeting in Nairobi this week. My company has business with some of them. By coming here I can kill several birds with one stone.'

'That all sounds very interesting . . . Calvin.'

'Not nearly as interesting as the work you're doing in Uganda, Sue. Now, tell me, how are things going here? I was so saddened by what I saw there – thousands of lives still badly scarred by that satanic Idi Amin and people dying every day in the continued fighting. Has Museveni's government brought real peace and put an end to all the suffering?'

Sue quickly got into her stride on her favourite subject and eventually it was Craig who brought the conversation to a close.

'Sue, this has been great, really great, but I guess you've got to get packed ready for your flight.'

They rose and shook hands.

'It's been lovely to meet you, Calvin.'

'The honour has been all mine, Sue. Goodbye, and God bless you in your great work. If there's ever anything a mere businessman can do, you have my card. Please don't hesitate to call me.' He made a quick, stooping bow and turned to steer a stumbling path among the tables.

Back in his hotel room Craig put a tape of Mozart's 'Jupiter' symphony on his portable cassette player, lay down on the bed and closed his eyes.

When the final chords had died away he got up, packed and went through to the dining room for lunch.

He prodded at his food without enthusiasm. It had been a wasted week, wasted and expensive. Now he would have to go back to the drawing board. Find some other way of making contact with Okello. He pushed his unfinished salad away.

A porter made his way among the tables ringing a bicycle bell attached to a pole. On top of the pole was a small blackboard. Craig saw his name scrawled on it. He called the man over.

'Mr Craig?'

'Yes.'

'Telephone call, bwana.'

At the desk he picked up the receiver.

'Craig here.'

'Oh, Mr Craig. I'm so glad I caught you. This is Sue Hayward. We met this morning.'

Craig quickly slipped back into the mannerisms of the courteous southern Baptist.

'Why, surely, Sue. Good to hear from you so soon. How may I be of service?'

'Well, I was just wondering, since you're in East Africa, whether you'd like to come to Soroti for a proper look at the hospital.'

'Why that's mighty kind, Sue, and there's nothing I'd like more, but I really do have to go back home today.'

There was a silence at the other end of the line.

'Hello, Sue, hello. Are you still there?'

'Oh, yes . . . Look, this is a bit awkward. The truth is, it's not just me who'd like to see you. I mentioned your name to Mr Okello – he's the Ugandan Minister of Finance. He said if you were coming through Kampala, he'd be pleased to meet you. I think he has some business he wants to discuss with you.'

Chapter Seven

Craig made the short flight on Saturday morning. He felt good. He felt even better when he discovered an official car waiting to convey him from Entebbe airport to his hotel in the centre of Kampala.

As they sped along the road, he noticed with detached interest the contrast between Uganda and the neighbouring country he had just left. Bands of soldiers in combat gear were much in evidence and the car was waved through two checkpoints where other vehicles were being detained. Twice Craig saw clusters of charred stakes amid the lush green foliage and knew them for the remains of villages. The streets of the capital were awash with aimless, raggedly-dressed men and boys. The humid air itself seemed heavy with insecurity and fear.

The shower in his hotel room did not work but the lunch was edible. The car returned at 2.30 p.m. to take him to the Government Buildings. As it passed the security check point and the twelve foot wire fence Craig thought, 'This is it. Everything – all the man hours of research and planning; all the expense; the careful selecting of personnel; risking the fatal displeasure of the Mafia – everything is riding on the next hour. Blow this meeting and it will all be wasted.'

His appointment was for 2.45. At three o'clock precisely a secretary put down the phone in the outer office and said, 'Mr Okello will see you now.' Craig smiled and said, 'Thank you' and thought, 'That's the last time you keep me waiting, Mr Okello.'

The minister stood up behind his large desk and leaned across to shake hands. 'Very good of you to come, Mr Craig. Please sit down.'

'It's a pleasure to meet you, sir. I hope I may be able to be of service.'

'Well, as to that, Mr Craig, I'm not sure. It was Dr Hayward, a very dear friend, who suggested that we should meet but I'm afraid I know very little about your company. What exactly do you do?'

Craig gave a slight sigh, as of one about to reiterate an oft-repeated prospectus. 'FFC is a well-established general commercial consultancy but we have in recent years established particular expertise in handling private investment to the developing world. There are certain institutions and individuals who regard themselves as having a moral responsibility to invest part of their funds on the other side of what the Brandt Report called "the North-South divide".'

He took off his spectacles and polished them slowly with a pocket handkerchief, gazing short-sightedly up at the ceiling as he continued. 'These individuals and institutions are not – and I must make this clear – in any way charitable benefactors. They are businessmen looking for a return on investment. However, they are prepared to take a smaller return on their capital than they could obtain elsewhere in order to assist worthwhile projects that might otherwise find difficulty in attracting development finance. FFC has been asked by an increasing number of potential lenders to identify such projects, and negotiate loans.'

'I see.' Okello's face was expressionless. 'Tell me, Mr Craig, why haven't I heard of FFC before?'

'We preserve a strict confidentiality over all negotiations, whether or not they come to fruition. Quite apart from anything else, the funds available, looked at in terms of global finance, are minute. If we were to advertise our services we would be inundated with requests we simply could not handle. Part of FFC's contribution to what we call in the house "Development Funding Programmes" is to charge very modest fees. If we had to take on more staff to deal with enquiries and evaluate projects we'd be forced to become ruthlessly commercial. We think we do a better job by keeping a low profile.'

'How do your activities fit in with loan schemes operated by IMF, World Bank and commercial banks?'

Craig chuckled. 'I guess you could say it fits into the corners those establishments don't reach. Major financial institutions are concerned with assisting developing countries through fiscal policy, trade balance adjustments and the like. They rarely get involved with specific schemes. In my experience, where they do they usually want to exercise too much control – but that's a personal opinion and quite out of order. The lenders we represent do not see themselves in the role of financial advisers. Once we recommend a specific project to a client he will satisfy himself that it is worthwhile and viable and that the loan details we establish are acceptable. Beyond that he does not wish to interfere with the company or government in charge of that project.'

'But your clients will require collateral before they agree to make substantial loans. I imagine that for some countries, already bled white by high western interest rates, this could be a problem.'

Craig thought, 'It's almost as though he learned the script.' He said, 'That's where we made a major breakthrough. We have developed a means of collateral security instrument programming. That sounds complicated but, in simple terms, it involves a major finance house or consortium acting as guarantor and taking over the repayment of principal and interest.'

Okello looked puzzled. Like a donkey staring at the dangled carrot, unable to believe his luck. 'Let me see if I understand you correctly, Mr Craig. Are you saying that if a country, like Uganda for example, negotiated a loan from one of your clients, someone else would actually repay that loan?'

'In effect, yes. But I must make it clear that we look to borrowers to provide their own security wherever possible. Our CSI programmes are only arranged to assist clients who are worthy of assistance but whose credit rating, for one reason or another is not high. You will realise that such clients have to be chosen with extreme care. We are talking about the movement of extremely large sums of money.'

The minister frowned his disbelief. Craig knew exactly what he was thinking. It all sounded too good to be true. No one simply gave away millions of dollars – however deserving the cause.

'Exactly how does this CSI programming work?'

Craig shook his head with a rueful smile. 'I'm afraid, Mr Okello, that we only release details in strictest confidence to *bona fide* applicants. I'm sure you will appreciate that we have to be very discreet in these matters. We have a document setting out the programming arrangements in full. This is released at the appropriate time so that potential clients can study it thoroughly before entering a commitment. To be frank, Mr Okello, I doubt whether we shall be setting up any more CSI programmes in the short term.'

'Oh, is the scheme running into difficulties?'

Craig laughed. 'On the contrary, Sir. Not unless you call over-popularity a difficulty. No, it's just that most available funding is subscribed for the next year or so. We don't like to commit ourselves too far ahead. We prefer to set up transactions quickly; to get the money moving and working. We find protracted negotiations help nobody. When a lender comes to us it's because he has money available *now*. He expects us to recommend quickly a project worthy of his support. He's not going to put his capital on ice for two or three years waiting for the right investment to turn up.'

Okello sat back thoughtfully and his chair creaked its protest. 'Can I offer you tea, Mr Craig?'

The American thanked him and his host took time over telephoning his secretary and ordering the refreshment. For the next few minutes the two men exchanged small talk.

It was only after the secretary had appeared, dispensed tea from a silver pot into bone china cups, and left the room that Okello said, 'We do have a project here in Uganda that might appeal to one of your clients.'

Craig expressed polite interest and the minister handed him one of the medical centre brochures.

'This is a project very dear to my heart and to Dr Hayward's,' Okello explained. 'I'm sure I don't need to tell you how important the provision of proper medical treatment is in this continent.'

For the next half hour he talked enthusiastically about the proposed centre while Craig examined the glossy prospectus and asked occasional questions.

Eventually he said, 'Minister, this is obviously an impressive and well-thought-out scheme. What are your cost projections?'

'A realistic estimate based on current inflation rates and assuming the work can be completed within three years is, we believe, one hundred and twenty-five million dollars. That would include the hospital, equipment, staff and the improved outlying clinic facilities.'

'Mr Okello, I'm impressed. Is this a project that you would like FFC to seek backing for?'

'Well, Mr Craig, my government does, of course, have other sources of potential finance but I certainly see no harm in your drawing this to the attention of any client seeking an opportunity to do something that will save the lives and improve the health of millions of Africans. When

81

you go to Soroti you'll see for yourself just how desperate the plight of our people is at present. The new medical centre is a top priority for my government.'

'I'm certainly looking forward to my visit to Soroti.'

Okello stood up. 'They're expecting you about midday tomorrow. I'll send a car to your hotel around 10.30. It will take you to the Air Force base where a helicopter will be waiting. Goodbye, Mr Craig. Perhaps we shall be doing business together before long.'

Craig was apprehensive about the Soroti trip. It was something he had not planned but could not avoid. He knew it would be hard to sustain the role of a born-again Christian businessman, when he had not prepared for it by studying the appropriate jargon and thought patterns. He also knew his stay at the mission would be uncomfortable. He had a vision of hard beds draped with mosquito nets, 'good plain food', rooms without air-conditioning, and no alcohol.

The reality was worse than he had feared. Sue Hayward welcomed him warmly and did everything possible to make him comfortable. She had put a vase of wild orchids in the guest room which was a small, whitewashed cube whose only other decoration was an old print of Holman Hunt's 'The Light of the World'. The bed *was* hard and creaked at the slightest movement of its occupant. And the food *was* atrocious, consisting mostly of indifferently cooked meat or fish accompanied by a tasteless maize mash known as *posho*.

But what was worse than all this was the attitude of one of Sue's colleagues. The other members of the mission team were pleasant and friendly. Dr Mike Summers struck Craig as a boorish young man with few manners. He regarded the guest with suspicion bordering on hostility, and had obviously set his mind against Okello's medical centre project. Mealtime conversation consisted largely

82

of a catechism of aggressively-phrased questions about politics and 'high finance' directed by Mike to the visitor.

'Don't you think it's irresponsible to encourage African governments to lavish money on prestige projects, Calvin?'

It was Sunday evening and they were having macaroni-cheese and baked beans as a special treat.

'It seems to me that a man in your position could have some influence – tell Museveni that foreign money should be spent on things that really matter like restocking farms and converting land from cash crops to food that the people actually eat.'

'I think such suggestions are more likely to carry weight coming from people like you, who have a real stake in the country. I know, for example, that Mr Okello thinks very highly of this little lady.'

Sue smiled wanly. 'It's not really like that, Calvin. European missionaries, doctors, engineers, agricultural advisers – we're all only here on sufferance. We have to be very careful what we say and do. Only a few days ago Sam Okello warned me to tow the line or be thrown out of the country.'

Mike nodded. 'We got ourselves into hot water last month for presuming to offer advice on the situation in Karamoja.'

'That's the north-eastern province, isn't it? Bordering Kenya and Sudan?'

'Yes, the people who live there are nomads, fine, tall, cattle folk with a way of life all their own. They've managed to keep out of most of the horrors of the last fifteen years, but they've had other problems. They've suffered terribly from successive droughts. Their herds have been decimated. The traditional way of making up cattle losses is to go on a raid and steal someone else's. It's been going on for centuries. But now there's a difference.'

'They've been sucked into the war and their suffering is absolutely appalling.' Sue took up the story. 'Karamoja is the last refuge of the deserted rebels. Guerillas fleeing from the NPA have set up camps and recruited the local people. They issue them with guns and help them in cattle raids. They promise them a brighter future once the government is overthrown.'

'Of course, it's their Libyan paymasters who are keeping the conflict going.'

Sue glared across the table. 'We don't know that, Mike.'

Her colleague smiled back. 'Sue, you're so innocent. Libyan "advisers" have been captured and there's a constant flow of arms and ammunition across the Sudanese border.'

'Well, anyway,' Sue continued, 'people up there are dying like flies. Those who aren't murdered or shot down in the fighting are killed by starvation, disease and gangrene. We made a report and sent it to Kampala. We urged the government to offer a truce and set up medical stations to treat the sick and wounded. Most of the Karamojong don't want to fight. Give them half a chance and they'd lay down their arms.'

'And what happened?'

'What happened, Calvin?' Mike's voice was hard-edged with bitterness. 'We were ordered to stop our own work in the area and we were accused of being a "disturbing influence".'

'So you've had to abandon the Karamojong?'

Mike laughed. 'No way. If we'd obeyed every order given us by different governments over the last fifteen years we'd have ended up sitting on our backsides doing nothing. No, we still make our regular trips to Karamoja. Tomorrow you'll be able to see the situation there for yourself.'

Craig did not like the sound of that.

Sue said, 'Oh, but I thought Calvin would prefer to rest tomorrow.'

'Rest?' Mike gave a scornful laugh. 'He hasn't come here

to rest, have you Calvin? He's come to see what really goes on. Well, you'll see that in Kaabong. Sue and I are going up there for our monthly clinic.'

Craig searched his mind for some excuse.

Sue said, 'Calvin, you do whatever you want. Don't mind Mike. He's in one of his angry young man moods. As a matter of fact, I was on the phone to Geoff and Kate Vickers of the Baptist mission at Magoro. I mentioned you and your church connections and they said they'd love to meet you and hear all the latest news from the church back home. They might drive over tomorrow.'

Craig decided that the frying-pan was marginally more comfortable than the fire. 'I guess Mike's right. I'd sure hate to lose the opportunity of seeing your work among the Karamojong.'

The next day was sheer hell.

It started at 3.00 a.m. Craig was roused with disgustingly strong tea laced with condensed milk. He helped to stuff boxes and bundles into the back of a Land Rover. Then he was jammed onto the front seat between Mike and Sue. Mike recited a prayer before starting the engine. Over the next three hours, as the aged vehicle shuddered and bumped its way over atrocious roads, Craig hoped that the God these people believed in was awake and listening.

The sun came up eventually over a barren, brown land. Soon afterwards they stopped in a place that seemed no more remarkable than the hundreds of empty square miles they had already passed through. Nearby was a large village of oblong, mud-plastered huts, and a wide *donga* with a trickle of water in the bottom around which a herd of scrawny, humped cattle were clustered.

The entire population turned out in welcome and were soon participants in what was obviously a well-established ritual. The first thing to be unloaded was an old, patched tent. When this had been set up Craig lent a hand carrying tables, chairs and boxes into the shade. Then, back already aching, he stepped outside the tent and received a shock. Whichever way he looked the plain was speckled with people. It was as though they had popped out of the earth. There were hundreds of them – men, women and children, old and young, some hobbling on makeshift crutches, some half carried by their companions – all converging on the clinic.

'No room for spectators, Calvin.' Mike thrust into his hand a bundle of old dressings, filthy with dirt and congealed blood. 'Start a fire and burn these.' Craig was already worn out. He had been deprived of sleep and subjected to unfamiliar physical exertion. Through it all he had had to keep up the pretence of being an enthusiastic Christian companion. Craig could not afford to let the mask slip. Even amidst the frantic activity of the next few hours Mike Summers kept him under scrutiny. And the American had little time to concentrate on creating the right impression. As the doctors and their two African assistants examined, treated and recorded, he was kept busy fetching, carrying, ladling medicine down the throats of those too weak to hold a spoon, gripping the skeletal arms of screaming children so that the missionaries could inject them. More than once the sights and smells almost made him retch.

It was the children who really got to him. He lifted one boy down from the examining table – pathetically light, his stomach horribly distended, flies clustered round the eyes set deep in their cavernous sockets. He looked like a frail two-year-old.

'That child is seven,' Sue said, pausing briefly to push the hair out of her eyes. 'It's a miracle he's alive at all. He's suffered from malnutrition ever since he was born.'

Craig saw another baby brought in wrapped tightly in blanketing. He took the inert form and unravelled it. The drawn, tiny features were those of an emaciated old woman. He handed the little girl gingerly to Mike. The doctor made a brief examination, shook his head and moved on to the next case. The mother received the lifeless form back with no show of emotion. She simply left the tent and set out on the long journey back to her village.

There was no end to it. All five of them worked without stopping for rest or food. They drank lukewarm orange squash from large plastic containers and sweated out as much liquid as they took in. Patients were dealt with quickly and efficiently whether they needed bandages, medication or minor surgery. Yet the queue outside the tent never shortened.

Even the approach of night did nothing to diminish the pathetic determination of the Karamojong to be treated. Going across to the Land Rover for another box of swabs Craig saw little beacons of light against the rapidly darkening sky. They were the fires lit by the ever-patient waiters.

Craig stumbled his way back to the tent and dropped the box by the table where, in the light of a camping-gas lamp, Mike was cauterising a long, abdominal spear wound.

'Had enough, Calvin?' The doctor looked up, briefly.

Craig forced a smile. 'No, Mike. As long as you need me I'm here.'

Never had Craig found a smiling lie more difficult. His shirt and trousers were soaked. His head was throbbing. Every muscle felt like frayed rope about to snap. A swarm of flies were his constant companions. His mouth seemed to be lined with sandpaper. His feet gave the sensation of being packed in live coals. And his emotions had been chopped in little pieces.

'Well, we'll have to stop soon. We're pretty well out of large dressings and penicillin. Tell Sue, would you?'

When he passed on the message Sue Hayward stifled a yawn. She walked with him to the front of the tent and peered outside.

'This is always the worst part of the day, when we pack up and drive away and all these people who haven't been treated go home again. By the time we get back here again next month some of them will have got beyond help. It makes you feel so useless. It's like trying to walk up a down escalator.'

She turned towards him. The light from the tent unkindly accentuated the lines and hollows of her face. 'It's a terrible thing to say, Calvin, but sometimes I wonder whether God's laughing at us. I expect you find that shocking, don't you?'

Words of bogus sentiment came readily to his mind but for once Craig could not utter them.

Chapter Eight

The following letter was posted in New York eight days after Craig's return.

CONFIDENTIAL   Fox Financial
                                  Consultants
                          Providence House
CC/KRE.3079/A   Broad St.,
                         New York 40350

Dear Mr Okello,

Further to our recent meeting in Kampala I have given the national medical centre project much thought. As I indicated, most available short-term funds are already committed. However, I have discussed your proposal with one of our clients and have stressed the importance of the facility, and its immense value to the people of Uganda and other African nations.

His initial reaction is favourable and he informs me that he is willing to consider financing the major part of the project at this stage. He feels that the construction and equipping of the hospital at Soroti should be the first priority and that the cost of this work should not exceed $100,000,000. He does not rule out the possibility of assisting with the provision of improved out-clinic facilities at a later stage.

If your government is prepared to proceed

with a modified programme my client is willing to open negotiations, subject to the following conditions:

1. Fox Financial Consultants shall be retained exclusively as negotiators.

2. All transactions shall be with the government of the Republic of Uganda, who shall be the sole recipients of funds provided by our client.

3. All funds provided by our client shall be made available through the Arab Overseas Investment Bank of Nassau, Bahamas, who shall hold such funds until authorised to transfer them to an account specified by the government of the Republic of Uganda.

4. Our client shall remain anonymous.

5. Our client shall receive written guarantees as to the repayment of principal and interest.

6. While not wishing to become involved in the execution of the project, our client shall receive full information concerning architects' plans and specifications, contracts with contractors and sub-contractors, and shall reserve the right to have the building site investigated on his behalf from time to time.

If these general arrangements are acceptable to your government our client is prepared to proceed with reasonable expedition since, as I understand it, you are anxious to begin work on the project as soon as possible. Our client has been involved in similar transactions in Asia and South America and I can confirm that those transactions proved most satisfactory to all concerned.

When we had our initial discussion the question of collateral was raised and I suggested that our office was highly experienced in the preparation of collateral security instrument programmes. In the event of your government making a formal loan application I shall be pleased to provide you with full details of this service.

Please do not hesitate to contact me if you require any further information or elucidation.

Yours sincerely,

CALVIN CRAIG
President

Craig was pleased with the letter. It achieved a perfect balance between the said and the unsaid, between information provided and information deliberately withheld. It gave Okello the opportunity to raise questions, make objections. That was important.

It worked. Ten days later Craig found the following message waiting on his telex machine in the dingy Providence House office.

Craig. My government unwilling to do business with anonymous client. We need guarantee concerning probity of funding source. Reply soonest. Okello.

'You b-b-blew it, Craig. I t-told you they'd smell a rat.' Kemp looked anxiously round the crowded bar of Frascatti's, hoping no one recognised him.

'Relax. Everything's going fine.'

'B-but Okello wants the l-l-lender's name. And we c-can't tell him because there *is* no l-l-l-'

'We can't tell him and we aren't going to tell him.'

'Well, if he p-p-pulls out, you're still going to have to p-pay me. I've p-p-put in a lot . . .'

Craig pushed a piece of paper across the table. 'I'm sending this telex to Uganda tomorrow.'

Kemp read:

Okello. Have had long telephone conversation with client who insists anonymity condition must stand. I am empowered to reveal that funding source is Middle Eastern and that Muslim laws on usury render complete secrecy essential. Failure to accept this condition will void negotiations. Advise soonest. Craig.

Kemp sat back, a frown of concentration scouring further ravines across the worried landscape of his face.

Craig smiled. 'You still don't get it, do you? Look, the Gulf States are awash with money – right?'

Kemp nodded.

'And where's it going? The sheikhs have long since acquired all the luxuries they could possibly want – palaces, cars, yachts, women, racehorses. Croesus never dreamed of wealth like it. Then they started spreading it round the world – houses they seldom lived in, estates they never visited, businesses they paid other people to run.'

'So?'

'So, that's all very well if you don't have powerful enemies constantly pillorying your western lifestyle, your un-Islamic activities, your flouting of the Koran. There's not one of these oil-princes that hasn't got a pack of Muslim fundamentalists snapping at his heels.'

Kemp was beginning to get the picture. 'Yeah, that's why Arab m-money's being hidden all over the place.'

'As everyone knows – even friend Okello.'

'And you think he'll really b-b-believe a slice of that m-money is coming his way?'

'He *wants* to believe it. He *needs* to believe it.' Craig gave the lawyer a wide, relaxed smile. 'He'll believe it. Now, you've got that letter explaining the Collateral Security Instrument

Programming?'

After more furtive glances Kemp produced from his briefcase four closely-typed sheets of A4. Craig read it through, chuckling.

'Brilliant, Will. It'll take Okello's lawyers days to understand all this.'

Kemp removed his glasses and rubbed them with a hand-kerchief. 'It's all p-perfectly p-proper legal language.'

'Yes, Will, that's the beauty of it – it really does have a meaning. And it does make sense. Accept the premise and everything follows with magnificent logic. And when it comes down to it all this,' he folded the papers and transferred them to an inside pocket, 'is the oldest con in the world. It offers someone something for nothing. It appeals to human greed.'

What the impressive-sounding Collateral Security Instrument amounted to was this: Fox Financial Consultants would recommend a finance house prepared to act as a 'private placement collateral issuer'. The anonymous lender would advance a sum *ten times greater* than that required by the government of Uganda. *Nine tenths* of that sum would be paid to the finance house for the term of the loan. They would satisfy the lender as to the security of his investment and they would guarantee the eventual repayment of the *entire* loan, together with all interest payments. The government of Uganda would thus receive the remaining *one tenth* of the total figure, completely unencumbered – *something for nothing*.

As Craig said, the swindle was concealed within an elaborate wrapping of what looked like sound financial common sense. Everyone got what he wanted: The mythical Arab prince found a safe, secret investment for his money. The equally mythical finance house received a large injection of medium term capital. The shattered economy of Uganda would benefit from what was, in effect, a no-strings-attached gift.

All this was padded out with legal jargon in the document which Craig rightly described as brilliant. There was not even any small print for Okello's lawyers to quibble over. Kemp had been quite up-front about the nub of Craig's advance fee fraud. Immediately *after* that section which baldly and matter-of-factly described how the 'recipient' (the government of Uganda) would be provided with $100,000,000 the following clauses appeared:

> '19. On signature of the contract the recipient shall pay to Fox Financial Consultants Inc a good faith deposit of £750,000. This deposit shall be forfeit in the event of the recipient subsequently cancelling the contract, for what reason soever. This deposit shall be deducted from the final instalment of the commission paid by the recipient to Fox Financial Consultants Inc.'
> 20. The recipient shall pay to Fox Financial Consultants Inc a commission amounting to two per cent of the total negotiated loan. Such commission shall be paid in two equal instalments. The first instalment shall be paid when the agreed funds are transferred by the funding source to the recipient. The second instalment, less the good faith deposit (see clause 19 above), shall be paid when three working days have elapsed after the aforementioned transfer of funds.'

Okello's advisers would quickly calculate that Uganda's financial commitment was $20,000,000. But of that only three-quarters of a million had to be provided up front. They could pay the rest out of the loan and, as Kemp's letter said, they could even calculate FFC's commission into the loan. They had nothing to lose.

A couple of weeks later Craig was smiling as he locked the Providence House office and descended in the elevator. In his pocket was Okello's letter accepting in principle the terms of the proposed deal and requesting a meeting to discuss it in more detail. The minister thanked Mr Craig for sending details of CSI programming and would also like to bring this up in their subsequent discussion.

'Hooked' Craig gloated as he emerged in the basement car park. All he had to do now was play his African fish – and in such matters he was very expert.

He was still smiling as he slid into the driving seat of his silver-grey Corniche. He turned the key in the ignition. He engaged the automatic gear. Another car pulled in front of him. Stopped. Two men got out. Craig immediately recognised the thug called Steve and the nameless black.

'Hi! Remember me?' Steve opened the door of the Rolls and beckoned Craig out.

Craig swung his long legs sideways and stood facing them. Frightened. 'Look, what do you want? I told your boss all I knew . . .'

Craig smirked. He was holding a flick-knife with a nine-inch blade. 'You sure get around, Mr Hartley.'

'What's that supposed to mean?'

'We like to keep our tabs on you.' He shook his head in mock solemnity. 'And you haven't been making that very easy for us.'

Craig watched the point of the knife as it rotated a foot from his face. They couldn't know about his trip to Africa. He'd covered his tracks too well. They couldn't know – could they?

'Where've you been, Mr Hartley?' The blade's tiny point touched the tip of his nose.

Craig glanced round. The car park was empty. Not that anyone would have come to the aid of a man being mugged. 'Travelling on business . . . South America . . .'

'Where else?' The pressure increased.

Craig felt the knife draw blood. He pressed his back against the car. How the hell much did they know?

'Germany . . . West Germany . . . Frankfurt.'

'Anywhere else?'

The blade now nudged Craig's midriff. He felt its sharpness through the jacket's worsted. 'No . . . nowhere else . . . I swear it.'

The young man's eyes gazed into Craig's, unblinking, probing. Craig stared back. He didn't blink. He didn't breathe. He didn't even think.

Without turning away, Steve called out, 'Georgio!'

The negro stepped forward.

'Hold him.'

The next moment Craig's left arm was jerked behind his back and his neck gripped in the crook of the black man's elbow. Steve stepped back a couple of paces, feeling the weight of the knife. He grinned. 'Goodbye, Mr Hartley.'

He lunged.

Craig closed his eyes. He felt Steve's hand brush past his right arm. Heard a grinding, scraping sound. And the men's laughter.

He turned and saw Steve gouging the Corniche's gleaming paintwork. He worked his way right round the car, crazing it with slash marks. He stepped back to admire his work.

'You know, I think it needed a new paint job anyway.' He laughed and Georgio joined in as he released his hold. 'We do like to know where you are, Mr Hartley. You won't make that hard for us, will you?'

The two men climbed into their car and drove off at speed, leaving scorch marks on the concrete and the smell of burning rubber.

Chapter Nine

What Craig discovered at the Bristol Hotel made him furious. He was already angry when he arrived in Paris. Everything was going wrong. He resented having to shuttle back and forth between airports to get the brotherhood off his trail. He was enraged by their threats. And more determined than ever to outsmart them. He was annoyed at having had to set up the meeting with Okello from his west coast apartment. He kept the Santa Barbara place strictly for vacations. But he had managed to arrange everything. Kemp was in London. Louise was on her way to Singapore. Okello and his delegation were due in three days. He had had to make labyrinthine plans to avoid any possibility of being seen with the Ugandan. He cursed the New York mafioso who were making his life so much more complicated. But he had salvaged the Ugandan Assignment from near disaster. He had fed all the new, unwanted data into the computer of his brain and come out with the right answer. And now, just when everything seemed back on course, Hafid had gone missing.

The Omani had recently returned to Paris after brief sojourns in Monte Carlo and Nice but when Craig called at the hotel he was informed that Monsieur Hafid had checked out three days earlier without leaving a forwarding address.

The Bristol, in the Rue du Faubourg St Honoré, is Paris's most prestigious hotel, a favourite haunt of the wealthy, including heads of state who have business with the president at the Elysée Palace, a stone's throw down the road. Its staff are, therefore, more discreet than most. Craig was only able to gather a few scraps of information and they cost him a thousand francs. M. Hafid, he learned, had departed suddenly after two of his countrymen had called at the hotel making enquiries.

Sitting in a cab that crawled, hooted and swerved its way to the Avenue Franklin de Roosevelt, Craig ran through his repertoire of maledictions. Even Hafid would have paled at the imprecations the American called down upon him. The Omani's disappearance had loused everything up. Everything was geared for the crucial meeting in three days' time. Craig could not put it off. He could not find and train another accomplice in that time. Ten million dollars down the pan! He could not, would not think it. Hafid must be found.

He almost ran into Ricci's. The manager of the exclusive gaming club was determined not to be helpful. Clients, he pointed out, relied absolutely on the discretion of his establishment. *Par conséquent, malheureusement*, he regretted he could be of no assistance. Monsieur would surely understand. They had not seen M. Hafid for some days. Beyond that he could or would say nothing.

Craig thanked him for his time. As he turned to leave the sumptuously decorated office, he had a sudden thought.

'Does Mr Ahmed Hassan still play here regularly?'

The manager was caught off guard, 'M. Hassan, I understand, is playing at the international backgammon championship in Istanbul.'

Craig went straight to the Air France office in the Champs Elysées. It was only a wild hunch but it was all he had. It cost him another thousand francs to get a look at recent passenger lists. It was worth it. Hafid had flown to Istanbul two days earlier.

Craig was on the next flight.

He checked in at the Hilton. It was the only hotel that

had a room left. The city was gripped by backgammon fever. Boys sat under trees offering to play passers-by for coppers. Men crouched over boards in all the pavement cafés. And the experts, from all over the Arab world and beyond, gathered in three officially-designated venues for the solemn business of winning and losing fortunes.

Craig obtained a list of competition centres from Reception and set off to do the rounds. As soon as he forced his way into the first salon he knew how hard his task was going to be.

Trestle tables were laid out in long rows and the players sat, almost shoulder to shoulder. The spaces between were crammed with excited spectators, noisily urging on their champions or jostling their way from game to game. Craig wondered how the contestants could possibly concentrate amidst the heat, the din and the stench of human bodies. He zig-zagged his way through the hall trying to scrutinise, not only the players, but also every face in the crowd.

Two and a half hours later he emerged into the evening street, sweating from every pore, spent another ten minutes trying, unsuccessfully, to hail a cab, walked to the nearest café, drank three glasses of iced Perrier water with two cups of thick Turkish coffee and indulged murderous thoughts on the subject of Aziz Hafid.

When he got back to the Hilton he had to cope with a bad case of jitters on the part of Kemp.

'C-Calvin? Is that you? Where the hell have you b-b-been? I've c-c-called a dozen times on that P-Paris number you gave me and got no a-a-answer.'

'Calm down, Will. There's been a slight change of plan. I'm in Istanbul.'

'Istanbul! What the . . . You're s-supposed to be s-s-setting everything up in L-L-London.'

'Everything's under control, Will. Don't panic. Now, what did you want to talk to me about?'

'We had a c-cable from Uganda a c-couple of days ago.

S-seems they're not happy.'

'What's the matter?'

'They want p-proof that the l-loan monies are really available. Now, there's no way we c-c-can p-p-p . . .'

'Relax, Will. That's no problem. Here's what you do.'

Kemp received his instructions in silence. When Craig had finished he said, 'Do you really th-think that will work?'

'I know it will work.'

'When are you going to b-be here? You should be-be here now.'

'I'll see you the day after tomorrow.'

'B-b-b-but . . .'

'Will, relax. Leave the worrying to me.'

Craig pressed the cancel button. He dabbed the perspiration from his forehead. Then he made another call. It was the first of nineteen calls to leading Istanbul hotels. None of them had the Omani on its books. There was nothing for it but to face the ordeal of the other two competition centres the next day.

At the first his pocket was picked. He had to walk to the American Express office and wait while his credentials were checked. Then an apologetic official informed him that the company could not issue a new platinum card until the theft had been reported to the police. So Craig had to spend another hour with the local constabulary, filling in a form and answering questions framed in execrable French. By the time all the necessary formalities were sorted out Craig could cheerfully have strangled Hafid with his bare hands.

That afternoon he drew a blank at the third competition centre. The meeting with Okello was now less than forty-eight hours away. Craig needed to think. He had to get away from the hot, crowded streets. He hired a motor boat for a trip up the Bosphorus. The cheerful owner launched into his usual tourist patter on leaving the moorings. Craig firmly and none too politely shut him up. He leaned on the rail watching the ramshackle waterfront dwellings and the minarets of the Dolmabahçe mosque drift away astern.

How would he behave, he asked himself, in Hafid's shoes? The Omani was fleeing from members of his own family, intent on preventing him living the kind of life he wanted to live. Yet he was not the sort of man to tolerate being a perpetual fugitive. He craved luxury and comfort and they were like a ball and chain to a man on the run. Craig gazed back at the city skyline pierced by domes and minarets. If Hafid was there somewhere, it was inconceivable to imagine him in a third rate hotel or one of the dingy backstreet houses with cards in the windows offering 'chambres' and 'zimmer'. He would be enjoying five-star luxury in one of the prime tourist resting places probably under an assumed name or renting a private apartment – perhaps one of those timber-built villas scattered along the western waterfront.

Craig admitted defeat. It was a rare experience and he hated it. Tomorrow morning he would have to return to London. Cook up some reason for postponing his meeting with the Ugandans.

Craig ordered the boatman to return. They had reached the narrow strait between the twin Ottoman castles of Rumelihisar and Anadoluhisar. They were of no interest to him. He stared steadily down into the swirling, thick green waters. Could the meeting be postponed? Could he reorganise Louise and Kemp? They were all keyed up to give convincing performances. They might very well go off the boil. Then there was Okello. If he was made to wait he might have second thoughts.

Craig told the boatman to land him at the üsküdar jetty from which the steamers depart for various points along the straits. He sat in the stern and began putting together a new plan.

At the wharf he paid the boatman, shook the hand the man insisted on extending and stepped ashore. That was when he saw Hafid.

A group of men were standing a few feet away deep in conversation. One of them, beardless and wearing mirrored sunglasses, glanced at the stranger and quickly looked away. It was that movement that drew Craig's attention. He stopped for a closer look.

The man glanced round, muttered something to his companions, and walked briskly away along the jetty. Craig followed. The man broke into a run. A ferry was just casting off. The man leaped aboard. Craig sprinted forward. There was already a gap between the boat and the quay. A crewman on the deck was waving his hands warning Craig not to jump. He jumped. The crewman caught him and said something uncomplimentary in Turkish. Craig muttered an apology and strode along the deck.

He found his quarry in the bows.

'Good day Mr Hafid. You and I have a business arrangement. Or had you forgotten?'

The Omani scowled. 'How did you find me?'

'With a hell of a lot of hard work. You have cost me a great deal of time and effort which I can't afford. I should be in London right now and I need you there.'

Hafid shook his head violently. 'No, the deal is off. I'm staying here.'

'Like hell the deal is off! I am paying you good money to do a pretty simple job and, by God, you're going to do it.'

'You don't understand. Things have changed.'

'Believe me, young man, I understand very well indeed. You're on the run from your own family and they very nearly caught up with you in Paris.'

'How do you . . .'

'I make it my business to know. I never work with strangers.'

'Then you realise why I can't go to London.'

'I realise that you can't do anything else.'

'What do you mean?'

'I mean that if you don't honour your obligations to me a certain gentleman in Muscat will receive full information about your movements, your favourite haunts and your present whereabouts.'

Hafid stared moodily across the water towards the square bulk of the old Selimiye Barracks.

'But in London . . .'

'In London you will be perfectly safe. I have very good reason to keep you safe. We will leave on the first available flight and you will stay with me at a modest hotel where no one will recognise you.'

He did not add that he, too, was hiding from would-be pursuers and could not use his own apartment. 'In a couple of days the job will be over and you can go where you like.'

Hafid spun round. 'No! You do not give me orders. I have some important games to play here. I will join you in London.'

'If you think I'm letting you out of my sight again, forget it.'

'I give you my word . . .'

'Stuff your word, Hafid.'

The Omani's whole body stiffened with anger. Craig thought he was going to lash out with his fists or perhaps even pull a knife. Instead, he muttered something in Arabic and said, 'In my country you would have died for saying that.'

Craig smiled. 'Then it's lucky for both of us we're not in your country, Mr Hafid.'

103

Chapter Ten

Craig was pleased with his arrangements.

The meeting had to be in London. London was familiar to Okello – a second home. He felt secure and relaxed there and that was important. But it was vital that he and Craig were not seen together, not even observed going into the same building. How can two men enter the same office through the same door without both being seen? Answer: keep moving the door.

Moonbeam was a yacht belonging to Viscount Lyven, the last representative of a family whose money had come from shipping in the eras of clippers and luxury liners. But those eras were long past and the third viscount possessed only three major assets. These he exploited to the hilt. His modest Jacobean mansion in Oxfordshire was frequently leased to multinational companies for top executive conferences. His yacht was hired out for fashionable parties and limited charter work. And his name graced several boards and occasional commissions of enquiry. That name appeared on the embossed letterheads of two of Craig's own companies and had been invaluable in lending some of the fraudster's activities a touch of respectability and class. Craig had not used the yacht before but now he realised that it was the perfect solution to his problem.

Craig boarded the boat at Greenwich early on 4 April, carrying an attaché case and a brown paper parcel. He put his luggage in the aft saloon then made a tour of inspection, determined to check personally every detail. He watched the caterers come aboard, approved the Batard Monrachet, the fois gras and the grouse but ordered fresher lettuce and a riper Brie. He inspected *Moonbeam's* three-man crew, making sure their blue jerseys and trousers were spotless. He had the brass fittings of the dining saloon repolished and made sure that the word processors and computer consoles arranged the day before in an adjoining cabin were working properly. When the two temps from the secretarial agency arrived he set them to work on a pile of phoney letters and documents on FFC's impressive headed notepaper.

Kemp came cautiously down the gangplank at 9.30 am, punctual and grumbling at having had to travel out of the centre of London.

Craig led him into the yacht's spacious aft saloon and settled him in one of the deep blue armchairs, with a large bourbon. He went back on deck and ordered the crew to cast off, then returned and poured himself a scotch. He raised his glass.

'Here's to a successful day's business.'

Kemp gulped the spirit and winced as it made a searing beeline for his duodenum. 'Yeah, well let's not c-c-count our chickens.'

'You've brought all the papers?' Craig sprawled on the sofa. The rectangular parcel was beside him.

Kemp hoisted his attaché case onto the low, fixed table in front of him and took out a bundle of files. He extracted various documents most of which ran to several typed pages.

'C-consulting Agreement. That establishes FFC as inter-mediary for the l-loan. Retainer Agreement. That n-n-nominates Inter-State Fiduciary Services as g-g-guarantor. And this one is the L-letter of Agreement and Institution for the Arab Overseas Investment Bank.'

'Setting up the account?'

'That's right, with instructions to make f-f-f-funds p-

105

payable to NatWest in Bread Street as the f-fiduciary bank n-nominated by the borrower.'

Craig spent several minutes familiarising himself with the salient points of the impressive documents. He said, 'Excellent, Will,' and he meant the compliment.

The lawyer scowled, 'Don't let's get over c-confident. I'm not sure the blacks s-swallowed our l-line about the mysterious Arab.'

Craig rose and refilled the glasses. 'You're forgetting human nature, Will. We've offered the Ugandans something for nothing and they want to believe it. Okello is desperate to believe it. He's at a crucial point in his career. If he could pull off a deal like this his standing would go up enormously in Uganda and in Africa. He hasn't come all this way to find flaws in our proposals.'

'O.K. but what's he going to d-d-do when he f-finds he has been t-taken for a ride.'

'That's the beauty of it. He's going to do absolutely nothing. His political survival will depend on the whole business being swept under the carpet and forgotten about. He'll be as anxious as we are to draw a veil of secrecy over the deal. He's not going to file reports with the FBI and Interpol, or stand up in open court and say, "Those are the men I gave $10,000,000 of my country's money to".'

The little lawyer drained his glass. 'Well I j-just hope we c-convince him today. Will this Hafid guy be OK?'

'No need to worry about him. I've been over his part with him several times. He'll carry it off superbly. He's a proud man and that helps his performance. He really only has to be himself. He hates my guts, of course. But he needs the money and he's also scared of me because of what I know about him. If he puts a foot wrong today he realises I could get him crated up and shipped back to the desert. And once he's there he'll be stuck there for life.'

'You enjoy having p-power over p-p-people, don't you?'

Craig pondered the question. 'Look at it this way, Will.

Loyalty is one of the most valuable things anyone has to offer. So it carries a high price, whether in love or money or power. If I want someone's allegiance I pay for it in whatever currency is appropriate – and I pay generously.'

He finished his drink. 'That's enough philosophy. We've got work to do.'

He picked up the parcel.

'What've you g-got there?'

'Just a little extra inducement for our honoured client.' Craig chuckled as he left the cabin.

Moonbeam was making her way up river on a drab morning which put a wet, shiny varnish on the deck without actually appearing to rain. Craig paused briefly to admire the grisaille cityscape emerging from the miasma ahead, then shivered and hurried to the dining saloon.

Centred on one wall above the mahogany and brass sideboard hung an indifferent painting of a steam and sail ship plying serenely across a turgid sea – presumably the pride of the Lyven Line a century ago. A few minutes with a screwdriver and Craig had it down. He unwrapped his parcel and drew from the paper and corrugated cardboard another picture. He tapped a small nail into the wooden panelling and hung the replacement.

Craig stepped back to admire his alteration to the decor.

Through layers of semi-opaque varnish peered the face of a young man. The refined, almost effeminate features and the plain wide, white collar were all that were visible. Everything else merged into blackness.

'Who's that?' Kemp has come in behind him.

'John Milton,' Craig replied. Then, receiving no response, 'Seventeenth century English poet,' he explained.

Kemp grunted.

Craig continued, 'There are very few authentic portraits of Milton.'

'Does that m-make this one worth a l-lot of money?'

107

Craig mused rather than replied. 'The Onslow portrait, as it's called, has been lost for over a century. It's only known from early engraved copies. Any serious collector would bankrupt himself to possess it.'

'So?'

'Okello is a serious collector.'

'You got a s-side d-d-d-deal going down? Going to s-s-sell it to him?'

Craig turned abruptly. 'Good Lord, no. That would be greedy. In this game you must always resist the temptation to be greedy.' He moved across to the door. 'Anyway, that's not the Onslow portrait – just an excellent forgery I commissioned in Paris.' He went out on deck leaving the little lawyer more bewildered than ever.

When *Moonbeam* reached Cadogan pier the Ugandan delegation was already waiting. Two Mercedes limousines were parked on Chelsea Embankment. From the first three, men in dark suits emerged and walked down the gangway. They were closely followed by Okello – and a lady. Watching from the aft cabin Craig was not pleased to recognise Susan Hayward. Why on earth had the African brought her?

Seconds later he was shaking hands and settling his guests in comfortable armchairs. Okello introduced his lawyer, Joseph Kiwanuka, and Craig presented Will Kemp, FFC's legal representative.

'Our quorum will be complete when we reach the City heliport,' he explained as *Moonbeam* headed once more downstream. 'Our client's agent, Mr Sulaiman, will be joining us there.'

He excused himself momentarily, went through to the office and dialled a telephone number.

Ten miles away, Aziz Hafid glared at an empty expanse of glistening tarmac through the rain-speckled windscreen of a small helicopter. A portable phone in the briefcase at his feet rang three times and fell silent. Hafid gestured to the pilot beside him. Slowly the rotar blades began to turn.

Rain was bouncing off the surface of the floating heliport as *Moonbeam* powered under Blackfriar's bridges, eased her engine and gently nuzzled up to the row of fenders made from old tyres. The six people in the aft cabin concealed their various anxieties beneath a veil of relaxed chatter.

'Well, here we are.' Craig extricated himself from the deep armchair. He walked across to the window. 'I hope this weather doesn't hold Mr Sulaiman up. No, I do believe that's his chopper coming in now.'

Okello came over and stood beside the American. They watched the machine's wheels settle in the middle of the large 'H'. They waited while the engine was switched off and the whirring blades slowed to a halt. By then a member of *Moonbeam*'s crew was beside the helicopter with a raised umbrella. Unhurriedly, the door opened and Aziz Hafid emerged, magnificent in white robes and Arab headdress. Slowly, majestically, he crossed to the yacht and descended the gangplank.

'My dear Mr Sulaiman,' Craig stepped forward as the Omani entered the saloon and made the slightest suggestion of a bow over the limply-proffered hand, 'how delightful to meet you again. I trust you had a comfortable journey. Now, please allow me to present . . .'

Craig made the introductions and Hafid with a slight smile of condescension shook hands with each of the other guests in turn. Very subtly the impression was created, without a word being said, that here was a man accustomed to deference and that if 'Mr Sulaiman' assumed the air of minor royalty, his superior must, indeed, be a highly important figure.

The party were served drinks by a white-coated steward, as the yacht left her moorings and eased out once more onto the tideway.

'A charming idea, Mr Craig, to hold our meeting in such . . . unusual surroundings. I salute your imaginativeness.' Sulaiman held up his glass of orange juice in a mock toast.

'I thought it would be pleasant and also ensure complete privacy.'

'Is the yacht one of FFC's assets?' Okello asked.

Craig laughed. 'Goodness, no. She belongs to Viscount Lyven, an old friend of mine. He has very kindly allowed me to use *Moonbeam* on several occasions. Sadly, this may be my last voyage in her.'

'Oh, why is that?' Sue had been gazing around wide-eyed ever since she came aboard. 'I hope such a beautiful and luxurious boat isn't going to be broken up.'

'I hope not, too, Sue. But I have a hunch, from one or two things Lord Lyven has said, that he's going to be obliged to part with her. She's an expensive toy to maintain.'

For half an hour or so everyone made small talk, sitting in the saloon or wandering on the deck to watch the procession of derelict warehouses and new dockland development.

Then they went into lunch. To reach the dining saloon they had to pass through the 'office' and Craig took the opportunity of pointing out the facilities available.

'Any data we may require is available here on computer disc. These good ladies will take care of documents or letters any of you gentlemen may want typed. Our meeting this afternoon will be minuted and transcripts will be available before you leave. The telephones are radio-linked to the British national system and, thus, to everywhere in the world should you need to contact your offices. Please feel free to use any of these services.'

Craig took the head of the table, seating Okello on his right and Sulaiman on his left. Okello was facing the fake portrait. Craig saw the connoisseur's quick double take. He saw Okello's eyes drawn back time and again to the rectangle of painted canvas.

Lunch was a great success to everyone except Kemp, who winced his way through each rich course and, at the end, swallowed a large dose of white medicine from a bottle in his bulging jacket pocket. By the time the company returned to the aft saloon for coffee everyone was relaxed and talking happily on first name terms. Everyone, that is, except Mr Sulaiman who kept an aloof profile. Craig, for his part, played the rôle of an attentive if over-fussy host.

At last he raised his voice and said 'Well, lady and gentlemen, I guess it's time we got down to business.'

He led the way back to the dining saloon, where the cloth had been removed and piles of notepaper, biros, bottles of mineral water and glasses now stood neatly arranged on the gleaming mahogany. They took their places, with Craig at the head of the table flanked by Hafid and Kemp. Once again Okello was placed facing the fake painting.

Craig cleared his throat. 'Well, now, we have no formal agenda but,' under the table he tapped Hafid's ankle, 'but I hope you'll trust me to structure our discussion. I thought we'd start . . .'

The Omani held up his hand. 'Pardon my interruption, Mr Craig, but there have been certain developments at our end with which I must acquaint the meeting.' He looked solemnly round the table. 'Our Ugandan friends have, I believe, been told the reason for the secrecy which must attend these negotiations. My country, like all other Arab countries, alas, is a prey to the scourge of Muslim fundamentalism. Its devotees interpret the Koran with a strictness never envisaged by the Prophet. However, their fanaticism, their extremism and the severe simplicity of their preaching have attracted a wide following. That means that the activities of governments and influential persons are coming under ever closer popular scrutiny. Now, there are two aspects of our current negotiations which, were those negotiations to become common knowledge, would provoke hostile comment. One is the question of usury. The fundamentalist imams oppose the taking of even modest interest. The other is the export of large sums of money to non-Muslim countries. The popular argument is that such funds should be expended exclusively for the benefit of the faithful.'

Craig nodded gravely. 'Mr Sulaiman, I'm sure our friends here appreciate the need for absolute discretion.'

Hafid continued, growing into his part with every sentence. 'No one regrets more than the prince . . . er . . . more than my principal this charade which imposes the need even for me to appear here under a pseudonym – I imagine that you will all have realised that "Sulaiman" is not my real name – I have no doubt that you are very sensitive to the position my principal finds himself in. Unfortunately, that position has worsened in recent weeks. You will have heard of the spate of assassinations throughout the Middle East and the scurrilous press attacks on certain governments. My principal feels that in the present climate of opinion to proceed with these negotiations might be . . . tempting providence.'

This bombshell was received in stunned silence: it was broken by Okello.

'Then it seems we are all wasting our time. Surely we should have been told of this change of heart by your client, Calvin.'

'Sam, I've had no intimation of this until this moment.' He turned to Hafid. 'Mr Sulaiman, can we try to look at this from another angle? In all the transactions FFC has been honoured to handle for your principal, has there ever been the slightest suggestion of an information leak? Now you know, I'm sure, just how much your assistance has meant to the people of Honduras and India.'

'Mr Sulaiman,' it was Sue who spoke from the far end of the table. 'I hope you will forgive a woman presuming to offer advice but I do know a little about Islamic law and the requirements of the Koran. Many of the people I work with in Uganda are Muslims and I have come to have a deep respect for their beliefs. As I understand it, the Prophet teaches that wealth carries heavy responsibilities. The rich should show compassion and charity. Your principal is obviously deeply moved by these considerations. He must know that the exercise of compassion can't be confined within national or even religious boundaries. If he could see the people I work among I'm sure that nothing, not even fear of assassination, would stop him coming to their aid. Mr Sulaiman, most of us round this table have seen those people. They are the reason we are here. Their sufferings are indescribable. There isn't one of them that hasn't been bereaved by the atrocities of the last few years, or by famine, disease or inter-tribal warfare. They've been reduced to mere animal existence. And, like animals, their only response is to breed vigorously. They don't realise that population growth only adds to their problems. They know nothing but the instinct of survival, the need to create new life. Anything beyond that makes no sense to them – education, health, hygiene, money, religion – all meaningless. The only thing they ask is the opportunity to live out their lives – like the other creatures they dwell amongst – cattle, gazelle, hyena. But these are people, Mr Sulaiman!' She raised her voice. It was unsteady with emotion. 'Not Muslims, not Christians, but brother human beings, degraded to the status of animals by natural disaster and the unspeakable cruelty of man. And there are millions of them throughout Africa. And we sit here debating whether or not to help them. I'm sorry, but I think that's almost obscene.' She came to an abrupt end and lowered her head.

There was another long silence. Then Craig said, 'Thank you, Sue. I'm sure that's helped us get things into perspective. Mr Sulaiman, I know, will take your words in the spirit in which they were intended. You, of course, imply no criticism of our client.'

Hafid nodded gravely. 'My principal is, indeed, a man of deep religious conviction, as you know Mr Craig. The very issues which Dr Hayward so eloquently raises are ones that are close to his heart. But his responsibilities are many and varied and require delicate balancing. He is, I think I may say in all honesty, somewhat perplexed in his own mind as to the right course to adopt.'

Craig nodded. 'We all appreciate that, of course. Perhaps you would prefer to adjourn this meeting until you have had an opportunity to confer with him?'

'No that will not be necessary. Perhaps I might use your telephone to acquaint him of the situation.'

'Of course.' Craig rose and led the Arab from the room.

In the aft saloon he clapped Hafid on the shoulder. 'Well done, young man. I must admit you had me worried for a while back there. I thought you'd gone over the top.'

Hafid frowned. 'You told me to put the wind up the Ugandans. That's what I did.'

'Yeah, well and truly. Fortunately, Sue Hayward gave us a way out.'

'She's some lady.'

'Yes, she certainly is.' Craig agreed with more reluctance than he showed. 'I'll go back now. Give it about five minutes.'

The atmosphere in the conference room was nervous and tense. Two of the Ugandans were talking in lowered voices; the rest sat in silence. After a while Okello rose and went over to look closely at the painting. Without asking permission, he took it down and turned it over to examine the back. He saw the labels and pencilled marks that indicated that the portrait had passed through provincial salerooms three or four times during the past century. He replaced it and returned to his seat.

It seemed an age before Hafid came back but, at last, the door opened and the lithe Omani moved gracefully to his chair. He looked round the table.

'I have spoken with my principal. He wishes me to apologise on his behalf for any alarm that may have been felt. He now believes that it would be right to proceed with the negotiations that have been begun and hopes that we can reach an amicable settlement.'

No one actually breathed a sigh of relief but the mood of the meeting changed radically at that point. Discussion moved along briskly because everyone was anxious to agree details and to avoid any further hitch.

Craig immediately raised the issue of the Ugandan delegation's desire for proof of the availability of funds. 'Will, I believe you have some documents to show our friends?'

'That's right.' Kemp extracted two sheets of paper from a file. 'Acting on our c-c-client's instructions I n-notified the Arab Overseas Investment Bank who in turn c-corresponded with the N-National Westminster Bank, Bread Street in the City of L-London. I have here a c-copy of that c-c-correspondence. You will s-see that NatWest have b-been asked whether they are w-willing to open an escrow account and hold in it one b-billion dollars on behalf of the g-government of Uganda until instructed to release it and they have agreed. He explained that one billion would be the total amount of the transaction if CSI programming was applied for. If the government of Uganda were providing their own collateral the figure would, of course, be one hundred million.'

He passed the papers to Kiwanuka, who read them through and held a muttered conversation with Okello.

The minister nodded. 'May we have a copy of these?'

Craig smiled at the secretary who had been sitting in a corner taking notes. 'Dawn, would you, please?'

She took the papers and returned almost immediately with photocopies.

Next, Kemp produced the Consulting Agreement and explained its terms. On signature Uganda was to transfer $750,000 dollars to FFC's account at the Banco Municipale in Zurich as a good faith deposit. In the event of negotiations being broken off 'with the full consent of all parties' this deposit would be refundable less FFC's legitimate expenses. If the Ugandans aborted the deal unilaterally they would forfeit this money.

'The n-next clauses relate to FFC's professional f-fees. We n-n-need to know the m-m-m-mechanics of the loan. Is it your i-i-intention to apply for CSI programming?'

Kiwanuka said that it was.

Kemp explained that, in that case, FFC's professional charges would be two per cent of the entire loan (one billion dollars) half of which was to be paid on the conclusion of all formalities and half on the transfer of funds.

'How exactly will these various transfers work?' Kiwanuka asked.

Craig made the explanation. 'On a normal escrow basis. When all the papers have been signed and the lender is satisfied that work on the project is ready to start he will pay one billion dollars into an AOIB escrow account set up for the purpose. At the same time your government will pay twenty million dollars into an escrow account at your fiduciary bank in London with instructions to release this in two stages to FFC's Zurich account. The banks will confirm to all parties that they have received the funds. All the monies will then be held until a previously agreed closing hour. At that closing hour the actual transfers will be made simultaneously by computer links between the banks. That is: AOIB will credit your NatWest account

116

with one hundred million dollars and the loan guarantor's account with nine hundred million dollars. At the same time NatWest will credit FFC's Banco Municipale account with ten million dollars – the first half of the consultancy fee. Three working days will be allowed for all parties to satisfy themselves with the transactions. Then NatWest will automatically transfer the second half of FFC's fee.

'Of course, we are jumping the gun a little because all this is dependent upon the satisfactory arrangement of CSI programming. I guess we'd better address ourselves to that question next. What I propose is that I put you directly in touch with a finance house prepared to handle the deal and you can discuss the matter with them direct. Is that OK, Sam?'

Okello nodded.

'Fine. I have taken the liberty of sounding out a company we've had a lot of dealings with. They're called Inter-State Fiduciary of Dallas, Texas. If it's OK with you I'd like to call them now.' He checked his watch. 'It's about a quarter after ten over there. Then you can talk to them and set up a meeting.'

He went to the side table and lifted the telephone receiver. He dialled a thirteen digit number. Seconds later he heard a female voice. 'This is Fox Financial Consultants. I'm sorry but the office is closed right now. If you would like to leave a message after the tone . . .'

Craig cut in, 'Hello, may I speak with Louise Traille, please? This is Calvin Craig . . . She is? Well that lady sure gets around. Say this is kind of urgent; do you have a contact address or number? . . . Yes, I'll hang on . . .' He grabbed a piece of paper and a biro from the table. 'OK, give it to me nice and slowly.' He scribbled down a number. 'Thanks a lot. You've been a great help.'

Craig returned to the table and handed the paper to Okello. 'The person you want to speak to is Mrs Louise Traille. She's the assistant M.D. Right now, apparently,

117

she's in Singapore but you can catch her at Raffles Hotel. That's the number. Let's see what time will it be there now? About half after eleven p.m. You should catch her. I know Louise well. She's definitely a night person.'

Okello passed the number to one of his aides who got up to put through the call. At the third attempt he heard a voice say something in Chinese and then, 'Raffles Hotel, can I help you?' He asked for Mrs Traille and after a few clicks and buzzes another voice came on the line. 'Hello, Louise Traille here.' The aide said, 'Will you hold on a moment please I have Mr Okello, Finance Minister of Uganda for you.' He passed the receiver across the table.

'Mrs Traille? Samuel Okello here. I believe our mutual friend Calvin Craig of FFC mentioned that I might be contacting you.'

'Why, yes. Delighted to hear from you, Mr Okello. How may I help?'

'I'd like to discuss the possibility of setting up a CSI programme for one billion dollars. Can we possibly arrange a meeting?'

'Why yes. Just a moment while I fetch my diary. Let me see. I leave here in three days for a meeting in Delhi. I could come on to Kampala after that. Say around the 11th. Would that suit?'

They arranged details of the meeting and said goodbye.

Kemp now went over the Letter of Agreement and Institution for setting up the AOIB escrow account and Sulaiman and Kiwanuka took copies to be studied and signed by their superiors.

Craig then asked what thoughts the Ugandans had about construction companies. Okello mentioned two names and Sulaiman made a couple more suggestions. It was agreed that all four should be invited to tender.

By the time the meeting concluded an hour later several other points had been covered and Tower Bridge was once more in sight. It was agreed that the lawyers would meet

118

again the following Tuesday to approve the final draft of the contract, copies of which would then be sent to the principals for signature.

Craig stood up. 'Well, I think we all deserve a drink.'

Everyone filed through to the aft saloon and the party split up into small groups.

Okello shook Craig's hand and thanked him for his excellent chairmanship. 'We certainly covered a lot of ground.'

'I hope everything works out satisfactorily.'

Okello lowered his voice. 'The painting in there. . .'

'Painting?'

'The portrait on the wall – do you know anything about it?'

'Not apart from the fact that it belongs to Lord Lyven.'

'One of his ancestors, perhaps?'

Craig shrugged. 'His place in Oxfordshire is full of them.'

'He's a connoisseur?'

Craig laughed. 'Hector? Oh I doubt that. I doubt that very much. He regards his inheritance as something of an encumbrance. Since he took over the title he's been quietly selling off whatever he can. Trouble is his mother is still very much alive and very – you know, old school aristocracy. "Must maintain our place in society. Must pass on our heritage intact." Very noble but not very realistic.'

'You think Lord Lyven might sell that old picture, then?'

Craig showed mild surprise. 'You're interested in it, are you?'

Okello made a show of nonchalance. 'It intrigues me.'

'Well, I'll certainly mention it to Hector when I see him.'

Craig chatted to one or two other guests and then made his way out on deck where he found Sue leaning on the

119

rail and sipping her orange juice. *Moonbeam* was now heading upriver again and was progressing sedately up Tower Reach.

'I'm afraid that must have been all very dull for you.'

She smiled. 'Mike said I was out of my depth in all this high finance and he was certainly right. My head's reeling. I don't think I understood a tenth of what you were talking about.'

'You made a very valuable contribution. Thank you.'

'I'm afraid I let my tongue run away with me – not for the first time. Mike sometimes says to me, "Sue, always remember, before switching on mouth, engage brain". I'm afraid I don't always follow that advice.'

'You're very fond of Mike, aren't you?' She avoided the question. 'He's very dedicated. You have to be, out there. I know he's a bit rough and ready but in our work you have to grow a pretty thick protective shell. You'd go mad otherwise.'

They looked across at the grey mass of the White Tower.

She let out a long sigh. 'It *is* good to be home.' She had a sudden thought and turned to him. 'What are you doing for Easter, Calvin?'

'Tying up all the loose ends of this afternoon, I guess.'

'That's not a very Christian way to observe the festival. Why don't you come and spend part of the weekend with Daddy and me? It's not very exciting down in darkest Dorset, but it's very beautiful. "Oh to be in England, now that April's there." Do say you'll come.'

All kinds of warning bells sounded in Craig's brain. He knew he should decline the invitation.

'Thanks, Sue. I'd like that.'

Chapter Eleven

Chepstone Magna was all that an English village ought to be – straggling, semi-thatched and tranquil. So tranquil that everyone seemed half asleep. Craig's car crawled along the congested high street while what must, surely, have been the village's entire population meandered about the highway as though the petrol engine had never been invented. Constrained to travel like a mechanised tortoise, the American had no difficulty in locating and turning into Palfrey Lane ('You'll see it between the butcher's and the Seymour Arms,' Sue had explained). Fifty yards along what only the English could refer to as a 'thoroughfare' he had to wait while a tractor driver concluded a conversation with one of the local beauties, leaning from the window of her boudoir. No sooner had he pointed his hired Rover up the hill towards the church than a flood of bleating sheep debouched from a gateway just ahead and once more brought him to a halt.

Craig watched the passing tide of stupid faces and wondered for the hundredth time that day what the hell he was doing here. Was it simply the attraction of opposite poles that drew him to Sue Hayward? Or was it the challenge of the ultimate test? Confronting someone so fervently honest was, in one sense, like taking candy from a child. But childish innocence could be a laser sharp weapon. One slip during the next few hours and Sue would realise, with astonished certitude, that the emperor had no clothes. The stragglers of the flock rushed past with a sheepdog at their heels and Craig engaged first gear.

Number four Seymour Cottages was the end dwelling of a row of old almshouses close to the church and Sue was at the door to greet him. She smiled a genuine welcome and enthused over the large bunch of carnations Craig had brought for her. She led the way into a small sitting room. What struck Craig immediately was how tidy it was. Obviously, Mr Hayward was a devotee of the old maxim 'A place for everything and everything in its place'.

The old man was seated at a table beneath the window, working at a word processor. He stood as soon as they entered and advanced towards them. His outstretched hand grasped Craig's firmly.

'Welcome, Mr Craig. Sue's told me all about you and the splendid work you're doing in the Third World. I'm honoured to have you beneath my roof.'

Craig saw an erect, dignified man a little above average height, his hair thick and grey, his eyes an intense blue.

Sue said brightly, 'Well, you two get to know each other while I make some coffee.'

'That's a fine daughter you have,' Craig observed as they sat. 'You must be very proud of her.'

'Little Suzie?' The old man smiled. 'I sometimes say she had Margaret, my wife, for her mother and Africa for her father. She's totally dedicated. There's never been any doubt with her. She always wanted to be a doctor and she always wanted to work in Uganda. As a girl and young woman she was never interested in the things members of her sex are supposed to be interested in. I long ago gave up the idea of having grandchildren.'

'Oh, it's early days for that, sir. Sue's a very attractive woman.'

'So everyone tells me.' The deep blue eyes smiled, disconcertingly fixed on a point somewhere beyond the visitor's left shoulder.

Craig made polite conversation, asking the retired missionary about his early life in Uganda. He learned that

122

Mr Hayward had served as an army chaplain during World War II, signed up with the missionary society and gone out to East Africa in 1948. For most of his thirty years in Uganda he had run a boys' secondary school just outside Kampala. 'It was obvious the country would be independent pretty soon. It seemed important to make sure that the future leaders were Christians – or, if not Christians, at least men of intelligence, integrity and honour. I don't seem to have made a very good job of it.' The Haywards had taught several of the men who had been in the political spotlight since the departure of the British in 1962. They had raised their only daughter in Uganda. They had lived through the early heartbreak years of Amin's tyranny. Their home had been looted several times. Pupils had been abducted and forced either into the army or anti-government guerilla bands. Once the school had been burned down by drunken soldiers. Several close friends had been butchered. Through all these horrors the missionaries had persevered, ever resisting a call from their London headquarters to pack up and go home. But eventually Margaret Hayward had broken under the strain. Ten years ago the couple had retired to England. Margaret's health had not improved. Reluctantly the old man had agreed to his wife being admitted to a psychiatric hospital where, eventually, she died.

'The Lord was gracious,' the old man concluded his story. 'Margaret's suffering was more than either of us could bear. So he brought it to an end and gave her her crown.'

Craig was spared the necessity of making a hollow, inadequate response by the appearance of Sue with the coffee. She fussed over him, proffering milk, sugar, biscuits, then turned to her father.

'Here you are, Daddy. It's already stirred.'

She set the mug on a table beside him, took the old man's fingers and placed them on the handle.

With a sudden shock, Craig realised that the profound blue eyes were sightless.

'How did your father come to be blind?'

It was after lunch and his hostess was taking him for a walk. They had explored the church and descended through well-cropped meadows to the bank of a small river.

'Overwork; too much study; bright sunlight; refusal to wear glasses or get professional treatment – they all played their part.' She spoke matter-of-factly. 'His eyes were very bad by the time he left Uganda but they might have been saved. By then he was too concerned about Mummy to take time seeing a specialist. Eventually it was too late.'

'How does he manage by himself?'

'He's learned to cope very well. In the house he knows where everything is. A lady in the village cleans and shops for him but he gets all his own meals. He's working on his memoirs and that's a useful therapy. You saw his word processor? That was a gift from the local vicar, who's a bit of a computer buff. Daddy's picked it up remarkably quickly. He puts everything on disc and the vicar spends a couple of afternoons a week with him, going over his mistakes.'

They paused by a packhorse bridge. Sue gazed over the low parapet at the river, swollen with spring rain.

Craig said, 'Excuse my saying so, but shouldn't you . . .'

'Stay here and look after him?' She turned quickly to face him. 'He wouldn't hear of it.'

'Too independent?'

'Partly that. But I think it's got more to do with his own sense of failure.' She paused, staring candidly into Craig's eyes. 'It's funny, Calvin, I don't know you very well but I feel I can confide in you. Back in Soroti there's no one . . .'

'What about your colleague?'

124

She laughed. 'Mike's a dear but we don't see eye to eye on many things.'

After a moment or two she went on, 'Daddy feels that what's happened in Uganda is largely the fault of the British and especially the missionaries.'

'That's absurd.'

'Is it? He says that most of the post-independence troubles could have been foreseen. There should have been more effort to break down tribal and religious divisions. They've certainly been at the root of all the bloodshed since 1971. It's been Baganda versus Acholi, Ankole versus Lango, Muslim versus Christian. No sense of a common nationhood. Not even of a common humanity. Daddy feels that by staying on in Uganda – as he would have wanted to do – I can repair some of the damage, help pull the country together.'

'That's a heavy cross to bear.'

'Yes, I feel that sometimes. But someone has to do something. You've seen what we're up against but that's only a fraction of the problem. You haven't seen the pile of skulls as the only marker of a village wiped out by Amin's troops. Or the little boys of seven and eight sent out with pangas to avenge their father's death. Or the deluded tribesmen sent into battle by their witch doctors wearing "magic cloaks" to protect them from bullets.'

'Sue, you know it'll take generations to heal all these social scars?'

'Of course.' She looked up at him brightly. 'That's why it's so wonderful to see the tide actually beginning to turn. The new hospital will do so much to rekindle hope and pride.'

Sue's enthusiasm alarmed him. He wanted to grab hold of her; steer her away from the pit he himself had dug. 'Sue's there's a long way to go yet. A lot can still go wrong. Don't set your heart on the hospital.'

She smiled. 'Oh but I just know it's all going to work out Calvin. I have faith in God – and in you.'

Over the next few weeks Craig pushed to the back of his mind the memory of his thirty-six hours in Dorset – the religious discussion long into the night with Sue's father whose mind was far too sharp for comfort; the fitful sleep shattered at last by the massed choirs of birds in the wood not a stone's throw from his window; singing hymns with feigned exuberance and sincerity in the packed church on Easter morn. But what he could not forget; what returned, unbidden, to his consciousness at frequent intervals; what became the only irritant in his well-oiled scheme was Sue's expression of childlike trust: 'I have faith in God – and in you'. It nagged at him. It annoyed him – the more so because everything was going so well.

Okello's legal advisers declared themselves satisfied with the arrangements and the delegation returned to Kampala. There, a few days later, Louise Sondemann called on the Finance Minister and drew up the terms of a contract whereby Inter-State Fiduciary of Dallas undertook to service a loan of one billion dollars on behalf of the Republic of Uganda. Craig awaited the outcome of the meeting with some anxiety but when Louise phoned, as arranged, it was to report that her well-rehearsed performance had been a success.

From that point Craig had little direct involvement. The machine he had set in motion ticked away steadily. Okello convinced his President that the hospital scheme was viable. The documents were signed. $750,000 – Uganda's good faith deposit – was paid into Craig's account with Banco Municipale. That meant that all his expenses to date were covered. If the worst came to the worst, he had lost nothing.

But the worst did not come to the worst. Hafid, installed in a suite at the Savoy, received a steady stream of visitors from the Uganda embassy. He examined the architect's drawings of the new hospital. He approved the tendering arrangements for construction work. He made a visit to Soroti to examine the site. The project gathered its own momentum as more and more innocent people – bankers, construction engineers, medical equipment suppliers, surveyors – were drawn in.

It was Okello who moved everything along at breakneck pace. He set a tight schedule for the tenders. Midnight oil was burned in many offices as competing construction companies hurried to meet the deadline. Okello also hustled his own lawyers to get the necessary documents drawn up and exchanged. As a result by mid-June the funding stage had been reached. The government was ready to place contracts and the chosen contractors were anxious to see the colour of their money. Okello and Kiwanuka therefore came to London for another meeting with Craig, Kemp and Hafid to finalise the financial details. Closing hour – the moment when all the funds would be transferred – was arranged for 2.00 pm, London time, on Tuesday, 30 June.

At 3.00 p.m. Zurich time Calvin Craig was seated in the manager's office of the Banco Municipale. The two men sat in silence. M. Florieux, a balding official in his mid-fifties showed his nervousness. This was not a normal transaction. It was perfectly legal and within the bank's rules. Nor was it for him to enquire into customers' behaviour. However it was not normal and M. Florieux would be glad when he was relieved of the responsibility.

Craig was just as nervous but concealed it behind the nonchalant, reassuring smile he directed across the desk. On the wall behind the manager a clock silently notched the seconds. Craig had already checked its accuracy. He calculated that he could safely allow no more than ten minutes. When NatWest Bread St. failed to receive the expected hundred million from AOIB they would phone Kampala for instructions. Okello would be waiting in his office, hopping from foot to foot eager for confirmation that the money was safely deposited with his fiduciary bank. The news from London would send him into a panic. What happened next would depend on how quickly the African got a grip on himself. He might try phoning the FFC office in New York. He might attempt direct contact with AOIB in Nassau. Both would prove fruitless. But what he would (or should) do straight away was try to alert the Banco Municipale that there was an irregularity about the transaction. He would have to go through his London bank to do this and they would then have to telephone Zurich.

The clock on the wall registered 15.01 – and twenty-nine seconds. Florieux's internal phone buzzed. The manager picked it up. Frowned.

'Plus tard!' he snapped. 'Je suis occupé.'

He replaced the receiver, smiled at Craig and shook his head. He dabbed at his brow with a large handkerchief.

15.02. Craig thought hard. There was nothing that could go wrong – was there? Was NatWest waiting for the receipt of the AOIB money before releasing the ten million? That would be highly irregular. Their instructions were clear. They had to make a transfer at two o'clock. What if some wretched computer operator were late back from lunch?

The clock's second hand had made two-thirds of its next orbit when the phone broke the silence again. Both men jumped slightly.

'Oui! Oui! Merci. Apportez cela ici, toute de suite!'

Relief showed on M. Florieux's face. 'They are bringing it now.'

Craig said, 'Would you like me to sign the receipt while we're waiting?'

'You will, surely, wish to count it, Monsieur.'

'It's a lot of money to count. I guess I'll have to trust you.'

The manager shrugged and pushed a sheet of paper across the desk.

As Craig bent over to sign the door opened behind him. A bank messenger entered with an attaché case in each hand. He laid them reverently before M. Florieux. From his pocket he took two keys and handed them to his superior. The manager fitted one in the lock of the first case. It would not turn. He dropped the other key under the desk, moved his chair back and, muttering to himself, bent down to pick it up. The clock behind him now showed 15.05.

At last the two cases were opened. Craig nodded his approval at the neat bundles of new Swiss francs. Florieux re-locked the containers, checked the receipt and handed over the money. Craig thanked him and shook hands. He walked slowly, unhurriedly out of the office, across the bank foyer and out through the swing doors.

He turned right out of the bank and took the first turning on the right. Fifty yards down the street he climbed into the BMW he had hired two days before. Three hours later he was in Strasbourg.

From there he flew to London. That night he paid off Hafid. He took the mid-morning Concorde to New York, travelling as Colin Hartley. The next day he settled his accounts with Will Kemp and Louise Sondemann. Then he went home to Somerset Cove to enjoy what he felt was a well-earned rest.

TAKE TWO

'. . . Dragons of the prime,
That tare each other in their slime,
Were mellow music match'd with him'
                                    Tennyson

Chapter Twelve

'Now, look at that, Mr Hartley. It's gotten so no one's safe anymore – not no one.'

Sunlight spilled across the table from the long windows and bounced back from polished mahogany, silver and cut glass. Craig reflected that it was good to be home. There was even something comforting about the waspish garrulity of Amy Sullivan, breaking his breakfast calm.

His housekeeper prodded a finger at the *New York Times* folded by Craig's plate so as to reveal the headline, HIT AND RUN DEATHS INCREASE – CALL FOR TOUGHER LAWS.

'It's nothing less than murder, I say. Brutal, unfeeling murder. I'd like to get my hands on them.'

'OK, Amy, I'll look at it in a moment. Right now I could murder some eggs.'

She returned to the kitchen and Craig sat back in the chair. He sipped orange juice appreciatively and gazed out on Melton's sheer lawns. It was at moments like this that he wondered why he bothered with a life of crime. Slipping into the persona of wealthy, respectable, enigmatic Colin Hartley was like relaxing into a warm bath. Perhaps, one day, Hartley would retire from his mysterious semi-government career and spend more time at Melton with his collections, his rosebeds and his friends. Perhaps.

He stretched, opened out the newspaper and cast his eye over the four column feature. Road accidents in the city showed a seven per cent increase, he read. Hit-and-run casualties were up by an alarming thirteen per cent. He yawned.

Amy returned and plonked a plate of lightly-scrambled eggs before him.

'Terrible, isn't it?' she demanded.

'Shocking.' Craig nodded and took in the details of urban carnage between mouthfuls of breakfast. Suddenly, he stopped eating, fork in mid air.

'. . . The recent tragic death of 38-year-old Louise Sondemann. Ms Sondemann was returning late last Tuesday to the Richmond apartment she shared with her son Simon, aged ten, when a car travelling at speed mounted the sidewalk and knocked her down. She was killed instantly. The car, described vaguely by the only eye witness as a black sedan, did not stop. This, the latest in a grim catalogue' . . .

'Why, Mr Hartley, whatever's the matter? You look as though you've seen a ghost.'

For a moment he did not answer. His mind had gone into top gear, computing the odds of coincidence.

That afternoon he emerged from the elevator onto the dingy twentieth storey landing of Providence House. He turned a key in the door on his right, a door which still bore in faded gilt letters on its frosted glass the name of some previous tenants, long since out of business. Craig looked round the headquarters of Fox Financial Consultants Inc.: two desks, two chairs, a battered green filing cabinet that he had inherited with the office, a telephone, an answering machine and a telex printer. Craig pocketed the cassette from the answering machine and checked the desk drawers. But there was nothing incriminating to remove. Within days the office equipment agency would come to take away their property and there would be no trace of Fox Financial Consultants Inc.

The phone rang.

Craig stared at it. It could only be the telephone company making arrangements to disconnect. No one else had the number. He lifted the receiver.

'Fox Financial Consultants.'

'Craig, is that you? Where the hell have you been. I've been trying to get you for days!' The voice was taught, high-pitched with near-panic.

'Who is this?'

'Aziz Hafid. Craig, I must see you.'

'Are you crazy! Any contact is out of the question. It's too dangerous. I told you that. Goodbye!'

'Hang up on me and you're a dead man, Craig.'

The receiver was inches from its cradle.

Craig paused. The Omani sounded hysterical. If he was not humoured he might do something really stupid. He tried a more soothing approach.

'OK, Hafid, calm down. Now just what seems to be the problem?'

'They've tried to kill me – twice. Once in Paris and once here in New York.'

'Now, look, Hafid, you must be imagining things. Your family wouldn't . . .'

'Not my family!' The Arab was shouting into the mouth-piece. 'Someone else. The Ugandans, I guess. They're onto us, Craig!'

Calvin's mind went into top gear. It was impossible! They couldn't have untied all those careful knots of bluff and double bluff. And even if they had . . .

'Craig! Craig, are you there?'

'Yes, I'm still here. Now, listen . . .'

'No, you listen. I've got to see you – now.'

'Hafid, that's not a very good idea. Why don't we . . .'

'Now!' The Omani screamed the word. 'I'm coming over to your office. Be there!'

'Not here, Hafid.' Craig tried to calm the other man with a tone of firm authority.

'Where then?'

Craig thought quickly. There was no avoiding a meeting but he had to be sure that the Arab was on the level. The venue would have to be in the open.

'Central Park,' he said. 'In one hour. Go in at the entrance by the Metropolitan Museum. Follow the path. I'll be waiting on a bench.'

Fifty minutes later Craig was standing in a small clump of trees on rising ground overlooking the broad expanse of tarmac running from the gallery towards the centre of the park. It was a hot afternoon. A few sun worshippers sprawled on the grass but most had chosen seats in the shade. Many benches along the path were vacant.

Craig fixed his eyes on the Museum end of the path and cursed his discomfort. Even beneath the trees it was hot and he was sweating inside his lightweight suit. He flapped angrily at the flies carrying out summer manoeuvres round his head. Repeatedly he checked his watch.

At 3.27 Hafid appeared. He wore a cream linen suit and an open-necked green shirt. He entered the park at his usual relaxed, unhurried gait and did not look like a man under stress. Craig watched him walk along the path, hands deep in pockets. He looked to see if the Omani was being followed. An old lady shuffled from the direction of the museum and eased herself onto the nearest seat. A young black in jeans and a T-shirt zoomed past her on roller skates his trance-like state doubtless induced by the rhythms pulsing through earphones attached to the personal stereo hung round his neck. He sped past the strolling Hafid. For fifty yards behind the Arab the path was empty. Everything seemed all right. Craig emerged from the trees and set off down the slope.

After three gangling strides he stopped.

The roller-skated young man had turned. As he drew level with Hafid he came to a halt. Craig did not see exactly

136

what happened next. The negro's back was towards him. But he heard three shots. While Hafid was still swaying, gaping down at the splatter of crimson on his chest, the assailant was racing away towards the park gates.

For what seemed several seconds, Craig stood shocked, unable to move. He stared at the sprawled figure. He took deep breaths to repel the nausea welling up in his throat. At last, he willed motion into his trembling legs.

He turned, regained the trees, and kept on walking.

From hazy, far-off peaks, pine-forested slopes and granite scarps step downwards, ridge after ridge, and finally drop sheer into the Adriatic. The coastline of southern Dalmatia is one of the most dramatic in the whole Mediterranean area. And the most luxurious spot to view it from is the terrace restaurant of the island hotel, Sveti Stefan. Here the Yugoslav Ministry of Tourism have created one of their great show pieces and foreign currency earners. They moved a little fishing community from its village, covering almost the whole island, and turned the red-tiled, stone cottages into smart apartments, luxuriously appointed in a manner designed to attract decadent, capitalist visitors. But only the wealthiest of them – men and women who can afford top prices to sun themselves on the beaches flanking the causeway which connects Sveti Stefan to the mainland.

It was a favourite refuge for Craig and he had come here to steady his nerves and do some hard thinking. The former had taken him forty-eight hours, several whiskies, three complete Mozart operas on cassette and the reassuring seclusion of his lovely surroundings. The latter still occupied his mind's every waking moment.

On the third morning after his arrival he sat on the rooftop terrace enjoying a late breakfast of black coffee, croissants and large, ripe peaches. Most of the other residents had already departed on visits to quaint, walled

Dubrovnik, or boat trips along the coast, or were water skiing or sunbathing close to the hotel. The only other eaters were a solitary Englishman, invisible behind a copy of *The Times*, and a pernickety middle-aged French couple who were giving the waiters hell.

Craig ignored them and assembled the facts in his mind for the hundredth time. Two members of the team had been killed – violently. The law of probabilities ruled out coincidence. Hafid had believed the Ugandans were on his trail. That was impossible. Unless Louise had given something away in Kampala. But she only knew what she needed to know. There simply was no thread that could be followed from the Omani to the out-of-work actress, or vice versa. Craig considered again the common features of the two murders. Both had been carried out efficiently. The victims had been tailed by someone who recognised his opportunity and used the most effective method for his crime. That pointed to a professional hit man. Then, there was the other, more alarming, shared factor: both assassinations had taken place in New York.

Whatever angle Craig looked from, he always saw the face of the man with the drooping moustache. He cursed himself for underestimating the mobster. The mistake would cost him dear. It would cost the delights of Somerset Cove and the comfortable persona of Colin Hartley.

He would have to break all links with the past. Find sanctuary in a new anonymity. He would have to seek a new base. Washington, perhaps. Or the west coast. Even Canada. He swore under his breath. Not until now had he realised how much Melton and all it symbolised meant to him. Suddenly he felt old. Old and too tired to be putting down new roots. He swore again – louder this time, so that the French couple turned to glare at him.

The Englishman, too, seemed distracted from his reading. He folded the newspaper, dropped his napkin onto the table and stood up. Craig noted with amusement the garb of the middle-class Briton on holiday. A blue-spotted handkerchief drooped from the pocket of his alpaca jacket. Dark sunglasses shielded his eyes from the glare of a 'foreign' sun and a panama hat protected his head.

The hat was doffed as its owner passed the husband and wife from France. Craig caught a glimpse of thinning sandy-coloured hair. Then he realised that the stranger was coming straight towards him. Sudden panic gripped him. Craig looked round quickly for a means of retreat. There was none. He was at a corner table. Behind him was the waist-high parapet. Beyond that a seventy foot drop to the sea.

'Good morning. Lovely here, isn't it?' The man was stooping forward beneath the sun umbrella.

Craig muttered a greeting.

'Thought you might like to see the paper.' He held out the neatly-folded *Times*.

'Er, no thank . . .'

'Awfully interesting story on page six. Picture too.' The Englishman smiled affably and laid his offering beside the bowl of peaches. 'Thought we might discuss it a bit later. Shall we say on the south beach in half an hour.' He raised his hat, turned and walked away.

When his pulse rate had returned to something approaching normal Craig made his way slowly, casually, back to his suite. There, he opened the newspaper. At the bottom of one of the foreign news pages he saw Samuel Okello's fat smile. The photograph showed him stiffly posed with other officials beside a large block of stone. The accompanying headline ran NEW HOSPITAL FOR UGANDA. The report was brief:

'War-torn Uganda yesterday took a significant step towards a more hopeful future. Finance Minister Samuel Okello laid the foundation stone of a large new hospital at Soroti, the first such project since the end of the colonial era.

'The multi-million pound complex is extremely ambitious. It will have beds for 200 as well as extensive out-patient facilities. When it is completed at the end of next year the hospital will be kept very busy. The daily toll in the continued fighting against rebels in the northern district of Karamoja is considerable and there seems to be no end of the conflict in sight.

'Mr Okello stressed, however, that priority would be given to tackling some of the country's more chronic health problems such as river blindness and malnutrition-related diseases.

'There is considerable speculation about the source of funds for this expensive project. Uganda is heavily in debt to the World Bank and inflation in the country is currently running at about thirty per cent. Mr Okello stressed his government's gratitude to "those who have made this great humanitarian advance possible" but he refused to be drawn by reporters into identifying his country's benefactors.'

Chapter Thirteen

'How good of you to come and how very sensible.' The Englishman, who had exchanged discreet jacket and flannels for discreet blue bathing trunks, reclined on a padded beach chair and waved Craig to another which shared the shade of a large, multi-coloured umbrella. 'A lesser man would have made a run for it. So futile. Such a tedious waste of everyone's time.'

Craig lowered himself onto the gaily-striped cushions. 'Your invitation intrigued me.' He did not say that he had considered – and rejected – the option of taking a speed-boat ride to some point on the coast where he could hire a car. As the man said, that would have been 'futile'. Anyone who could track him from New York to a tiny European resort must have the organisation and resources to follow him anywhere.

Then there was the challenge of a new situation. Craig had always been the hunter. Now he was the prey. Well, if he was to stand any chance, he would have to find out what he could about those who were stalking him. Why were they not running to form. If this Englishman was a hired assassin why had he not done his job during the last few days? There had been plenty of opportunities. Craig sensed in this Anglo-Saxon a worthy adversary. His only chance of preserving his skin lay in outsmarting that adversary.

'I don't know your name,' he said.

'Oh, do forgive me.' The Englishman sat up and extended his hand across the low table standing between them. 'Pierrepoint Adam. Bit of a mouthful, I'm afraid. The Pierrepoint bit is a family name that we keep up generation after generation for no very convincing reason. I normally answer to "Adam"; it makes life easier all round.'

He sank back on the cushions and gazed up into the vivid canopy above.

'Funny things – names. Our parents make a decision – perhaps to please a wealthy relative, to honour a statesman or a pop star, or just to satisfy a passing whim – and we're stuck with it for the rest of our lives. There's no way I can escape from the name "Pierrepoint" – not even by deed poll. It's "an ill-favoured thing, but mine own". I must live with it. Ah, drinks!'

A waiter set down a tray bearing a couple of glasses and a jug of an orange liquid crammed with ice and cubed fruit. Adam sat up and poured.

'You will join me, won't you? I don't know what's in it and it's called something quite unpronounceable, but it's very refreshing.'

He sipped his drink appreciatively. Only when Craig had watched him do so did he follow suit. Adam reclined again and took up his reverie.

'Shakespeare was wrong. All that stuff about a rose by any other name smelling as sweet. There's definitely a connection between a man's name and his character. I'd have grown up quite differently if I'd been called Charlie or George.'

'Look, this is all very interesting . . .'

Adam ignored the interruption.

'Did you know that medieval necromancers believed a man's soul resided in his name? Knowing a man's name gave you power over him – or so they thought. I wonder if there's any truth in that.' He turned his disarming smile on Craig. 'I imagine you must be inclined to believe it.'

Craig stared back, his face a blank mask. The man was playing with him, using words as elaborate camouflage. Craig knew the technique. He had used it often himself. It was disconcerting to find himself on the other side.

'Perhaps we could get to the point,' he said.

'The point is, my mysterious friend, I know your name – or, rather, your names. All those aliases, and the identities that go with them. Such a fascinating cast of characters that you've slipped in and out of over the years. Craig Appleby, Craig Anderson, Colin Hartley, Count Carnotti, the Reverend Alberich Craven. But you know, Calvin Craig is definitely your most inspired *nom de guerre*. It suggests a certain austere, single-minded, intellectual brilliance. You and the great reformer are, if I may say so, birds of a feather. Calvin reduced theology to a system. He even put God into pigeonholes. You have done the same for fraud. I salute your genius.'

There was a sardonic twist to the Englishman's lips as he raised his glass.

Craig was too seasoned a trickster to be seduced by one of his own techniques – flattery.

'Look, Mr Adam . . .'

'Just "Adam", please.'

'Look, Adam, you seem to have gathered a great deal of information, much of it spurious. Now, I don't know who you are and frankly I resent your interest in me.'

Three young children rushed past down the beach shouting to each other in excited Italian, pursued by their mother, picking her way gingerly over the shingle. Craig, glancing at her bulging, overfed flesh, reflected that the bikini was a mistake.

Adam also followed her progress with casual interest. 'As to our intelligence, I assure you it is highly accurate. I hate to think how many man and computer hours have gone into unravelling your complex affairs, Calvin. You don't mind if I call you "Calvin" do you? It's really a compliment. As to your resenting my interest, I do hope I can persuade you to change your mind. You see,' he turned to look at Craig, all trace of humour now vanished from his face, 'in the whole wide world I am the only man who can keep you alive.'

Craig stared straight back at him. 'And why would you want to do that?'

'We'll come to that later. For the moment we will concentrate on your position. As you know, your life is in danger and two of your associates have recently been assassinated.'

'Even supposing that were true . . .'

'Craig, don't underestimate my intelligence!' The words crackled as though with static electricity. Adam had dropped any suggestion of casual bonhomie. 'You're a cold-blooded crook who's grown very fat off other people's misery and degradation. I could quite cheerfully stand by and watch while you got your come-uppance. As it is, I advise you to believe that, against most of my finer feelings, I find myself offering you help. What I know about you could put you behind bars in any one of half a dozen countries. So, don't try my patience with any evasive nonsense. Now, as I was saying, two of your associates have recently been assassinated. Do you know, by whom?'

'I presume by you or your paymasters, whoever they are.'

A surprisingly light ripple of laughter trickled from Adam's throat as he sank back in his chair. 'Would that I could solve my problems quite so simply. Come now, have you really not worked it out, Calvin? Not even after those brushes you had with some nasty gentlemen in New York? You disappoint me. There must be a faulty microchip in that computer you call a brain. Well, let me ask you another question: where do you suppose Okello got the money for his hospital?'

144

'I've had no time to think about that.'

'Then start thinking now. Consider two apparently un-related facts. Fact number one: what we are pleased to call the developing nations are desperately in need of cash. Most of them have run up enormous debts with IMF, the World Bank and international commercial banks and they haven't a hope in hell of meeting their commitments. Ever since OPEC quadrupled the price of oil in 1973 and sparked off mammoth inflation the non-manufacturing countries have plunged deeper and deeper into the red. Partly through no fault of their own they've been forced to borrow until their credit has run out. Now, when they come like Oliver Twist asking for more, they go away empty-handed.

'Of course, Calvin, you know all this. You've been cashing in on it for a long time. So let's move to fact number two: organised crime is on the run in Europe and the USA. The Mafia has been decimated in Italy by informers ever since Tomasso Buscetta began naming names in 1984. In America several gangland leaders have been put behind bars. Of course, the mob is hydra-headed; lop off one and two more appear in its place. But several criminal organisations have been smashed and a number of international syndicates have had their activities severely hampered. In particular they're finding it increasingly difficult to launder dirty money. Now are you beginning to see the picture?'

Craig gazed out across the glimmering water. Some fifty yards offshore a group of teenage boys and girls were engaging in horseplay on and around the diving raft. Their shrieks, shouts and splashes drowned the sibillant ripple of the tired wavelets crawling up the shingle.

'There's nothing new about the mob supporting corrupt regimes.'

'Of course not!' Adam flapped impatiently at a hovering mosquito. 'But I'm not talking about wholesale bribery or black politicians up to their smelly armpits in drug-running. The scale has changed. What we're up against now is a criminal organisation systematically buying political power throughout Africa and Asia.'

Craig stared at the other man and knew that he was quite serious. Yet what he was saying was scarcely credible. Craig considered the organisation, the funds that would be involved in such an operation.

Adam broke into his thoughts.

'Mind boggling, isn't it? Gives a whole new dimension to the word "imperialism". If these men are not stopped they'll create a new political grouping, a vast territorial power base. I call it the Devil's Empire.'

'And you're saying this process is well under way?'

'Very much so. Given the financial resources it's easy to set in motion. Imagine a third-world government, hanging onto power by its fingernails. Threatened by the political unrest created by famine, poverty and corruption. Guerrilla forces growing in strength, armed by China, the Eastern Bloc, Libya or some other self-interested busybodies. Their need for foreign exchange is desperate. How else can they buy food and weapons or fund showy development projects to enhance their prestige? If someone offers the chance of unlimited resources they're going to grab it. What matter if there are a few strings attached? So they take the money for a hydro-electric plant, a guided-weapons system, a hospital. In return they abrogate all extradition treaties, change a few laws, appoint "advisers" to the army and police, replace a few top civil servants and politicians. Before they know it they've sold their sovereignty. The real power is held by a bunch of foreign criminals and their stooges. The hydro-electric plants and the hospitals never get built. Instead, money is spent on cannabis plantations, airfields for the movement of arms, drugs, political dissidents and young girls for the brothels of New York, Rome and Amsterdam. Banks are set up for backing terrorist elements in other countries. Worst of all, the ordinary people go on suffering, wasting away with malnutrition and hideous diseases – just to satisfy the greed and power-lust of a few human vermin.'

Now, there was passion in his voice – venom. Craig realised, with relief, that this man cared. It was a tiny chink in Adam's armour. For all his apparent omniscience and confidence, the man was vulnerable. Craig stored the fact away in his mind and concentrated on the incredible picture the Englishman was painting.

'Forgive me, Adam,' he said, 'but all this talk of criminal organisations trying to take over the earth – it does sound a bit like something out of Ian Fleming. In the real world there are ways of combatting this sort of thing – international political pressure, the UN, the CIA, other intelligence agencies, Interpol.'

Adam drained his glass and refilled it.

'In the bad old days of the Empire, or even the badder old days of American economic imperialism that was true. The West could act as a benevolent big brother, making sure these political simpletons didn't make asses of themselves. Not so, now. Try giving friendly advice to some black leader whose ancestors swung down from the trees a couple of generations back and what happens? Formal protests or complaints at the UN about interfering in the internal affairs of a sovereign state. Get caught using intelligence agents and you risk a diplomatic incident, closure of your embassy, retaliation from neighbouring states. That plays right into the enemy's hands.'

'Then let these gullible governments stew in their own juice.'

'And ignore the domino theory? Impossible. If this organisation isn't checked, it will go on adding one-horse nations to its empire. We shall find ourselves fighting drug-traffic, terrorism, gun-running and vice on an unprecedented scale.'

147

Craig did not reply. He needed to learn all he could about Adam. The man obviously liked the sound of his own voice, so the best plan was to let him ramble on.

After a few moments' silence Adam asked, 'Can you swim, Calvin?'

Craig laughed. 'You mean there's something you don't know about me?'

'Look at those kids.' The Englishman pointed towards the diving raft.

A well-built, darkly-tanned lad had gained possession of the gently-swaying platform and was busily engaged repelling half a dozen others who were trying to clamber aboard.

'The syndicate behind the Devil's Empire are pretty damned sure of themselves. They defy governments and international organisations. There's only one thing they're sensitive about – competition. They're quite ruthless about keeping rivals off their patch. Rather like "Charles Atlas" over there. Only they don't just push people away; they drown them. So I hope you can swim, Calvin.'

'Those mobsters in New York . . .?'

'Just a part – a small part, as it happens – of the syndicate. They were detailed off to keep an eye on you. You see, our infernal imperialists were almost ready to move on Uganda when you blundered in. Naturally, your appearance created a great deal of angst. My guess is that you came within a whisker of being terminated when they realised exactly what your little game was.'

'They found out what I was doing?'

'Oh, yes. Don't imagine for a moment that your evasions hoodwinked them. They're not that stupid. All they had to do was lean on your stuttering lawyer friend to discover every detail of your sordid – very clever, but nevertheless *sordid* – plan.'

Everything the smug Englishman said made sense – pulled into focus those parts of the picture which had been

148

a puzzled blur. But not for a moment did Craig drop his guard.

He said, 'OK, if that's true, why didn't they get rid of me? I guess you know they tried to scare me off.'

Adam tut-tutted. 'Isn't that obvious? They didn't kill you – *then* – because they realised you could unwittingly be useful to them. Once they knew what you were up to they decided to let you go ahead. They only had to wait until you had jilted Okello and then catch him on the rebound. The poor man was in a desperate state. Suicidal. You had destroyed him. Dismissal and public disgrace was the very best he could hope for. Then, like a fairy godmother, enter a certain Italian gentleman, brandishing banknotes. There was no way he could refuse the money. He has been bought lock, stock and barrel. In a few months they'll make him head of state. Then there'll be no holding them.'

'Killing Hafid and Mrs Sondemann – that was a kind of revenge?'

'Yes, partly that.' Adam had returned to his casual, reflective tone. 'Partly to tidy up the loose ends. And partly just sheer, bloody-minded viciousness. Of course, you're the one they're really after. And they won't stop until they've found you.'

'So, who is the man behind this – Devil's Empire?'

'The man who wants you dead? I think that's a card I'll keep up my sleeve for the moment.'

Craig tried a different approach. 'You still haven't told me your interest. Just who are you? And why do you care what happens to me?' Adam sat up and yawned. 'All this talking is so enervating. I think I'll take a dip.' He removed his sunglasses and stood up. He looked down at Craig and smiled.

'I want you to do a job for me.'

'And why would I do that?'

'Because in return I offer immunity from prosecution and a chance to stay alive. In the pocket of my beach robe you'll find a card with a phone number on. Call me next Tuesday.'

'Don't count on it, Adam.'

'But I am counting on it, Calvin.'

'I'm an American citizen. My passport says so. You can't touch me here.'

'My dear Calvin, I can have you picked up just like that. But I don't need to. I can have you traced wherever in the world you choose to hide. But that's not necessary. You will co-operate because you have a terrible enemy and because I'm the only man in the world who can protect you from him.'

He turned and walked down to the rippling Adriatic.

Chapter Fourteen

If Craig had been the sort of man who crumpled under pressure he would not have been a successful fraudster with several million in the bank to prove it. There was no question of his submitting to the mysterious Adam's demands. The Englishman was a puzzle and Craig enjoyed puzzles.

That evening, he hired a car and drove the hundred twisting kilometres to Titograd. There he made three international telephone calls from a hotel pay phone. He checked out of Sveti Stefan the next day. He took a flight from Belgrade to Vienna and another from Vienna to Istanbul. He never left Yesilköy Airport. Nor did he collect his baggage. He made a last minute booking on a flight to London, using a different identity. From Heathrow he took a taxi to Harrods. There he equipped himself with new clothes and an expensive camera, paying cash for all purchases. He travelled by underground to the pleasant suburb of Harrow and booked into a small hotel under the name of Clark Chambers. He was, to all outward appearances, just another American tourist of modest means, vacationing in Britain.

Craig did not underestimate Adam's ability to keep track of him but he was determined to make the task as difficult as possible. He needed time – time to carry out his own investigations to equip himself with as much information as possible. If he could panic Adam into thinking that he had made a run for it, that would be a bonus.

The next three days were busy. He had a long, expensive lunch with a young lady of his acquaintance who worked as a freelance TV researcher. He spent an evening in a Clapham pub with a small-time crook. At both meetings money changed hands. But most of Craig's time was spent at the Central Reference Library in St Martin's Lane, sitting in front of a microfilm scanner, reading back copies of *The Times*.

At night Craig worked into the small hours in his hotel room, reading and re-reading his sheaf of notes and photostated documents. His researches had borne fascinating fruit. Pierrepoint Adam, he discovered, had been to the right school and university and had entered the Metropolitan Police Force after gaining a first in Oriental Languages. He had risen rapidly and, in 1972, had become Commissioner of the Hong Kong police. Four years later saw him as head of C11, Scotland Yard's Criminal Intelligence department. He remained there until 1984 and for much of that time he had also been British consultant to ICPO, the Interpol General Secretariat in Lyon. It was the next step in Adam's brilliant career that intrigued Craig.

In July 1984 amidst minimum publicity and maximum security, a high level conference took place in one of the Oxford colleges. Among the 170 participants were police chiefs and attorney generals from over fifty countries, as well as highly-placed officials from Interpol, CIA and British Intelligence. Ostensibly, the purpose of the gathering was to achieve greater international co-operation in the fight against major financial swindles, a category of crime, Craig discovered with some satisfaction, which had been alarming the authorities by its rate of increase. Conservative figures published by the Metropolitan Fraud Squad indicated a five-fold growth in international fraud in the decade 1973–83. Governments, multi-national corporations and major banks had been cheated out of untold billions by criminal syndicates and individuals, most of whom were still at large. The delegates at Oxford had agreed that a new, heavily-resourced organisation should be set up to integrate information on top-level criminals and organise joint action against their activities. The result was ISIF, the International Syndicate for the Investigation of Fraud. Its Director was Pierrepoint Adam.

ISIF, it seemed, was not all it purported to be. Bizarre rumours about it were persistent in journalistic circles and the underworld. Rumours about its funding. The organisation's headquarters were almost ostentatiously modest – a clutch of offices in an old Lombard Street building in the heart of the City. The staff was small – a dozen assistants, secretaries and clerks, recruited from police and intelligence departments. To all outward appearance ISIF was just another shoestring government department. So how was it that Adam and his deputy could afford almost non-stop, first class travel round the globe? And where had the money come from for the conglomeration of extremely sophisticated computer hardware installed in Lombard Street – including a private satellite communications system?

Then there was the question of ISIF's power and accountability. To whom was it answerable? When an opposition member of parliament had tabled a question to the Home Secretary on this very matter he had had to be content with a written reply saying that the minister had no information because ISIF was not a government department. Adam apparently experienced no difficulty over manpower resources. He only had to ask and the world's best police brains were diverted to his investigations. The word on the street was that the Syndicate enjoyed an independence and lack of restraint that made the KGB look like a Politburo rubber stamp. And Adam had complained about *Mafia* empire-building!

Which brought Craig to the Englishman's story about

a Ugandan takeover. Was it feasible? He knew it was. The mob had the money, the political influence and the ruthlessness to do it. Craig recognised the simple logic behind the scheme. With independent, inviolate bases throughout the Third World they could make the words 'international crime' take on a whole new meaning. And *that* really was a frightening prospect. If that was the ball game Craig had got himself into, the odds on his reaching hoary old age must be very long. Even assuming Adam was as powerful as he hinted, what was his supposed 'protection' worth? Craig remembered Johnny Saltire, an ebullient little man he had known briefly in Valparaiso. One night, after several hours drinking in a bar, Johnny had confided how seven years before, he had put one over on a member of New York's Bonanno family. Three days later Johnny's head was found in a trash can. The letter 'B' had been carved on his forehead. They never found the rest of him.

Craig examined his situation; on one side *cosa nostra*, on the other, a scarcely less sinister private force of crime busters. Whichever way he looked at his options they always dwindled to one.

An old proverb came into his head, 'Who sups with the devil should use a long spoon'. When Craig made his phone call to Adam on the following Tuesday, he did so from Paris. He took a mid-morning flight and dialled the number from a booth at the airport.

Adam wasted no time on preliminaries.

'Things are moving faster than we'd expected. Come to my office as quickly as you can.'

'Said the spider to the fly. Don't try to hustle me, I know all about hustling. I'm a pro.'

There was a short silence at the other end of the line. Then, irritably: 'Where are you?'

'Since you can trace the call, there's no point in not telling you. I'm at Charles de Gaulle Airport – Paris. And

I can be away from here in any one of a dozen different directions before you can say "Sherlock Holmes". I've been several jumps ahead of you ever since our last encounter. I intend to keep it that way.'

Another silence. Adam sounded genuinely worried when he spoke again.

'It's not me you should be afraid of. Phone some of your friends in New York. Then get straight back to me.' There was a click and the phone went dead.

Craig wasted no time in getting through to Greg Bronson, a director of Chase Manhattan and a regular golf partner. Greg's wife, Jean, answered the phone.

'Colin? Is that you? Oh, thank God! Wait while I get Greg. He's having breakfast.'

Craig knew from her high-pitched staccato that something was very wrong. Seconds later the banker was on the line. He was almost as agitated as his wife.

'Colin, it's good to hear you. We've been so worried. The police have been trying to get hold of you for a couple of days. You've spoken to the police?'

'Greg, just calm down and tell me what's happened.'

'What! You mean you don't know. Oh, Jesus, Colin I hate to be the one to have to break it to you.'

'Break what to me?'

'About Amy Sullivan. It was Sunday. A friend called for her. Seems they always went to mass together. She got no answer. Then she saw that the curtains were drawn. They were still drawn a couple of hours later when she came back. She called the police. Oh, God! It was awful. Poor Amy. She was tied to a kitchen chair. She was . . . Colin, I'm so sorry . . . She was dead. Murdered.'

'Murdered! How?'

'Strangled.'

'My God, that's awful!'

Craig thought quickly. The silence registered an appropriate sense of shock and horror. He *was* shocked, but he had other things on his mind. He needed to get information without appearing callous.

'Did the burglars ransack the place?'

'The police don't think it was burglars. Whoever it was, they went through your desk and all your drawers but they don't seem to have taken anything of value. Your golf trophies and your snuff box collection are OK. Of course, only you'd know. The police will want you to check. You are coming right back, aren't you, Colin?'

'What's that?' Craig was trying to think and make the right responses at the same time. 'Er . . . yes. Yes, of course. Just as soon as I can. What about poor Amy's funeral. Have her people been contacted?'

'Yes, I think so. But they may not release her for burial just yet. The pathologist . . .' Greg fell silence, then blurted out. 'Oh, God, Colin, there's no easy way to tell you. Poor Amy . . . They gave her a hell of a time. Before they killed her, they tortured her and raped her.'

'Tortured!' The word came out as a gasp from Craig's dry throat.

'I talked to the lieutenant on the case. He told me how they found her. She was stripped and there were cigarette burns on . . . parts of her body . . . Colin! Colin, are you there?'

'What? Yes, yes, I'm here. It's just that this is a terrible blow. Who would want . . . Have the police any idea . . .'

'I don't know, Colin. I don't think so. The only thing the lieutenant would tell me is that it looked like a professional job. Colin, Jean and I are so sorry, so very sorry. If there's anything . . . Let us know your flight and we'll pick you up at the airport.'

'Thanks Greg. Yes, I'll do that. Thanks, I'll be in touch later. Goodbye!'

Craig found a bar and ordered a large cognac. Then another. By the third he had the shakes under control and had begun to discipline his thoughts.

156

'Think! Think clearly. Don't clutter yourself up with emotions.'

'But I'm angry – and scared.'

'All the more reason to pull yourself together. Survival – that's the name of the game. If you're going to get yourself out of this you'll need a clear head.'

'But, Amy. To do that to a helpless, harmless . . .'

'Obviously, they wanted her to tell them where you were. Could she do that?'

'No. Of course not. I never tell her my plans.'

'Looks as though they've come to a dead end, then.'

'Never underestimate them.'

'What then? Carry on running? Or take up Adam's offer?'

'Hobson's choice.'

Craig put through the London call.

Adam's voice, still urgent, came clear down the line.

'Are you convinced now?'

'Let's say I'm prepared to hear what you have to say.'

'Right, listen carefully.'

Adam gave his orders succinctly and rang off.

Dean's Yard is a little enclave of peace reached by an arched gateway close by Westminster Abbey. The buildings of different periods and styles are occupied by government departments, church officials and Westminster School, whose pupils use the large square of grass as a games field. But on a warm August evening there were no boys in blue shorts running around the tree-lined green. The secretaries had gone home. Their bosses were already packed onto suburban trains or drinking in their nearby clubs. Dean's Yard was almost deserted. The only signs of life were two elderly clergymen, crossing the grass slowly, deep in conversation, and the driver of a Post Office parcels van who was slumped over the wheel of his parked vehicle.

Big Ben intoned the half hour as Craig entered the square. 'Dean's Yard. 6.30 on the dot. You'll be met.'

Those had been Adam's instructions.

Craig walked slowly along one side of the green. He kept well clear of doorways, eyes and ears alert for any movement. He turned the first corner, past three empty parked cars and the red van. Turned the second corner. Someone emerged from a doorway ahead and walked towards him. A man, mid-thirties, tall, fair hair, dark suit. He came on briskly. Craig maintained a leisurely pace. The stranger approached, passed, walked on. Craig realised his heart beat was sprinting. He took some deep breaths and continued steadily. He completed one circuit of the square. Then another. He sat for a few moments on a bench, thought better of it and continued his monotonous round. He cursed Adam. If this was an example of the man's efficiency, he was not impressed. Big Ben pounded out the third quarter.

As he approached the Post Office van for the third time he saw that the driver had bestirred himself and was clambering from his cab with a couple of empty mail bags. He smiled as Craig drew level.

'Lovely evening.'

'Yes, it sure is.' Craig returned the pleasantry without pausing in his stride.

'Ah, one of our American friends. Over here on holiday?'

Craig stopped and turned. He was standing between the van and an expanse of windowless wall.

'Just a brief stay.'

'Well, I hope you like the Old Country.'

'I'm sure I . . .'

Craig felt his arms pinned from behind by very strong hands. The 'postman' snatched up one of the sacks and threw it over his head. Instinctively Craig opened his mouth to shout. There was a firm pressure on his face. Something sweet mingled with the dry smell of the mail bag. Craig felt his body going limp but being supported by others. Then all sensation ceased.

Chapter Fifteen

Craig's first impressions were of lying on something uncomfortable with a bright light burning his eyes. As he opened the lids and gazed upwards he saw a naked bulb suspended by a long flex from an elaborate ceiling rose. He sat up, head still throbbing from the drug. Slowly he looked around him, eyes at first focusing with difficulty.

He seemed to be in a large, old-fashioned drawing room – Victorian probably. He took in dark panelling, brown velvet curtains, a tiled fireplace surmounted by a fussy overmantel, unyielding sofas and chairs of solid design, a scattering of occasional tables and a vast ebony grand piano with bulbous legs. As details became clearer he realised that the glory of this imposing salon was a faded glory. Carpets were threadbare, table tops undusted, horsehair poked through tears in the upholstery and discoloured rectangles around the walls showed where pictures had once hung.

Craig rose cautiously from the leather covered *chaise-longue*. Supporting himself on its elaborately scrolled back, he took a few uneven steps on legs which felt weak. He stumbled slowly across the room to a tall pair of double doors and grabbed the tarnished brass handle.

He expected to find the door locked but it swung easily inward. He looked into a wide, tiled hallway into which coloured light from the setting sun tumbled down an uncarpeted staircase through tall windows filled with armorial stained glass. Craig peered round towards the front door and quickly withdrew his head. Two men were playing cards at a small table.

He closed the door and went over to the heavily-draped french windows. He pulled back the velvet and looked out on a desolate vista of nettles, weed-cracked terraces and overgrown shrubbery. He tried the handle. This time any pressure was firmly resisted. Craig turned at a noise behind him.

Through the open doorway someone was wheeling a trolley laden with food. It was the 'postman', cap and grey uniform now replaced by baggy trousers and an open-necked shirt. Adam entered the room behind him. He looked pleased with himself.

'Ah, Calvin, recovered just in time for dinner. Excellent.' He turned to the other man. 'Cartwright, put everything there, on that hideous brass-topped table.'

The man called Cartwright unloaded two plates of cold ham and chicken, a bowl of salad, french bread, butter, cutlery, two wine glasses and a bottle of hock. Adam arranged a pair of balloon-back chairs on either side of the round table, seated himself on one of them and motioned Craig to the other.

'Fall to, Calvin. A modest repast, I'm afraid, but Cartwright's culinary repertoire is not very extensive.'

The younger man smiled. 'The job description didn't say anything about cordon blue cooking, sir.' He wheeled the empty trolley from the room.

Craig sat and was glad to do so. His legs were still weak. But he did not eat. He glared angrily across the table. 'What the hell was all that cloak and dagger stuff about? You didn't need to do that!'

Adam poured wine. 'A little melodramatic I agree, but not without point. It is vital that you disappear completely. If even you don't know where you are the chances of anyone finding you are reduced to a minimum.' He sniffed at his glass and made a slight grimace. 'Besides we have

160

to keep the location of our little hideaway quite secret. By the way, that's why you'll find you can't leave the premises. You're free to wander about the house and the grounds but, as you will observe, there's an electric fence inside the perimeter. Crude, perhaps, but we find it more effective than the elaborate paraphernalia of TV cameras. Please keep well away from it. Although, as I've indicated before, your death would cause me no loss of sleep, right at this moment you are worth more to me alive. Now do eat up. You're going to need all your strength.'

'And just what am I going to need it for?' Calvin helped himself to salad. He suddenly realised that he was very hungry. He certainly was not going to sit and watch Adam feeding himself with such obvious relish.

'As to that, I'm afraid I'll have to ask you to wait just a little bit longer. Your briefing will begin after dinner.'

Craig felt much better with food inside him and his head was considerably clearer as Adam dabbed his lips with a pocket handkerchief. The ISIF chief walked over to the door, muttered something to someone outside, then turned back to face Craig.

'Cartwright will show you around. We'll have our introductory planning session in ten minutes. *À bientôt!*' He disappeared and was replaced by Craig's erstwhile hijacker.

The cheerful, loquacious Cartwright led Craig upstairs and gave him the benefit of a non-stop commentary.

'Feeling better, now? Sorry we had to manhandle you. Orders are orders.' He opened a door into a large, sparsely furnished bedroom. 'These'll be your quarters. It's no five star hotel but the bed's comfortable. Thank your lucky stars it's summer. This place is like a bloody deep freeze in winter. Bathroom's next door. You'll find clothes in the wardrobe and chest of drawers. I think we got your sizes right but they're no designer styles – just best Marks and Sparks.'

'I'm here for a long stay, then?' Craig broke into the monologue.

Cartwright shrugged. 'Couldn't say. That's up to the boss. Ours not to reason why.' He led the way from the room. 'There's only more bedrooms on this floor.' He returned to the staircase. The clatter of their footsteps on the bare boards echoed round the hall.

'Recreation room!' Cartwright ushered his guest into a chamber which was positively luxurious in comparison with the rest of the accommodation. It was obviously the original library and the bookshelves which lined three walls, though not full, were surprisingly well-stocked. Easy chairs of modern design were scattered around. There were standard lamps and tables littered with magazines, packs of cards and, on one, a chess board and pieces. At the far end, by the long, curtained windows, there stood a table tennis table. A row of computer game machines completed the diversions provided for ISIF staff.

'You've made yourselves pretty comfortable,' Craig observed.

'Sometimes we're cooped up here for weeks at a time. We'd go round the twist without something to take our minds off the job.'

'You don't get out into the village?' Craig asked the question casually.

Cartwright smiled, not taken in.

'Village, sir? What village would that be? I'll show you the office now.'

The next room they entered was full of activity. Half a dozen men and women sat at desks in front of computer consoles or answered telephones. Maps and charts filled most of the walls. Cartwright led the way to a desk where an attractive blonde in her later twenties sat frowning at the display on the orange screen before her.

'Sara's the queen of the place. Anything you want to know – but anything – ask Sara.'

The young woman looked up, ignoring Cartwright and scrutinising the newcomer as though he had some obvious and particularly repellent skin disease.

'Oh yes, Mr Craig. We know a great deal about you.'

Craig smiled. 'I look forward to hearing a lot about you.'

'I doubt that will be necessary. I'm here to obtain information. If there's anything you need to know, then ask me. If Adam clears your request I'll do my best. We have some pretty sophisticated equipment here.'

With that she turned back to the screen and gave it her full attention.

Outside in the corridor Craig said, 'Obviously the star pupil in the Pierrepoint Adam charm school.'

Cartwright shrugged. 'Sara's not very broad-minded when it comes to criminals. Can't blame her really. Straight out of college she married a young cop. Two months later he was killed trying to stop some bank robbers making a getaway. She sees her work with ISIF as a sort of personal crusade.'

'Hasn't anyone ever told her that life goes on?'

'Pretty difficult to tell Sara anything – like most clever women.'

'She's clever as well as beautiful.'

'Brilliant is the word. Brain like a razor blade. Double first at Cambridge – whatever that is. She's what's called a mathematical genius, which puts her in a different league to mere mortals like me. I understand women who like Mills and Boon, and dancing and go gaga over babies. Sara keeps herself much to herself. All I've seen her do in her spare time is play chess and read Russian novels, this thick.' He made an exaggerated gesture.

'Poor kid.'

Cartwright shrugged. 'Yes and no. She'd get more sympathy if it wasn't for her sharp tongue. Most people

163

here ignore her. It seems to be what she wants.' He chuckled suddenly. 'Still, pity to think of that great body going to waste, isn't it?' He checked his watch. 'Well, time to report to the boss.'

He led the way back to the hall and through a door opposite the room in which Craig had originally found himself. It was laid out like a small lecture hall. Fifteen or so chairs were arranged in rows facing a table. On the wall behind it there was a screen and Craig noticed an array of film and slide projectors ready for action. Half the chairs were already filled and other members of Adam's entourage were rapidly assembling. Cartwright showed Craig to a chair in the front row and sat beside him just as Adam entered and marched straight to the table.

'Everyone here? Hurry up, Fletcher! We've a lot to get through.' This to a young man who sidled in through a side door, obviously hoping not to be noticed.

'First of all I'd like to introduce Mr Calvin Craig who has been persuaded to help us with this operation.'

Craig thought, 'You're presuming a hell of a lot, Adam,' but he said nothing.

'You have all read the synopsis of Calvin's remarkable career. He is, like all of us, a specialist and a highly accomplished one. His rôle is going to be absolutely crucial.' He smiled at Craig. 'Calvin, I won't introduce you to the whole team. You'll get to know them quickly enough.'

'OK, first we're going to run over most of the information we've gathered. This is principally for Calvin's benefit but it'll do none of you any harm to refresh your memories. Lights!'

The room was plunged into darkness and at the same moment a beam from the film projector illuminated the screen. The first image was of a man in ecclesiastical robes, a mitre on his head, eyes closed, hands clasped in front of him. The camera back-tracked and Craig realised that the figure was dead, lying in state in a chapel. Two Swiss

Guards, with pikes flanked the catafalque and a procession of mourners shuffled past.

'We start with an interesting little montage of scenes,' Adam explained. 'This is the late Pope John Paul I, called by some "God's candidate" and by others "the thirty-three day pope". The official cause of death was a heart attack on 28 September 1978. If he had not died he would have carried out a fearless enquiry into the corruption of Vatican finance and its connection with the Mafia.'

The next picture was of a very different kind of corpse – clothes crumpled and stained, eyes wide, a cord still fastened round its neck. Craig had seen it before and was searching his memory when Adam took up the commentary again.

'Roberto Calvi, found hanging under Blackfriars Bridge on 18 June 1982, with twelve pounds of bricks stuffed in his pockets. Official verdict: suicide. Calvi was over here talking with Interpol agents. He was ready to spill the beans on various underworld financial dealings in the hope of keeping his Banco Ambrosiano afloat. Calvi posed a severe threat to an awful lot of people. His bank had a network of finance houses and companies all over the world. These were laundering money for crime syndicates, channelling billions of unofficial aid to fascist dictatorships in Latin America, financing assassinations and drug running.'

A succession of faces and places appeared on the screen.

'The collapse of Banco Ambrosiano after Calvi's death should have been a godsend for police forces which had been working for years to collect information about Mafia dealings. It was the biggest break they'd ever had. Unfortunately, the bank's records were shredded.' Adam's voice had an edge of bitterness. 'It seems too many top people were involved. The two men in this clip are Mafioso John Rosselli and CIA agent Ewan Jackson. Back in the sixties they jointly planned an assassination attempt on

Fidel Castro. That failed but American Intelligence was more successful in its backing of the plot to overthrow this man, President Allende of Chile, in 1973. Money for the military coup came from the Italian Mafia, via Banco Ambrosiano. In the 1970s syndicated crime had one thing in common with right-wing regimes in South America, the CIA, and certain elements in the Vatican and U.S. and European politics – a determination to suppress Communism at all costs. This resulted in some very strange bedfellows: Cardinal Marcinkus, head of the Vatican bank; Graham Maretin, U.S. Ambassador in Rome – he diverted ten million U.S. dollars to right-wing parties in Italy – Alexander Hurd, Commander of NATO forces in Europe and later Reagan's first Secretary of State; and this man, Milan-based, Mafioso Paolo Sylvestri. I'll come back to him later.'

Craig examined the figure, obviously filmed with a hidden camera in front of an impressive building which looked like a city palazzo. He saw a small man, perhaps five foot six or seven, in his mid-sixties, dressed unobtrusively but expensively, walk with firm, decisive movements, the short distance from the columned portico across a courtyard to a waiting black Mercedes, that Craig assumed to be armour-plated. Craig had trained himself to form instant impressions. Everything about Sylvestri spoke power and willfulness. The kind of man to be avoided if possible and, if not, to be handled like nitro-glycerin.

The image changed. Now, newsreel footage revealed a scene of bloodshed and carnage. As an excited Italian commentator gabbled away, the camera panned across a concourse littered with broken glass, strewn luggage, bodies quickly covered with coats. Polizei were trying to tape off the area where a bomb had obviously exploded, a task made difficult by hysterical women and obtrusive pressmen. Adam let the horror speak its own message before adding a few statistics.

166

'The Bologna railway station massacre in 1980 killed 85 men, women and children and injured a further 182. The world, and particularly the Italian electorate, was meant to believe that the bomb was planted by communist terrorists. We now know that this indiscriminate slaughter of innocent people was a political action designed to discredit the left-wing and keep Mafia friends and associates in power. The organiser was this man.'

A police photograph of a dark-haired man with anxious eyes and a Groucho Marx moustache appeared on the screen.

'Licio Gelli. He was arrested in 1983 in Switzerland. Before he could be extradited to Italy he was sprung from jail and spirited away to Uruguay, where he now lives in considerable luxury on a ranch near Montevideo. Gelli was Paolo Sylvestri's right-hand man. His exile was a severe blow to the Milan organisation. But worse was to follow.'

Craig had no difficulty recognising the subject of the next film clip – a dark-haired man in sunglasses descending the steps from an airliner under heavy police escort.

'Buscetta.'

'That's right.' Adam sounded like a teacher encouraging a diffident pupil. 'Thomasso Buscetta, not a big fish in the international *cosa nostra*, but he knew who many of the big fish were. When he was extradited from Brazil in July 1984 he began to name names. Money men, hit men, front men. Once he started, there was no stopping him. Police on both sides of the Atlantic were kept busy for months and months. Jails bulged with mafiosi – big ones and little ones. Throughout '85 and '86 there were spectacular trials. Massive sentences were handed out. So were promotions. It was like a never-ending Christmas in the criminal investigation offices in New York and Rome. It was certainly the biggest bombshell ever to hit the nerve centres of organised crime. Other supergrasses clambered on the Buscetta bandwaggon. New jails and courtrooms had to be built, more police recruited. Some over-enthusiastic simpletons even talked about the death throes of the Mafia. They were wrong, of course. Lights!'

People shuffled and coughed as the show ended but Adam continued after the merest pause.

'They were wrong because the Mafia is too big, too well organised and too diffuse. As fast as leaders were roped in new ones appeared to take their place. Some even boasted that the Buscetta débâcle had been a necessary pruning away of dead wood. The ones who survived, or even profited, from the crisis were those who had the imagination and the vigour to re-organise their operations. And that brings us to Paolo Sylvestri. Sara, you have the file for Mr Craig?'

The blonde superbrain came forward from her seat at the back of the room and handed Craig a red folder. It was well filled.

'Bedside reading.' She gave him the merest hint of a smile.

'That's right,' Adam nodded. 'You'll need to have mastered that by tomorrow morning. It'll tell you just about all we know about Sylvestri and his operations. I won't waste time by repeating it. I'll just say that his is now the biggest Mafia operation in Italy and one of the top three in the world. They call him the White King, and that's got nothing to do with chess. He is the largest single dealer in *La morte bianca*, the white death – heroin. Last year he distributed over five tons of the stuff in America and Western Europe – and God knows how much cocaine on top of that.'

Craig was fascinated, despite himself.

'If you're so damned clever and you've got all this dope on Sylvestri,' he tapped the red file, 'How come you haven't pulled him in?'

Adam sighed deeply and Craig noticed, for the first time, the lines around the man's eyes that unmistakably indicated stress. 'Paolo Sylvestri has another nickname – *Il Flagello*, the Scourge. He is *totally* ruthless. If he so much as suspects that someone might be in his way he has him removed. Politician, policeman, banker, rival mobster – it doesn't matter. In the last eighteen months five men have been assassinated simply because they were in a position to point the finger at the White King. Not one of them would have dared turn informer. But to Sylvestri that's irrelevant. He knows the only silence that can be guaranteed is the silence of the grave. Does that deal with your question?'

Craig nodded.

'And it prompts another one I don't want to ask.'

'Well, I'll answer it anyway. Sylvestri is the man I was telling you about last week. He's moving his operational base to East Africa. Once he's done that, there'll be no stopping him. Uganda will be like a feudal barony, a no-go area for international law enforcement. That's why we have to put a swift end to his career. That's why we have to use unorthodox methods. In short, Calvin, that's why you have to pull off the biggest con of your life against one of the most dangerous men in the world.'

Chapter Sixteen

Craig was mentally winded. Till now he had felt himself to be almost level on points in his bout with Adam. But this was below the belt. Everyone in the room was looking at him. They were expecting him to stagger, to grope for the ropes, to show defeat in a display of frightened, angry bluster.

With an enormous effort he remained outwardly calm. In the thick silence he forced his mind to work: 'The enemy is most likely to be off guard in the moment of victory'. 'The unexpected . . . always use the unexpected.' 'Keep the other guy guessing.'

He tilted his chair back and stared for a long moment at the ceiling. The stage was his and the audience on the edge of their seats. The showman in Craig responded. At last he smiled and gazed at Adam with disarming candour.

'A few weeks ago I was happily minding my own business, making a quiet dishonest living.'

Adam returned the smile.

'And now you have a unique opportunity to do your little bit for the western alliance. As a patriotic American I'm sure you'll jump at the chance.'

Craig made a deprecating gesture.

'Since you put things like that, what can I say? I'm flattered by your confidence. If you really think I can help, I'll be delighted to do what I can.'

He noted with satisfaction the involuntary, surprised flicker of Adam's eyebrows. Someone behind Craig gasped.

Cartwright fumbled for a packet of cigarettes, thought better of it, and returned it to his shirt pocket.

Adam took his time replying. Now it was his turn to circle his opponent, re-appraise his resilience. Craig watched him, trying to read his mind. He would know that he had not broken his prisoner; had not raised him to that pitch of fear where he could do nothing but co-operate. He had no idea whether he could trust Craig and Craig intended to keep it that way.

Adam stood abruptly. He returned Craig's smile. 'Splendid, Calvin. Splendid. We have every confidence in you. With your skill and the resources at the disposal of our little organisation, I'm sure we can carry this operation to a successful conclusion. Now, ladies and gentlemen, the hour is late. We'll postpone the detailed briefing till tomorrow. Back here at 9.30 a.m. everyone, please.'

He strode from the room.

Craig joined the little crowd filtering through the main doorway. In the hall he saw Sara, her green eyes fixed on him intently.

'You're very good.' The words were a statement of fact; nothing more.

'I'm glad you approve.'

'Oh, I don't approve. I most emphatically don't approve. I regard you as just about the lowest form of human life.'

'I bet you say that to all the men.'

She pursed her full lips and two tiny grooves appeared between her eyebrows.

Craig thought, 'A hit; a palpable hit!'

He said, 'In my case, of course, you're quite right. My only redeeming feature is that I play a very good game of chess. Would you like to pit your holy zeal against my low cunning over the little chequered board?'

Sara smiled very faintly. 'As Adam said, it's late. I need my beauty sleep.'

She turned and preceded Craig up the staircase.

He surprised himself by sleeping very well. In the morning he bathed, changed into a casual shirt and trousers and went in search of breakfast. This event took place in a large basement kitchen, where he sat with members of Adam's team, round a scrubbed deal table of immense proportions. The cooking, he discovered, was done on a rota basis by the ISIF men and women, as were all the other household chores. The house, known as the 'manor' by its inmates, was a totally closed community. No outsiders ever entered its cloistered seclusion. Craig found the 'monks' and 'nuns' polite, pleasant but reserved. He assumed they were under directions from 'father abbot' not to fraternise too closely with their devious American guest.

Back in the lecture hall, now flooded with light from large windows, giving onto a vista of horticultural neglect, Adam assembled his entourage on the dot of 9.30.

'Good morning, everyone. All rested and fit for the fray?' He wore militarily-creased flannels, a white shirt with the sleeves rolled up and a Old Wykehamist tie striped in blue, brown and red.

'This operation, as I'm sure we all realise, is going to be the most difficult we have so far undertaken. Those of you who go to Italy and Uganda – and especially you, Calvin – are going to be scrutinised by Sylvestri's people. If they suspect, even for a moment, that you're not kosher, it'll be a case of "goodbye cruel world". Yes, Calvin?'

Craig had held up his hand.

'I take it your plan involves my dealing with Sylvestri face to face.'

'That's right.'

'Hasn't it occurred to you that he's bound to recognise me?'

'That is a risk, certainly, but one we've calculated very carefully. Sylvestri's organisation is large. Winding

172

up your activities will have been left to his American subordinates. To the White King you are nothing but a name, an item on one of his many hit lists. He's never seen you. It's unlikely that he's even seen a photograph. We shall, naturally, be taking precautions. You'll have a new identity, which will stand up to the closest scrutiny and your facial features will be . . . rearranged.'

'If you mean plastic surgery, forget it!'

Adam laughed, hugely enjoying Craig's alarm.

'I doubt it will come to that. A few adjustments here and there. That's all. But you don't need me to tell you about that sort of thing. You're a positive character chameleon, Calvin.'

'Why don't I find your confidence reassuring? Well, what is this identity you've dreamed up for me?'

Adam resumed his lecture.

'Through Okello, Sylvestri is trying to win the confidence of the existing Ugandan regime. It's costing him a lot but he regards it as money well spent and he believes the government is basically secure. What we have to do is sow a few seeds of doubt in his mind.'

The folding chair creaked its protest as Craig shifted in a vain effort to achieve a little comfort. He said, 'Men like Sylvestri don't panic easily. They're good at their business. They plan thoroughly. They've got immense resources.'

Adam nodded.

'Absolutely right, Calvin. But in this case we think that very fact may be Sylvestri's Achilles heel. He's committed to the Ugandan move – totally. He is personally supervising every aspect of it. Bringing it off successfully is vital to the very continuance of his whole organisation; and time isn't on his side. Someone is going to blow the gaff on him before long – lead the police to one of his heroin-manufacturing laboratories; arrest one of his lieutenants before he can be silenced. Italy is getting too hot for him. Moving records and personnel to another country; re-routing exports and imports – it's a major operation. Once a waggon like that is set rolling it's well-nigh impossible to put the brakes on. If we present Sylvestri with a major snag, he'll have to take it seriously. He'll have no choice.'

'And what "snag" have you guys dreamed up?'

'Fletcher!'

In response to Adam's summons, a solemn-faced young man with black hair and beard made his way to the front of the room. He was carrying awkwardly a bundle of large display cards. While he was arranging these on an easel, Adam explained.

'Fletcher is our African affairs expert – and a brilliant one. The Foreign and Commonwealth Office were furious at losing him. Isn't that so, Fletcher?'

The young man smiled shyly and immediately launched into his presentation.

'Uganda is a land-locked state.' He pointed to a map of north-eastern Africa by way of proof. Then, with the aid of lovingly-prepared charts, he dilated for thirty-five minutes on the historical, geographical and political realities of that troubled country.

What it came down to was this: to settle internal squabbles the existing government relied on the goodwill, or at least the neutrality of neighbouring states. But, at one time or another, Tanzania, Kenya and Sudan had all either intervened directly in Ugandan affairs or provided asylum for ousted leaders. Thanks to the numerous changes of regime that had taken place since independence, this latter category now consisted of scores of politicians and generals who had had a taste of power and wanted more. Like exiled Hapsburgs, all of these men had their devoted followers within Uganda and their friends without. President Yoweri Museveni had been more successful than most in pushing guerilla forces across

174

the state boundaries and evoking from most tribal areas an exhausted acquiescence to his rule. But no informed observer would be prepared to take bets on the dawning of a new era of peace in that shattered, hate-infested land.

Fletcher thankfully resumed his seat and Adam took up the narrative again.

'The spanner we propose to throw into Signor Sylvestri's works is the threat of a major invasion across Uganda's northern and eastern borders.'

Craig snorted his incredulity. 'For God's sake! You're going to martial an army in the Sudan!'

Adam's face showed fleeting annoyance. 'I said the *threat* of a major invasion, not an actual invasion. Saunders, come and explain, will you?'

Saunders was bald, stocky, pallid, middle-aged and had 'ex-cop' written all over him. Adam pulled a face but said nothing as Saunders perched on the edge of his table. He made his contribution in the flat, disillusioned voice of a weary infantryman in the war against crime.

'Drugs, terrorism, arms traffic – the three corners of the eternal triangle of modern, major-league crime. Sylvestri's involved in all three. Gun-running isn't a big part of his operation but we know he's supplied weapons to both guerilla forces and legitimate governments in Africa and Latin America. Anyone who wants to start a bloody revolution anywhere in the world and needs the hardware will have Sylvestri's name on his shopping list.'

He paused for effect and gazed slowly round his audience. 'We are going into the market.'

Craig listened intently. He approved this man's economy with words; it made a refreshing change to Adam's self-congratulatory pomposity.

'When I say "we" I mean Juventus Ltd. It's a front company dealing in computer games. For the last seven years its real activity has been the illegal movement of sophisticated small arms, mainly to the Middle East and the wealthier terrorist organisations. The man behind Juventus is Corrigan Dentwood-Smithe – with an "e".' Saunders' lips twitched with contempt. 'One of those privileged Englishmen who's channelled the benefits of an expensive education into a criminal career.'

Saunders produced another thick, red file and tossed it to Craig.

'Dentwood-Smithe is your new alias. You'll find all you need to know about him in there. If you don't, ask.'

.'Just hold it right there.' Craig dropped the folder on the empty chair beside him. 'There's no way I'm going to impersonate a real man. It's too tricky. If I'm going to be checked out by Sylvestri I have to be one hundred per cent convincing. I make up my own rôle, or the whole thing's off. Anyway, what's the real . . .' He looked at the file cover '. . . Dentwood-Smithe with an "e" got to say about all this?'

Adam explained. 'Mr Dentwood-Smithe, known to his intimates, apparently, as "Corrie", has been persuaded to take an all-expenses-paid holiday at one of our locations abroad, where he is, and will remain, totally incommunicado. Meanwhile, we have "borrowed" his company.'

'What about his employees and business associates? They'll smell a rat.'

'Corrie runs a commendably slim organisation. And we've taken the liberty of making a few staff changes. In point of fact, you won't have to meet any of his established contacts.'

'Too damned right, I won't.'

Adam ignored the protest. 'It's out of the question to invent an arms-dealing company. As you say, Sylvestri will check up on you very thoroughly. When he does he'll find that you have an established organisation and a proven record.'

'But . . .'

Adam interrupted, raising his voice just enough to make his point. 'This is the only plan that will work. This is the plan we've spent months perfecting. And this is the plan we're going to activate. OK, Saunders, carry on.'

Craig put on a scowl and listened sullenly as the elaborate fraud concocted by Adam's team was unfolded. Inwardly he congratulated himself on his bluff. He was sure from Adam's covert glances that the head of ISIF believed that his star was gradually being won over to the rôle designated for him.

As he heard what the rôle entailed, Craig was more determined than ever to extricate himself from ISIF and all its works at the first possible moment. Adam's plan was hazardous, ill-conceived and hadn't a cat in hell's chance of working. It was a fantasy concocted by someone who had been watching too many British World War II movies. The whole set-up – secret H.Q. 'somewhere in the country'; the 'briefings'; the *esprit de corps* of a little brotherhood pledged to the defeat of the 'enemy' – it all smacked of a script written for David Niven, Jack Hawkins and John Mills. The only trouble was that Adam believed it, and that made him dangerous. Trying to keep out of the Mafia's clutches was one thing. Trying to outsmart them on their own territory was quite different. If he had any chance of survival, Craig decided, it lay in working solo.

After lunch Craig did a reconnaissance. He took the two red files with him and, under the pretence of doing his homework, wandered around the grounds. Not even the bright sunshine could lift the gloom of neglect. The estate was a wilderness. An area of 'lawn' was kept roughly mown and was sprinkled with the partially-clad bodies of off-duty ISIF operatives. It was fringed with a tangle of rhododendron, buddleia, nettles and brambles that combined with once-decorative trees to form thickets of Amazonian density. There was a vestigial tennis court,

177

its hard surface buckled and crazed by weed. A few paths had been cut through the jungle. They led, as Adam had indicated, to a ten-foot high, electrified fence completely concealed by the undergrowth, which extended unbroken beyond it. Craig found the drive and strolled casually along it. Fifty yards from the house it bent sharply to the right and was immediately blocked by a meshed gate.

Craig gave a casual wave to the security guard in his little hut and turned back along the drive. As he did so a small pick-up truck with a canvas cover came towards him and stopped at the barrier. Craig recognised Cartwright as the driver. He hurried round the bend out of sight of the gate. Then he stepped quickly into the undergrowth. He forced his way through shoulder-high ferns and creepers that grabbed at his ankles, to reach a vantage point where he could watch the egress ritual. He saw Cartwright show his pass, saw the guard solemnly check it, then take out his keys and unlock the gate. The whole process took twenty seconds or so.

Casual conversation over dinner disclosed that Cartwright went out for supplies most afternoons. Next day Craig made a careful scrutiny of the area close to the gate. He found that he could reach a point which bordered the drive but was hidden from the house and the guard hut. He calculated that, from this base, he could, with luck, reach the back of the pickup and climb in while the driver was waiting and the guard was busy with his keys. Like all the best plans it was simple.

In his room that night Craig reviewed progress. The 'jail-break' was easy enough. There were one or two details to be attended to; such as making sure Cartwright did a shopping run on the day Craig chose for his attempt. He already had some ideas about that. What he needed to work out now was how to keep his freedom once he'd gained it. An impecunious Yank would be pretty conspicuous in an English village. Adam had, of course,

178

confiscated Craig's passport, cash, chequebook and credit cards. Somehow, Calvin had to get to London undetected. There he had bank accounts Adam could not possibly know about. There he could buy a new passport, a new identity. Somehow, he had to lay his hand on some money – fifty pounds would do; a hundred would be better. Craig reflected on the irony of his situation. Here he was, a multi-millionaire who had long since given up trying to calculate how much he was worth, trapped in a ridiculous situation for want of a few paltry English pounds. Well, he told himself, he wouldn't be trapped for long. One way or another, he would finance his escape.

Meanwhile, he gave every appearance of learning with resigned application the rôle Adam had assigned him. It was hard work. Adam was a perfectionist. It was the one thing the two men had in common. Craig was convinced that the whole operation was insane and its foundations weak. But he could not but admire the intricacy and precision of the structure that Adam had built upon them. Nor was the Englishman satisfied until Craig was word perfect on every location, every timing, every element in his concocted story.

Each day at the manor was divided into four work periods. From 9.00 to 11.00 Saunders and Adam himself went over and over with Craig the minutiae of the plan. 11.00 to 1.00 Craig spent on his identity. That meant being grilled by two of Adam's men on every aspect of Corrigan Dentwood-Smithe's upbringing, career, family life and business activities. It meant being subjected to lessons in English 'county' pronunciation by an elderly, female version of Attila the Hun, ('What the heck, Mrs Fennel, Sylvestri's English is a lot worse than mine.' 'A debateable point, Mr Craig. Now, once again, "Nain thaousand paounds for a faim haouse in Hempstead"'). It meant a complete change of appearance. His spectacles were replaced by tinted contact lenses. He had to grow a thick moustache and wear his hair longer. Both were died black, as were his eyebrows, which were augmented with false hair to give them a bushy appearance. He had silicon pads inserted in the walls of his mouth to bulge his cheeks. His jackets, which bore Savile Row labels, were also padded and he had to practise walking, slightly slumped with a casual saunter to disguise his height.

Three till five every day was occupied in lectures, tutorials and demonstrations on the subject of small arms. In a few days Craig had to become an expert in the latest automatic rifles and pistols and hand-held missile launchers. He had to be able to use them, dismantle them and quote performance specifications in detail.

The final session, before dinner, was an illustrated Who's Who of international arms dealing. The real Corrie knew personally the major handlers. He was familiar with all the techniques for getting consignments of contraband goods through customs. He had mastered the art of 'shuttling' cargoes from port to port and providing false bills of lading in order to conceal their true point of origin or destination.

It was a punishing regime and if Craig had had any intention of going through with Adam's plan he would have demanded more time to prepare for his rôle. But the professional in him responded to the challenge. Craig was good, probably the best individual con artist in the business. He managed the double bluff with consummate skill. Charm and persistence even penetrated Sara's crisp coating of cynical detachment. After four days of pestering she agreed to a game of chess.

It was very revealing. Craig learned more about her in one hour of intense concentration over the chequered board than he would have done in days of guarded conversation. The cautious human computer, doing everything by the book was a fraud. Sara played an open, attacking, some-times reckless but always ruthless game. Within minutes, the board had been denuded of most pawns; the opponents had exchanged knights and Craig was a bishop down. Sara made her moves decisively and without hesitation, obviously playing for a quick and humiliating victory. Craig allowed himself to be put under pressure, hoping to lure his adversary into a mistake. When her pieces were well spread, he made a feint against the white queen but, with a quick smile, Sara recognised the ploy, castled, and secured her king's side. She foiled two more breakouts but maintained a defiant advance, consolidating what appeared to be an irresistible attack, spearheaded by queen and queen's rook. Craig gave the appearance of being nonplussed. His hand hovered to and fro over the board like a kestrel vainly seeking its prey. He advanced a castle, then had second thoughts. But while Sara was watching these bewildered manoeuvres, Craig was watching her. A lock of hair hung, unrebuked, over her eyes. She bit her lip in eager anticipation of the kill. At last, Craig sidled his remaining bishop into a protective position close to the king. Sara pounced on it with her queen.

'Check!' she announced triumphantly. Then, 'Damn!' as she saw, too late, the trap she had slipped into.

The black king's rook swept her majesty from the board and the whole game swung round.

Now came the most difficult part of the contest for Craig. He saw that he could win in four moves. He knew that Sara could see it, too. He also knew she would resent losing to him. With elaborate care he contrived a 'mistake' that looked like the result of over-confidence. He lost a knight and castle in quick succession and, after three more moves apiece, he and Sara agreed to abandon the game as a draw.

'Thanks a lot. You play quite well.' The condescension was deliberate and Sara reacted.

'Quite well for a woman, I presume you mean.' She brushed the hair from her forehead with a quick, angry gesture.

Craig tilted his chair back and yawned.

'Well, there has to be a reason why there are different world championships for men and women.'

'It couldn't have anything to do with male chauvinism, of course.'

Craig considered the point calmly, apparently oblivious to Sara's mounting indignation.

'What you need to be really successful at this game is a controlled killer instinct. The female of the species simply doesn't have it.'

That was too much for his lovely opponent.

'You damned, arrogant Yank. Come on, set the pieces up again. I'll show you a woman prepared to go for the jugular.'

Craig stood up and treated her to a smug smile.

'Rule one, never play chess when you're angry. Anyway, much as I'd love to have another game, I must decline. I have to know the finances of the Sylvestri arms deal backwards by tomorrow morning and it's late already.'

'Chicken!'

'Not at all. It's a case of business before pleasure. Isn't that the motto of this place?'

A group of half a dozen had gathered to watch the closing stages of the game and were now enjoying the argument.

Sara got to her feet and glowered across the table.

'Tomorrow, then. Same time. And perhaps you'd care to back your confidence in male superiority.'

'You forget, I have no money.'

Your cash is in the safe and I have the combination. I'll just help myself to my winnings.'

'Suppose you lose?'

'I'll put the money in your wallet.'

'And the stakes.'

'Ten pounds?'

Craig laughed.

'Is that the value of your confidence? Let's make it a thousand. Best of three games.'

Sara sneered.

'Oh, very clever. You know I can't possibly match that.'

Everyone in the room was now following the exchange like spectators at a tennis match.

Craig shrugged and turned to leave. Then he stopped and faced Sara once again.

'OK. Tell you what I'll do. A thousand pounds . . . against one night of unbridled passion.'

The look she directed at him would have done credit to Medusa.

'Don't be stupid.'

Craig lifted his hands in an expansive gesture and addressed his audience.

'See what I mean; no killer instinct.'

Everyone joined in the laughter as Craig sauntered from the room. He had reached the door when Sara's voice cut through the air like a wind from the Urals.

'Very well. Nine o'clock tomorrow, then.'

Craig turned, smiled, nodded.

He could still hear the ribald cheers as the door closed behind him.

Chapter Seventeen

'Can I come in?' Bob Cartwright's cheerful face appeared round the door.

It was half an hour later and Craig was lying on his bed, going over several pages of A4 notes. Cartwright entered, laughing, and propped himself against the marble-topped washstand.

'That was bloody marvellous, Calvin. Took our snow maiden down a peg or two. Brought a bit of life to this place, as well. It's the only excitement we've had in ages. You should see 'em downstairs, now. Proper gambling den it is. Barney Low has opened a book and everyone's having a flutter.'

It was what Craig had expected, counted on. He said, 'What are the odds?'

'I'm afraid our Sara's still favourite. Barney's only offering evens on her. He reckons you've made it impossible for her to lose.'

'And what can you get on the Yankee?'

'Three to one at the moment.'

'OK. Put a hundred on for me and I'll split the winnings with you.'

'You mean it?'

'Sure, it'll add a bit of spice to the contest.'

'A night with the lovely Sara would be spice enough for me.'

'Oh, I wouldn't really want to humiliate her. But don't tell anyone I said so. In fact I'd like to lay on a little dinner for her the day after tomorrow as a gesture of friendship. If

I gave you a shopping list could you buy the food and wine? Charge it all to my account, of course. That wouldn't be breaking the rules, would it?'

'No, I don't think so. I'd have to check with Adam, but I can't see that there'd be any objection.'

'OK. But ask him to keep it secret. I'd like to surprise Sara. Now, if you don't mind, I must get back to these figures.'

Throughout the next day Craig kept to himself as much as possible, concentrating on his preparations for the match. Winning it was a vital part of his plan to escape from Adam's madhouse. Yet winning it would not be easy. Sara was a better player – just. But she was under pressure – demoralised by her defeat, angered at losing face in front of her colleagues and worried about the terms of the wager. Craig reckoned that she would also be distracted by the crowd that would assemble to watch the match. He was banking on her concentration being badly upset. That was why he had insisted on three games. It was on the cards that Sara would keep cool enough to win a single contest. Craig was gambling on being able to erode her mental and emotional stamina as the night wore on.

Apart from work and meals he stayed in his room, using Yoga-type exercises to relax his mind and body. After dinner he completed the process with a long, calming, hot bath. He dressed and checked his watch and deliberately went downstairs ten minutes late.

Craig entered the recreation room to a chorus of sardonic cheers and desultory hand claps from the twenty or so people seated on chairs in a circle round the table where Sara and thirty-two black and white pieces waited. He bowed lightly to his adversary and waved affably to the audience.

'Sorry to keep you waiting.'

'Well, now that you are here, perhaps we can make a start.' When Sara spoke it was as though someone had opened a refrigerator door.

Craig noted, with approval, that she was smoking a cigarette and that two stubs already lay in the ashtray beside her. He sat down, picked up a chess piece of each colour and moved his hands, briefly, below the table. There he switched the white piece for a, previously palmed, black and held out both closed fists to his opponent. She pointed to the right one and Craig opened it to disclose a black pawn.

'Me to start then,' he said cheerfully, replacing both legitimate pieces on the board. Having the opening move in two games out of three gave him a slight advantage.

He was to need it. Sara played the first with teeth-gritting concentration. It turned into a protracted war of attrition. Craig deliberately extended it further by taking a long time over each move. But he was careful not to give the impression of hesitant uncertainty. While Sara crouched over the board and hardly ever moved her eyes away from the battlefield, Craig sat back in his chair, occasionally chatting with bystanders and giving every appearance of being totally relaxed. The game had been in progress over two hours when he realised that his position was hopeless but he waited another twenty minutes before conceding.

Craig did not relax his concentration but Sara did – marginally. Before the second game was more than a few moves old, Craig sensed that she was reverting to her natural, aggressive style. He countered with an Alekhine defence. He let her occupy the centre of the board in the hope that she would confuse occupation with control. With pawns advanced to K5, Q4 and QB4, white appeared to have a commanding position. In consolidating this apparent advantage Sara weakened her king side. Suddenly, with a nonchalant gesture, Craig advanced his bishop to take a pawn and announced quietly 'Check'. Now Sara was hustled into a series of improvised defensive moves and discovered that her own central pieces were in the way. Craig changed the tempo of his game. A series of swift moves drove a corridor through white's ranks. At last Craig said, 'Mate in three, I guess.' Sara nodded angrily. She sat back and looked at her watch.

'Gone midnight. Shall we postpone the final game till tomorrow?'

Craig had no intention of not pressing his advantage.

He grinned. 'What? Disappoint our fans?'

One of the bystanders said, 'You can't stop just when it's getting exciting, Sara.'

Another added, 'Yeah, I can't wait to count my winnings.'

'Nor can I,' Craig said, and everyone laughed.

Everyone except Sara, who blushed deeply and busied herself setting up the pieces on the board.

Craig watched her as she lit another cigarette to steady her nerves. Like a leopard confronting a cornered prey, he could smell her fear, could savour already the taste of victory. Yet not for one unguarded instant did he allow his mental muscles to relax. He brought every element of sophisticated gamesmanship into play to keep Sara flustered.

The final game was scrappy. Black lost a pawn and a knight unnecessarily in the opening moves; then countered with a badly-planned attack, in an attempt to put white under pressure. Craig hit back against black's exposed queen's side. With her pieces badly scattered, Sara could only fight a long, defensive game.

Eventually, she glowered her hatred at her opponent. She said, coldly and struggling for self-control, 'Congratulations, Mr Craig.'

'Thanks for the game, Sara. I enjoyed it.'

He stood up, stretched, yawned.

'Well, I guess the sandman's calling. Adam won't forgive me for being half asleep on parade in the morning.'

Sara looked up, suddenly hopeful. 'You mean you're not . . .'

'Not tonight, Josephine.' The joke brought a few guffaws from the onlookers. 'I'm afraid I wouldn't be at peak performance right now. Let's make it tomorrow night, shall we?'

Sara stood up and left the room without a word.

Craig turned to his audience. 'Gee, I hope she's as good on the mattress as she is on the chessboard.'

The next morning Adam called a general meeting. His announcement was brief and to the point.

'Ladies and gentlemen, you'll be pleased to know that our preparations and training are complete. You've all worked hard and I'm satisfied that we're as ready as we ever shall be. Three days ago we made contact with Sylvestri. His organisation lost no time checking out Juventus Ltd and, I'm delighted to say, they took the bait. Our friend Corrie has been invited to a meeting with Paolo Sylvestri. So,' he beamed round at his charges like a headmaster announcing an extra half-holiday, 'we go tomorrow.'

The announcement was received with a skitter of applause and an outbreak of conversation. Adam held up a hand for silence.

'This is a big one but if we all keep our heads and stick to the plan, we can pull it off. Oh, I might just add that, in the best military tradition, I've given the plan a codename. For various reasons, I thought the most appropriate title would be "Operation Checkmate".'

As the laughter subsided, Craig got to his feet.

'May I just have a word?'

Adam nodded.

'I only wanted to say that I've found the last week instructive and even enjoyable. You may find it difficult to believe but the idea of setting a thief to catch a thief appeals to me. If I have a debt to society, I'd sure as hell prefer to pay it off this way, rather than spend ten years in some state penitentiary. So you can be assured I'll play my part to the best of my ability. I'd planned a kind of celebration dinner for this evening. Seems it's going to be a farewell dinner, too. I look forward to seeing you all then.'

He sat down to polite applause.

Craig thanked whatever gods watch over successful criminals that his own plans had been perfected in the nick of time. He prayed that his luck would hold till he was safely away from the manor.

It didn't.

Adam insisted on a final run through of all the major elements of the plan. That lasted till 12.50. Then Craig went in search of Cartwright and could not find him. Someone suggested that he had already gone into town and Craig's heart missed a beat. At last he ran to earth (literally) the organisation's gofer in the stable yard. Cartwright was lying underneath the pickup, tinkering with the engine.

Craig gave Bob a list of provisions and found out that he was going out straight after lunch. He also collected his £150 winnings from the young man.

Craig did not feel like eating but he went into lunch to avoid any possible suspicion. He left the table as soon as he could and went to his room. He changed into the clothes he had already chosen for his escape – rubber soled shoes, dark trousers and jacket, and a lightweight jumper. He was about to leave when there was a knock at the door.

It was Sara. A different Sara. Not the self-assured, granite maiden of a week ago. She slipped into the room and stood just inside the doorway. She stayed there not looking at him, not saying anything.

'Well hello,' Craig made the greeting warm and encouraging. At the same time he glanced at his watch.

'Look, Mr Craig,' she faced him and he read hope, despair and revulsion in her eyes. 'You've had a big enough triumph. You don't need to humiliate me further.'

'Meaning that you don't want to go through with your side of the agreement.'

'It was stupid of me to accept your terms.'

Craig walked to the window and glanced down at the drive. There was no sign of the van but it could only be a few minutes before Cartwright drove out. He turned, striving to appear calm, unhurried.

'And now you've suddenly remembered you're not that kind of girl?'

'You can't seriously intend to go through with it. You wouldn't . . . A gentleman wouldn't . . .'

Craig laughed. 'I've been called many things in my time but seldom a gentleman. Let me ask you something. If you'd won our bet, would you have taken the thousand pounds?'

Sara fumbled in her handbag and pulled out a small bundle of notes.

'Let's settle this thing with money. Here's £150. It's all I can manage at the moment.'

It was tempting. More cash in the pocket would make things easier over the next couple of days. But Craig resisted. It was important to maintain the impression that he had every reason to stay at the manor. He looked again at his watch. Almost two o'clock. He had to get rid of the woman quickly.

'Keep your money. You've got something else you value more highly. And so do I. See you tonight. Now, you really must excuse me. There are one or two final points of detail I have to attend to.'

He strode past her, opened the door and went out. As he reached the head of the stairs the word 'Bastard' echoed along the passage behind him.

Walking as fast as he dared, he crossed the hall, let

himself out onto the terrace, descended the steps and crossed the drive at an oblique angle. He was about to enter the shrubbery when two men came round the corner of the building. He turned sharply and strolled nonchalantly along the weed-infested gravel. Seconds later the van swung into view around the back of the house. Bob gave a smile and a wave as he passed. Craig stared hopelessly after the vehicle. Momentarily he thought of sprinting after it and scrambling into the open back. He abandoned the idea immediately as impracticable.

In desperation he rushed into the undergrowth bordering the drive. Brambles snared his clothes as he forced his way through to the path he had trampled down days before. But he knew it was pointless. He had watched Cartwright's departure four times. The pickup had never waited at the gate more than twenty-three seconds. Breathless and muttering curses Craig arrived at his vantage point.

The van was still there. He heard the guard's voice.

'You're sure you don't mind, Bob? I wouldn't ask only they're photos of my daughter's wedding. I promised I'd send them off as soon as they were ready.'

Through the bushes Craig saw the man unbutton a pocket in his tunic and take out a wallet. He heard Bob say, 'That's all right Arthur. Give us the ticket. Chemist on the corner of Bridge Street, is it?'

'That's right. They said they'd be ready today. Very good of you, Bob.'

Craig waited till the man had handed a slip of paper in through the cab window and turned towards the gate. He heard the clunk as Cartwright engaged first gear. He looked quickly around to make sure no one else was in sight. Then he stepped lightly across the packed gravel, put both hands on the van's tailboard and vaulted into the shaded interior.

There was a large wooden crate at the far end and some sacks scattered on the floor. As the pickup began to move, he lay down and pulled some of them over him. In the darkness Craig smiled.

'So long Adam,' he thought. 'Don't call me: I'll call you.'

The van had picked up speed. Suddenly it slowed and came to a halt. Craig strained to hear external sounds while the blood pounded in his ears. He heard creaking metal. A voice called out, 'OK, Bob. On your way.' The engine roared and they were moving again. Staring through a chink in the sacking, Craig saw tall iron gates swinging shut as the pickup turned onto a public road. Two lines of defence? He admired Adam's caution. He admired himself more for triumphing over so wily a foe.

Through the open back of the van he looked at the retreating road. It was a quiet lane, flanked on both sides with woodland. No other vehicles were in sight. Craig decided to get out as soon as the driver slowed for a junction or turning.

He sat up, his back resting against the large wooden box, waiting for his opportunity.

He was suddenly aware of a faint sound immediately behind him. He half turned. The crate lid was raised. He struggled to his knees but someone gripped his shoulder. He wrenched free but the man was now standing behind him. A powerful arm encircled him. A hand came up to his face. Craig tried not to breathe in the familiar sweet-smelling fumes. But his lungs had to have air.

Chapter Eighteen

Slowly, painfully Craig came to realise that the whining drone was not inside his head. He opened his eyes and read the words, 'I'M NO MOLE SAYS PALACE AIDE'. He squeezed his eyelids shut, then tried again. Now he could see that he was staring up at the front page of the *Sun*. As he moved his head to take in more of the scene, the newspaper was lowered to reveal Cartwright's smiling face.

'Well, well,' the smile widened. 'Who's a naughty boy, then?'

Craig groaned. 'Where the hell am I?'

'To coin a phrase.'

'Spare the witticisms.' Craig eased his protesting body into an upright position.

Cartwright folded the paper. 'Well, Mr Dentwood-Smithe, we're aboard your private jet somewhere over the Alps and, in about an hour, we'll be landing at Pisa.'

That explained the noise. Craig's head was now clear enough to recognise the sleeping quarters of a luxuriously-appointed executive jet. The bed, upon which he had been lying, had the monogram 'DS' worked into its royal blue counterpane as did the little matching curtains drawn back from the windows. The implications of his whereabouts took a few more seconds to register. Then Craig felt as though something hard and very heavy had hit him in the solar plexus.

'You don't mean you're going through with this God-awful charade!'

Cartwright got to his feet.

'You'd better freshen up. Toilet's through there. I'll go and tell Adam you're back in the land of the living.'

In the mirror of the tiny washroom Craig gazed at the now-familiar face with its dark, perfectly-trimmed moustache and flaccid features. He gulped down a couple of beakers of iced water from a dispenser beside the royal blue basin and took some deep breaths. Neither did much to still the armed insurrection in the region of his lower intestine.

'Come on through Corrie. Sit down.'

Adam beckoned him to an armchair in the aircraft's lounge. He and Cartwright were seated on either side of a low table with drinks on. In a chair by herself, Sara gave the appearance of being totally absorbed in a very thick paperback.

Craig took the initiative.

'Look, Adam, this entire plan is crazy., It's got more obvious holes than a Brooklyn brothel.'

'You should have thought of that before.' Adam's face showed no emotion. 'We've been over everything dozens of times. You've had every opportunity to raise detailed objections.'

'Listen . . .'

'No, you listen.' Adam's voice rose a few decibels. 'We haven't much time. Get this very clearly into your head: you're not as smart as you think you are. It was precisely because you didn't raise scores of objections that I guessed you had some little plan of your own. That meant two things. First of all I had to have you watched every waking minute. Secondly, I had to do your thinking for you – look for those little flaws that only you, as the front man, would spot. At one stage you had me fooled – but not for long. I saw through you.' He leaned forward and tapped the table to emphasise his next words. 'And so will Sylvestri – unless you apply your not inconsiderable mental powers

194

one hundred per cent to this project. From now on, until I tell you otherwise, you are Corrigan Dentwood-Smithe. I've invested a hell of a lot of blood, sweat and tears into getting this mafia excrescence behind bars. You put one little toe out of line, and if he doesn't kill you, I will.'

Craig glared, beaten. 'Damn you, Adam. Damn you to hell.'

Adam's response was as quick as an echo. But it was not Craig's *words* that angered him.

'Drop that American accent! Now! You *are* Dentwood-Smithe. For God's sake show a bit of professionalism.'

He turned to Sara.

'Go over the itinerary for Corrie's benefit, will you.'

She put aside the novel she had not been reading, took a shorthand notebook from a smart briefcase beside her, opened it and read, in a bored secretary kind of voice.

'11.15 – arrive Pisa airport. Meet car to drive to the Villa San Angelo – that's a hotel in the hills about 15 kilometres from the city. ETA noon. Move into our suite and wait. Sylvestri will contact us there.'

Craig frowned. '"We"? "Us"?'

'Ah yes.' Adam looked faintly uncomfortable. 'I've had to make a slight change to your entourage. You need the best back-up we can provide. So Cartwright will be your minder, as planned. But I've substituted Sara as your PA. That may not please either of you but it helps my peace of mind.'

Craig shrugged. 'She's efficient. That's all that matters.'

Sara said nothing. On the drive from the airport she spoke to Craig for the first time.

'You ought to know that the Villa San Angelo belongs to Sylvestri. He'll have us under surveillance from the moment we arrive.'

'Room's bugged?'

'Very likely. We'll check of course, but we must behave as though we suspect nothing. Our performance has to be convincing down to the last detail.'

'What about this car?'

They were riding in a discreet Mercedes 380; Cartwright next to the chauffeur; Sara putting as much distance as possible between herself and Craig on the back seat.

'It's safe. Owned by a Juventus subsidiary. The driver's one of ours.' With hair drawn back and wearing a cream pleated skirt with a matching silk shirt and a wide crimson belt, she looked like exactly what she was supposed to be; a correct, unflappable, expensive confidential secretary. She resumed her icy silence.

After a further five minutes travelling in their emotional refrigerator Craig told the chauffeur to stop the car.

'Bob, Sara, let's step outside and admire the view.'

The other two exchanged glances but followed him as he got out of the car and walked a few paces up the road. They stopped, looking down on a landscape of terracotta roofs and a haphazard scattering of vineyards each laid out with mathematical precision.

Craig said, 'What happened back at the manor – there was nothing personal in it. I tried to get out of this . . . 'Operation Checkmate' escapade because it's crazy and dangerous and it hasn't a cat in hell's chance of coming off. You're both intelligent people. Surely you can see . . .'

'You used us!' Sara spoke in a hostile whisper.

'Sure I used you. I'm good at using people. I majored in it. So did Adam. That's what this game is all about. Probing people's weaknesses. Exploiting them. Adam's trouble is that he's confused the nasty busines of using people with a Boy Scout obsession for doing good deeds. The two don't mix. They're oil and water.'

Cartwright shook his head. 'I've been with ISIF just over a year. I've done a couple of jobs. One was a complete success.'

'And the other?'

'It didn't go completely according to plan. We lost a couple of good men. But we did make a big hole in a high-society cocaine ring.'

'Well, perhaps you don't mind ending up as a notch on some hit-man's gun butt. But that is definitely *not* the way *I* plan to go out.'

He turned to Sara. 'Look, you're a very intelligent woman. You must see that we can't beat a man like Sylvestri.'

She faced him squarely for the first time that day.

'I see that a man like Sylvestri must be beaten. I see that he makes a mockery of the police and the law. The people he can't buy, he kills. I see that Adam is right in fighting fire with fire. And right now I see that if the operation fails it'll be because you haven't the stomach for it.'

'And you, I suppose, will be at my side, reporting every word and gesture to Adam on a mini-transmitter, hidden in your powder compact.'

Sara's eyes half closed in a superior smile. 'Oh, Adam will be kept fully informed.'

Craig gazed from one to the other. He read wariness and mistrust on each face. He shrugged, acknowledging defeat.

'One thing I'll never understand about you British is your passion for futile gestures. I just hope you know what we're getting ourselves into. Well, at least I tried to make you see sense. OK. Forward the Light Brigade!'

He led the way back to the car.

The Villa San Angelo was an imposing edifice. An eighteenth-century classical façade concealed a range of quattrocento conventual buildings around a colonnaded cloister. At its centre, where monks had once paced the lawns in contemplative silence, scantily-clad women bronzed themselves beside a large swimming pool. And the suite allotted to Mr Dentwood-Smithe's party was bugged.

For two days Craig played at being a successful international businessman. He spent an hour or so each morning on the phone to his London office giving instructions about non-existent deals. He dictated letters to Sara about the delivery of non-existent merchandise to fictional customers. And Sara dutifully typed these letters, brought them back for signature and posted them. They spent the afternoons sight-seeing and the evenings sampling Pisa's limited night life.

There was no sign of Sylvestri.

On the third morning, the hotel porter delivered an envelope. Craig ripped it open and read a brief, typed message.

'Saturday. 11.00. Lay-by on Strada No.556, two kilometres east of Londa. Be alone.'

Cartwright fetched a map and located the place on a winding road running from Florence up into the hills of Umbria.

'Pretty lonely spot,' he observed.

Craig spent the rest of Friday going over and over the proposition he had to put to Sylvestri.

He got little sleep that night.

Craig pulled the Mercedes into the lay-by and switched off the engine. He checked the dashboard clock with his watch. He was eight minutes early. Eight minutes to compose himself. Slow the racing heartbeat. Dry the sweat trickling down his temple. Eight minutes to make himself think clearly. He got out of the car and leaned against the parapet, gratefully breathing in the cool air that wafted up from the scramble of woodland, scrub and parched grass dropping steeply into the valley. There should have been something soothing about the timeless, mottled landscape; the lumpy hills and the stuccoed villages, clinging possessively to their summits; the dusty, ochre tracks and the regimented lines of poplars dividing fields of maize from hectares brown with the stubble of harvested grain. But it failed to calm the thin man, desperately clutching for its peace. Unbidden, a line of De la Mare came into his mind and would not leave: 'Look thy last on all things lovely every hour'.

He turned as, with roars and shouts, two overloaded Lambrettas appeared round the bend of the road. Their young drivers were intent on racing each other up the hill but the girls perched behind were not too absorbed to give him a cheerful wave as they swept past. Nervously, Craig fingered his new moustache and ran a hand over his dyed hair. He blinked in the strong sunlight, his eyes still not fully accustomed to the contact lenses.

He climbed back into the car. Two minutes to eleven. He slipped a cassette tape into the player – the Mozart K 503 piano concerto. The confident C major chords blazoned forth as Craig closed his eyes and sank into the soft leather. The piano welled up quietly through the orchestral undergrowth like a clear, sparkling spring. But the music failed to work its accustomed magic. Craig opened his eyes – and found himself gazing down the barrel of a Walther PPK.

The man behind the gun gestured Craig out of the car. In a few curt words of Italian he ordered him to spreadeagle over the bonnet. A colleague frisked Craig expertly. Then the one with the gun – a young man in denim jeans and jacket – marched Craig back up the road, while the other climbed into the driving seat of the Mercedes. Round the first bend Craig saw a white Cadillac with tinted windows. Two more of Sylvestri's guards occupied the front seats. A rear door stood open. Craig got in. The man in blue slid in beside him and sat, holding the automatic in his lap. The Cadillac eased out onto the road and Craig's car fell in behind.

Fifteen minutes of winding upwards through vineyards and olive groves brought the little convoy to a pair of tall iron gates in a high wall. The driver of the Cadillac sounded his horn and the electrically operated portals swung open. The drive dipped down towards the house, a long, low villa of gleaming white stucco, which seemed poised on the edge of a precipice, so steeply did the hillside descend beyond it.

The cars came to a halt to let the passengers out, then drove on towards a separate garage block. Craig was ordered round the side of the house and emerged onto a terrace where tables and deck chairs were scattered around a semi-circular swimming pool. Craig had no difficulty recognising the lithe figure of Sylvestri seated at one of the tables, deep in conversation with two other men, one wearing the cassock of a church dignitary. The youngster in blue denims went over to report.

Craig scanned the view of terraced slopes plunging dramatically towards the plain where the haze-covered town of Djocomano could just be seen and reflected that the house and its setting were a realtor's dream. If Sylvestri was being forced to leave all this he must be pretty sore about it.

Without even a glance at his latest guest, Sylvestri issued a brief order. In pursuance of that order Craig was taken to the house. He was shown into a room expensively and tastefully furnished. In one corner stood a comprehensively-stocked bar. He was invited to make free with it. A man entered with Craig's briefcase and placed it on a long, low, glass-topped table. Beside it he laid a fat, leather covered album.

'Mr Sylvestri would like you to read this while you are waiting.'

The guards withdrew and Craig heard the key turn in the lock.

He poured himself a generous brandy and was annoyed to see that his hands were shaking. He flopped into a deep armchair and drank the spirit slowly. 'Get a grip on yourself,' he muttered. 'This guy's only doing what you've done with every con you've ever worked – softening up the opposition. He wants to get you in the frame of mind to do business on his terms.'

He gazed steadily at the large volume on the table before him. Only after pouring himself another brandy did he turn back the cover. What he saw took his mind straight back to the briefing room at the manor. In stark black, white and grey a man was lying half in and half out of a car. The window of the open door was shattered. Black rivulets streaked the asphalt. The caption and newspaper article accompanying it described the assassination of Rome magistrate Vittorio Occorsio on 10 July 1976.

Calvin turned half a dozen pages. GUILIANO SLAIN was the glaring headline above a photograph of the draped figure of a police chief being carried from a Palermo café on 21 July 1979. Another page of the macabre scrapbook was dedicated to the funeral in August 1982 of Milan businessman and mafioso Giorgio Gambarini. And so on through scores of glaring headlines and lurid pictures of assassinations, 'suicides' and 'accidents'. There were even photographs of the Bologna railway station outrage – bodies and bits of bodies strewn everywhere like broken discarded dolls in the nursery of some petulant, spoilt child.

Craig closed the album and let it fall on the table. For what seemed like minutes he sat quite motionless, staring down at his host's autobiographical statement. Sylvestri was trying to frighten him. And succeeding. Yet another part of Craig responded differently to this gross overkill. The sham Dentwood-Smithe had come into this room with only one thought in his mind: to keep his skin intact. Now he knew there was something that mattered more. There was a picture in his mind, more vivid than the shock-horror press photographs accumulated by Sylvestri. The picture of a little Karamojong girl lying dead in his arms.

The White King kept him waiting for an hour. When he entered the room, at last, Craig was calm and confident, looking forward to the contest. Able now to regard *Il Flagelo* not as a terrifyingly formidable adversary but as a mark, a sucker, ripe for the picking. Sylvestri came up to him, hand outstretched, features expressionless. Now that he saw the Italian close to for the first time, Craig realised how small he was, but his physique was that of a younger man. He walked with short, bouncy movements. When he spoke his voice was hard; his words terse, economical, to the point.

'Welcome, Mr Dentwood-Smithe. We lunch in fifteen minutes. You will want to freshen up first. Gregori will show you where. After lunch I will give you one hour exactly for a preliminary discussion. I don't do business over meals.'

Abruptly, he turned and walked away.

Lunch was served in a room whose large, sliding windows were fully opened onto the terrace. There were seven men at the table. Craig found himself sitting at the bottom opposite his host. On his left was the ecclesiastic he had noticed earlier. Craig discovered that he was a member of the papal curia and obviously very influential. That was about all he did discover for the man had no English and Craig's Italian was soon used up on conventional pleasantries. He fared only slightly better with his other neighbour, a Milanese banker. There was sufficient overlap in their knowledge of each other's languages to make conversation possible with occasional recourse to French phrases. It was an effort and after a few minutes the banker turned with obvious relief to the local businessman on his right.

Craig addressed himself to the food and wine, which were excellent. The *fettucine all'uove* was fresh and pungent and was followed by a dish of raw veal slices marinaded in olive oil, herbs and vermouth. It was accompanied by a delicate Montecarlo which, as the cardinal pointed out in a rare burst of eloquence, came from Signor Sylvestri's own vineyard near Lucca.

But Craig could not devote all his attention to the meal. He was aware that he was under constant scrutiny from the other end of the table. Sylvestri watched him without any polite effort to cover up the fact. So Craig watched back. He saw a man who listened without appearing to listen. Sylvestri seemed oblivious to the conversation flowing around him but occasionally he dropped in a sentence, or a mere word, that showed that he had missed nothing. Craig also noted that the little Italian never smiled. When one of his guests made a joke that evoked titters from the others, his only reaction was a nod of appreciation. Craig concluded that Sylvestri's mind was active on several layers simultaneously. He kept a notepad beside his plate and twice during the course of the meal he jotted a message down and handed it to one of his men. Yet, whatever the host was doing, it seemed to Craig that his gaze hardly ever deviated. Determined to appear relaxed, the American ate slowly and with every sign of enjoyment. But he did find it necessary to help the mouthfuls down with plenty of wine and mineral water. And he was relieved when the plates were eventually cleared away.

Sylvestri rose abruptly.

'Mr Dentwood-Smithe, we will have coffee in my study.'

He led the way to a surprisingly small room which was half filled by an ornate eighteenth-century desk. He seated himself behind it and waved his guest to a low, leather armchair. When the coffee had been served and the two men were alone, Sylvestri leant forward, once more staring at his guest.

'Just who the hell are you, Mr Dentwood-Smithe?'

Chapter Nineteen

Craig launched into his well-rehearsed routine. 'I'm merely an agent, Mr Sylvestri. I act for principals in various negotiations where secrecy is . . .'

'Bullshit!' Sylvestri snapped the word out without raising his voice. 'If you were a major arms dealer I'd have met you. I've checked you out. You've got a small time outfit. You're getting out of your depth.'

Craig held his ground. 'My proposition is absolutely kosher. If you didn't believe that, you wouldn't have asked me here.'

Sylvestri maintained his unblinking scrutiny. 'The fact is, however, that I don't know you. And if I don't know you, I don't trust you.'

'Then you don't have to do business with me, Mr Sylvestri. I'm offering you a share in a four billion dollar deal. If you don't want to be part of it, I can go elsewhere.'

'You're not going anywhere.'

With slow, elaborate care the Italian selected a cigar from a box on the desk, clipped it, lit it and took a long pull at it.

Through the drifting smoke he said, 'You read my *Brown Book*?'

Craig nodded.

'Then you realise the importance I place on absolute trustworthiness. If I decide you're on the level then maybe we can do business. If I have any doubts about you, you're dead.'

Craig decided that frightened bluster would be Corrie's most likely response.

'Look, old chap, there's no need for threats. This is absolutely on the up and up. I've been in this business for seven years – and never a disappointed customer.'

'Prove it!'

Craig picked up his attaché case. In opening it he deliberately fumbled with the locks.

'In a business like mine documentation is, of course, kept to a minimum.' He extracted a thin file of papers and opened it. 'But here you can see the way a typical shipment is arranged.' Craig enumerated the documents and placed them, one at a time on the desk. 'Ministry of Defence permit for the export of a part consignment of machine guns to Oman for army use. Cargo manifest for these weapons cleared from Southampton to Matrah. And this is a forged manifest for gaming machines Marseilles-Durban. The goods were, of course, trans-shipped in Marseilles and the crates re-labelled. The guns were delivered promptly in South Africa for the use of right-wing rebels in Mozambique. They were actually paid for through a bank in Muscat and the British manufacturers' records show what is, on paper, a completely kosher deal.'

Craig smiled at the mafioso, who remained expressionless.

Sylvestri gave the papers no more than a cursory glance. 'These prove nothing. They could all be forgeries.'

Craig drew a hand nervously across his brow. 'But, I assure you . . .'

'Mr Dentwood-Smithe, I'm beginning to think you're wasting my time.'

'No, no, you can trust me.' Feigning panic, Craig pulled a leather-bound notebook from his pocket. 'Look, if you don't believe me, phone Tony Morelli in New York. You know Tony? Or Yukio Taito in Tokyo. You must have come across him. He's the biggest name in illicit arms dealing. Either of them will vouch for me. I have their numbers here.' He held out the pocket-book with a trembling hand.

Sylvestri did not take it. He sat back in his chair, savouring the cigar.

'I know how to get hold of them. And I will.'

He was silent for several moments, gazing up at the swirling smoke.

Craig watched him, like an angler gazing at a trout who is suspiciously scrutinising an attractive fly. He willed the Italian to rise out of the secure depths of his caution. He knew he would.

At last Sylvestri said, 'Four billion is a lot of money for a small operator like you to be handling.'

'The customer has a very big problem to solve.'

'Who is the customer?'

Craig laughed. 'Come, now, Mr Sylvestri, you know I can't reveal that. In a deal like this absolute secrecy is essential. The fewer the people who know the details the better. I will personally guarantee that you get paid. I can assure you, I wouldn't dare to double-cross you – especially now that I've read your *Brown Book*.'

The Italian leaned forward. He pointed his cigar at Craig. 'Listen, and get this clear, Paolo Sylvestri doesn't go out on blind dates.'

Craig played flustered and really scared. 'No . . . really . . . I realise your position of course but . . . really . . . I can't possibly divulge . . . There are very big names involved. International statesmen . . . really, I can't say any more.'

For the first time, Sylvestri smiled, enjoying the other man's discomfiture.

He said, 'Well, when I want the information I'll get it out of you – one way or another. But let it stand for the moment. What sort of deal are you proposing?'

Craig cleared his throat and mentally picked up the

script, memorised and laboriously reproduced for Adam's benefit at the Manor.

'My clients require the most sophisticated weapons for an army of 20,000 men, fighting a guerrilla-type campaign. They need fully-automatic rifles, night-sighting equipment, ground-to-ground and ground-to-air missiles, hand-held launchers, helicopters, explosives and radio-controlled detonators.'

'Is that all?'

'It is a major undertaking. That's one reason why I'm bringing together a consortium of experts to handle it. The other reason is that all this military hardware has to reach its destination by different routes. There must be no possibility of anyone suspecting a build-up of arms in the region.'

'And what's your cut?'

'A project of this size obviously demands enormous organisation – and risk. I have to set up supply routes from sources in both East and West, arrange all the complicated documentation, bribe officials – there's a hell of a lot of work involved. And my customers want delivery within six months. It's going to take . . .'

'How much?'

'Twenty-five per cent.'

Sylvestri looked at him in silence for several seconds.

'OK, Mr Dentwood-Smithe, you've outlined your proposals. Now, I'll tell you mine. First of all I check you out thoroughly, and you tell me precisely who wants these weapons and why. If I decide to go ahead then I deal with them directly and exclusively. There will be no consortium. You will handle all the arrangements. You will be working for me. And if I am satisfied, I will pay five per cent on the deal.'

'Mr Sylvestri, really . . .'

'Those are my proposals and they're not up for negotiation.' He pressed a button on his desk. 'Now you run along back to your hotel and I'll be in touch.'

The door opened to admit blue denims. Sylvestri turned to him.

'Jacomo, escort our guest to his car.'

Craig opened his mouth to make a protest but the little Italian impatiently waved to him to leave. When he reached the door, Sylvestri called after him, 'You'd better pray that my enquiries turn out satisfactorily.'

Craig spent the first half of the journey back to Pisa cursing Adam and his whole hair-brained plan; the second half looking for a way out of his predicament. By the time he reached the hotel he had realised that there was nothing he could do. He had to see Adam.

Slamming the door behind him, he strode into the apartment, flung his jacket onto a chair and called out, 'Sara!'

She came through from the balcony and immediately sensed that something was wrong.

Craig said 'That letter to E.F.R.; have you typed it yet?'

He shook his head as he spoke.

'No, Corrie. You said it wasn't urgent.'

'Well, I've changed my mind. Be an angel and do it now, will you? Then run into town and post it.'

Sara went through to her own room and was soon rattling the keys of the typewriter. Craig sat at a table and wrote a report on his conversation with Sylvestri. He put it into an envelope then scribbled a note on another sheet of paper: 'Get this to that smart-ass boss of yours and tell him I want a meet tomorrow morning'. When Sara came back he handed her the letter and the note. She nodded, put them in her bag and left.

Shortly after ten o'clock next morning Craig and Sara climbed the 296 steps to the top of Pisa's campanile. There were three shirt-sleeved tourists on the gallery, taking photographs of the cathedral and friends in the piazza below. Two of them were Japanese. The other was Adam.

Craig leant against the inner wall, getting his breath back.

'You certainly have a passion for the theatrical,' he muttered.

Adam closed his camera case. 'Can't come to Pisa without climbing the Leaning Tower,' he said.

Craig got straight to the point.

'I told you you hadn't covered all the angles; hadn't considered all the things that could go wrong. Your creaking tub of a plan started to fall apart as soon as it hit the water.'

Adam shrugged off the criticism.

'Sylvestri took the bait; that's the main thing.'

'Oh, yes, he took the bait – *and* the line, *and* the rod, *and* the goddam angler!'

He crossed to the overhanging parapet, gazed down into the square, and promptly wished he hadn't.

Adam said sharply, 'Exaggeration isn't going to help.'

Craig faced him, anger flaring.

'Exaggeration? For Chrissake; this sadistic bastard only wants to deal direct with the customer – the top man!' Craig had slipped into his own voice. Now, he reverted to the cultured English tones of Dentwood-Smithe, which somehow were better suited to sarcasm. 'Now, since the top man knows nothing of this phoney arms deal – since he's never heard of Juventus Ltd or Corrigan Dentwood-Smithe – we just could find ourselves in the teensiest spot of bother.'

Adam frowned. 'Yes, well I have been giving the matter some thought. Couldn't you head him off, so that he doesn't pursue his enquiries?'

'When I am "reluctantly" forced to reveal the client's identity, as per our plan, Sylvestri's going to be shattered.

209

That's the whole point of it. Now, the first thing he'll do is go straight to the source to check out the facts.'

'Then you'll have to stall.'

'Stall? Are you crazy? Or perhaps you actually want me delivered in little pieces to Dentwood-Smithe's "widow"? It's all very well for you, looking down from a great height.' He gestured to the piazza below. 'But I'm one of the poor bloody "ants" actually down there involved in the action.'

Sara intervened. 'What about our CIA backup?'

Adam nodded. 'I'll activate that immediately. We'll convince Sylvestri through his own sources that western intelligence is seriously worried about escalating military activity in East Africa. If you can avoid mentioning names, he'll have to check back with those sources.'

Craig shook his head. 'He may decide it's easier to beat the shit out of me.'

The look on Sara's face suggested that she found that idea quite appealing.

'If he does get rough with you, he daren't go too far. As long as he thinks you have information and contacts vital to his interests, he'll keep you alive.'

'Why don't I find that thought comforting?'

Adam said, 'Just play hard to get for as long as you can.'

'Play it by ear,' Sara added. 'That shouldn't be difficult. Opportunism is your strong suit.'

A clattering of footsteps below heralded the approach of another group of tourists. Adam began to descend the steps.

'You'll think of something. I've every confidence in you. Just stick as close as you can to the script. Otherwise none of us will know where the hell we are.'

It was two days later that Craig received another of Sylvestri's terse invitations.

'Tomorrow. Same time. Same place. Pack a suitcase.'

This time the White King granted an immediate audience. He took his guest on a tour of the villa's grounds which consisted largely of terraces and parterres on a variety of levels, linked by ornamental stone stairways and avenues sentinelled with cypress. It was no stroll. Sylvestri set a brisk pace and two of his men followed a dozen paces behind. He came straight to the point.

'OK. Mr Dentwood-Smithe . . .'

'Corrie. Please call me Corrie . . . everyone does.'

'Right, Corrie. You can call me Mr Sylvestri. Everyone does. As I was saying, you check out. So, perhaps, you really have come to offer me a deal.'

Craig slipped into a mood of ingratiation.

'As I remarked before, it would be foolish of anyone to try to deceive you, Mr Sylvestri.'

'So what's it all about? Where is this 20,000 strong guerrilla army?'

'Naturally, Mr Sylvestri, you will want as much information as possible. Four billion is a great deal of money even for someone in your position. That is one reason why my associates thought it would be advisable to spread the financial load. As I mentioned before, our customer is a rather impatient man. Not to put too find a point on it, he is a rather dangerous man. If he felt there was a hold-up over arranging the finances he could behave . . . unpredictably, irrationally. He has agents everywhere.'

Sylvestri stopped suddenly and turned to Craig.

'I think you've forgotten that I'm a dangerous man, too. You've got yourself between the devil and the deep blue sea, my friend.'

He resumed his energetic progress.

'Now, give me facts and names – fast.'

Craig felt the perspiration oozing out on his forehead, and dabbed at it quickly with a handkerchief. 'All very well for Adam to talk about stalling,' he thought, 'his life isn't at the mercy of a raging psychopath.'

'What we're talking about is a certain East African country which has seen several changes of regime in recent years . . .'

Sylvestri stopped in his tracks. Craig read suspicion and anger in his intense gaze.

'Do you mean Uganda?'

Craig nodded.

Sylvestri grabbed his lapel and jerked him almost off his feet.

'What the hell's going on here?'

The man seemed to have gone suddenly berserk. Craig tried to look frightened, which he was, and puzzled, which he wasn't.

The Italian's grip did not relax.

'I want to know who's interested in Uganda – now!'

Craig knew precisely how much he was going to 'blurt' out. But before he could open his mouth one of Sylvestri's minders hurried up holding out a radio phone.

'Call from New York, Mr Sylvestri. It's Joey.'

Sylvestri took the handset over to a small arbour where there was a stone bench. He sat down and spent several minutes in agitated conversation. Craig and the others watched as the little man's features registered mounting anger. At last he dashed the phone down on the paved path. The plastic splintered. He strode towards the house, shouting in Italian as he went.

'Carlo, find out all this guy knows about Uganda!'

Carlo – six foot two and broad with it – grinned at the prospect. He came slowly towards Craig, who backed up against the hedge, gibbering.

'OK, I'll tell you whatever you want to know! No need to get rough!'

Carlo was not to be so easily deprived of his sport. He swung a blow to the side of Craig's head that sent him sprawling on the ground. Then he kicked him in the stomach.

212

Craig doubled up, gasping and retching. A heavy foot smashed into the side of his face and he tasted blood. He struggled to his hands and knees, trying to gasp out words to make this sadist stop.

Strong arms hauled him to his feet, then lowered him onto the stone bench.

Carlo jeered down at him.

'You talk what Mr Sylvestri want to know.'

'Yeah, yeah,' Craig gasped. 'Only for chrissake stop hitting me.'

Carlo frowned.

'Yeh, you talk like a Yank.'

Craig mentally kicked himself.

He said, in the plummiest English accent he could manage, 'You'd talk funny with a bruised and bleeding lip, you sadistic bastard.'

The sadistic bastard laughed, probably not understanding completely. Craig wondered how he was going to communicate with this simpleton, who had little English. How could he tell the man what he wanted to know without taking a fresh beating. Carlo was like an animal who had tasted blood and was hungry for more. He took some deep breaths, which was painful. He spoke slowly, partly to make it easier for Carlo and partly because breathing was difficult.

'Look, why don't we go to Mr Sylvestri and I'll tell him *everything*.'

'Mr Sylvestri say you tell me everything.' Carlo took a pistol from his belt. He gripped it by the barrel in his upraised hand.

Craig cringed.

'OK, OK. I tell you.'

The next half hour stretched to a painful eternity. Craig felt like a man in a semi-coma, desperately trying to communicate with a world which couldn't or wouldn't understand. He went over the salient facts half a dozen

213

times in half a dozen different ways. He used words of one syllable and a nursery school vocabulary. When Carlo understood, he nodded and smiled. When he didn't he resorted to violence therapy. Sometimes it was a fist, sometimes an open hand, sometimes the gun butt, occasionally a foot. One of Craig's eyelids was swollen. Every part of his body was sore. With his good eye he tried to focus on trees and hedges which kept swirling around. Just when he felt a friendly unconsciousness about to embrace him, another man came and talked to Carlo. Then the two minders, one each side, lifted him from the bench and half-carried, half-dragged him to the villa.

Craig was taken to a room and pushed inside. Dimly he saw shuttered windows, rugs on a polished floor and a wide bed with a pink counterpane. He staggered towards the bed, like a drunk trying to reach the bar. About half way his knees buckled and his body, at last escaping from pain, crumpled insensible to the parquet.

He came to on the bed in the same room. The shutters were open and the vivid blue of the sky hurt his good eye. There was a tightness in his chest. Looking down Craig saw that his jacket and shirt had been removed and his torso bandaged. He eased himself into a sitting position and passed out again as pain prodded his body in a score of places.

His next awakening was abrupt. The splash of icy water on his face brought him spluttering into consciousness. He saw Carlo standing over him, grinning, an empty jug in his hand. Beyond him Sylvestri stared down, sullen, impatient, angry.

'You've got twelve hours to get yourself fit enough to travel. We leave for Africa this evening.'

Chapter Twenty

The twin-engined jet slanted into the night sky, levelled at 30,000 feet, swung in a wide arc and headed south over the Tyrrhenian Sea.

Inside Sylvestri sat opposite his unwilling guest and surveyed him through the smoke of his cigar.

'OK, Corrie, I now understand the general scenario. I'll put it to you and you can fill in the details.'

Craig, sitting very still and upright in his padded chair because the smallest movement was painful, nodded.

Sylvestri exhaled a cylinder of smoke and watched it twist, expand and then flatten as it was caught in the flow from an air-conditioning nozzle.

'Ugandan politics have seen more twists and changes than a TV soap opera until Yoweri Museveni appeared on the scene. He drove out the previous government, dealt with most rebel groups and has given the country more stability and peace than it's had in years. He seems to be pretty popular.'

'Popularity in these African countries always has a tribal basis, that's why governments are so unstable.' Craig shrugged, and promptly wished he hadn't. 'Who can say how much support President Museveni has. His own roots are in the west of the country. Elsewhere he is accepted because his army is strong, his enemies are exhausted and the people are sick of civil war.'

'That sounds like a good enough recipe for restoring peace. But you reckon a new war is about to blow up – one Museveni can't handle.'

'The forces ranged against him are powerful, well-organised and heavily-financed.'

Sylvestri nodded. 'Yes, my own sources confirm that. Just who are these characters combining against him?'

'It's a formidable coalition of former Ugandan leaders in exile. Idi Amin has done more than anyone else to bring the various parties together.'

'But Uganda would never accept the return of a man who slaughtered over a million people?'

'No, I think even Amin realises that. He's kept a low profile. His representative is a Belgian mercenary who calls himself General Foncet. He's in charge of the guerrilla army and is the chief arms negotiator.'

'You've met him?'

'Yes.'

'And the politicians who have made their peace with each other and Amin?'

Sylvestri checked a list of names written in his notebook. 'Orema Allimandi?'

'Prime Minister under Obote until 1983. He leads the outlawed Uganda People's Democratic League and has a big following in the North.'

'Colonel Dominic Ogania?'

'He's an Iteso from the eastern region. He heads another proscribed party, the Uganda National Front. Then there's Tom Mumeni of Fedepa – the Federal Democratic Party. He's from Buganda, in the South, the traditional political heartland. There are others but those are the principal activists. They make up a pretty impressive team.'

'And what are their military prospects?'

'Uganda's a hard country to defend. It's small but it has a long frontier. Most of it runs through open bush. It can be crossed at a thousand points. A well-equipped, expertly-led army, making co-ordinated attacks from the North and East could strike to the heart of Museveni's little empire before he knew what had hit him.'

'That would require the collusion of neighbouring states and strong political backing. If your information is correct that's where the new movement has made its biggest breakthrough. They've got the active support of Colonel Gaddafi. Now, tell me, why should he put his money and political effort behind . . . what fancy name have these people given themselves?' Sylvestri squinted at his notebook. 'The UUM?'

Craig nodded, 'The United Uganda Movement. As to Gaddafi, the man has messianic delusions. Over the years he's tried to "liberate" Chad and Egypt and to pose as the leader of united Islam. He and Amin have megalomania in common. They speak the same language. It was inevitable that Amin should turn to the Libyan leader for help. And he has been immensely valuable to the UUM. He's given them massive financial backing and supported their secret negotiations with the governments of Kenya and Sudan.'

'That's another thing I don't understand. Why should Kenya and Sudan be interested in destabilising Uganda?'

'They don't much care for Museveni. There have been too many border incidents since he came to power. Gaddafi seems to have convinced them that the UUM will exercise greater internal control.'

'And will they?'

'I don't know, Mr Sylvestri. I only provide the hardware. Politics I leave to other people.'

Craig shifted his position and grimaced at the pain in his chest.

Sylvestri smiled. 'Still uncomfortable, Corrie?'

Craig grunted. 'It wasn't necessary to have Franken-stein's monster work me over. I'd have told you all you wanted to know.'

'Would you? I wonder. In my experience a little encouragement saves a lot of time.' He took a long pull at his cigar.

Craig asked. 'Am I allowed to know where we're going?'

Sylvestri nodded. 'Of course. I've checked your story with my own international sources. Now I'm going to double check it – on the ground. We're going to Tripoli so that you can introduce me to your Libyan contacts.'

Craig felt a new pain that had nothing to do with the beating he had taken from Carlo.

'If you show up in Tripoli Gaddafi's people will smell a rat. Negotiations are at a very sensitive stage.' He watched anxiously for the Italian's reaction but Sylvestri's face remained emotionless. 'Besides, most of the negotiations are done through General Foncet.'

Sylvestri shook his head. 'Foncet looks after things in Uganda. I'll get to him in good time. Right now I'm interested in the Libyan end. What did you say the name of your contact was?'

'Mouriba,' Craig muttered.

'Then we will call on Mr Mouriba first thing in the morning.'

Craig thought, 'That'll be difficult.' Mouriba was one of the balder patches of Adam's threadbare plan, as he had pointed out to the damned insouciant Englishman. The Libyan simply did not exist. Nor did the address which had been invented for him. Craig closed his eyes and forced his tired mind to think. Could he deflect Sylvestri from searching for this fictional Libyan? Failing that, had he any hope, in his condition, of escaping before the mafioso discovered that he'd been double-crossed? One thing was for sure, Craig realised: he was well and truly up the creek without a paddle. There had been no way to get a message to Sara before he left the villa. If there was a way out of this mess he would have to figure it out for himself. He had no ideas and none came to him before the short flight was over. From the airport they were driven straight to the Hotel Mediterranean. Sylvestri led the way immediately

218

to the lift. Their rooms were on the second floor. Before entering his own suite Sylvestri said, 'Breakfast at eight.' Carlo escorted Craig to his own room, unlocked the door for him, and kept the key.

Craig lay on the bed and waited. After an hour he opened the door softly and peered out. Carlo was sitting on a chair six feet away, reading a girlie magazine.

At 2.15 am Craig looked out again. The guard had been changed. Another of Sylvestri's henchmen lounged against the wall smoking a cigarette and looking very much awake.

Craig went back to the bed. He had already checked the window. Escape by that route would have been dangerous for a fit man. For someone in Craig's condition it would have been suicide. In the darkness he roundly cursed Adam and all his works. Then, because there was nothing else to do, he slept.

He woke early, ran a bath and gingerly lowered his aching body into the soothing water. For an hour he lay there, looking at the problem from every angle and finding no answer. All he could do was keep his wits about him and grab the first half-chance that offered itself to get away.

On the dot of 8.00 a.m. Carlo let himself in. He escorted Craig along the corridor to the sitting room where Sylvestri was already seated at a table drinking coffee. He motioned Craig to join him and the American was surprised to discover that he had an appetite.

They ate in silence for a few minutes, then Sylvestri looked up at Carlo and said 'Map!' The hulk produced a visitor's guide to Tripoli. Sylvestri made space on the table and opened the fold-out map section at the end.

'So where does this Mouriba hang out?'

Craig stared at the meaningless network of unfamiliar streets. 'Stall. Don't commit yourself. Put off the moment of truth.'

He said casually, 'He's in one of the government ministries but I've never been to his office. Our meetings are always secret, usually in a back street café.'

So how do you contact him?

'By phone.'

Sylvestri waved to a telephone which stood on a table by the balcony window. 'Be my guest.'

Craig looked at his watch. 'No good calling before nine. Mouriba's not exactly an early riser.'

Sylvestri stared hard at him. Craig saw the suspicion that was never far from the surface of the mafioso's mind. But this time the little man said nothing and Craig knew that he had gained a slender half hour. Sylvestri poured another cup of coffee, carried it to the window and looked out on the city.

'What a stinking hole this is. Arabs are like the desert they live in. They creep over civilisation and choke it. First the Romans. Then the Italians. Trying to teach these people how to live with comfort, style, dignity. You might as well teach pigs table manners.'

The phone rang. Carlo answered it, laid the receiver down and went over to whisper something to his boss.

Sylvestri looked at Craig. 'It's for you. Seems your friend is up and about a little earlier this morning.' He strode towards the adjoining room. 'I'll be listening on the bedroom extension.'

Craig picked up the receiver. 'Hello,' he said cautiously.

The voice that answered was deep, rich, affable. 'Corrie, what a pleasant surprise. How are you, my dear friend.'

'Fine. How did you know I was here?'

There was a throaty chuckle at the other end of the line. 'My dear Corrie, we have to keep a close watch on all our more distinguished arrivals. Now, tell me, why this welcome but . . . unscheduled visit? Nothing is wrong, I hope?'

Craig thought quickly. Whoever this character was, Adam must have dredged him up at short notice. He could not have been fully briefed.

'No, nothing wrong. I have someone with me who is interested in taking up some of the equity and wants to know more about the company.'

'The Italian gentleman? He is known to us, of course. But,' the voice had lost its friendly tone, 'you realise that our managing director does not like plans to be changed without consultation. You were to handle personally all negotiations with potential shareholders.'

'I realise this is a departure from our agreed procedure but my client has a very attractive proposal which he wishes to put in person.'

'My dear Corrie, you must be aware that we cannot contemplate a change of strategy at this late stage. If you do not wish to carry on as planned we shall be regretfully obliged to employ a different intermediary.'

'I think the proposal is at least worth listening to. Since my client is here in Tripoli don't you think you could, at least, meet him?'

There was a pause at the other end of the line. Craig guessed that 'Mr Mouriba' did not relish the prospect of a personal confrontation. Sylvestri, on the other hand, would be satisfied with nothing less.

He said, 'My client is *particularly* anxious to meet you and explain what he has in mind.'

Mouriba sounded doubtful. 'I will talk with my MD but I think it unlikely he will agree. Stay in your hotel. I'll call you back later. Goodbye, Corrie.'

Sylvestri stormed through from the bedroom.

'Who the hell does that guy think he is and what do you mean by grovelling like that?' He was shouting now. 'I am Paolo Sylvestri! I go cap in hand to no one.'

Craig countered with quiet, sweet reasonableness. 'Gaddafi is a highly volatile man. This is his country. Therefore,

221

we are at his mercy and it will be as well if we show respect.'

Sylvestri glared, eyes bulging. 'Me! Show respect to some half-crazy wog!'

Craig thought, 'Yes, you evil, little bastard; even you!' He said, 'That half-crazy wog happens to be paying the piper and he expects to call the tune. Not that it matters much. We've probably blown the whole deal. That won't worry you, but I've put a lot of time and money into this project.'

He sat down in an armchair.

'Well, all we can do is wait for Mouriba's call.'

Sylvestri stared at him.

'Like hell we do. Carlo, get packed! We're leaving.'

Craig swore inwardly. Sylvestri's petulant megalomania was driving him to the edge of rationality. Somehow he had to pull him back.

'If we got as far as the airport, we certainly wouldn't get any farther. Every move we make will be watched. We'll be allowed to go when Gaddafi says so; not before.'

Sylvestri went back into the bedroom without replying. Craig picked up the guide book and began nonchalantly leafing through it. But his mind was working fast. So far things were going a hell of a lot better than he – or Adam – had any right to expect. 'Mouriba' would, of course, agree to a meeting and, if he knew his job, would hold out to Sylvestri the faint chance of a deal. It was a cardinal rule of all con tricks to make the mark fight hard to be swindled. Sylvestri had to talk himself into providing arms for Gaddafi's guerrilla army.

But Sylvestri was no ordinary mark. If he even half-suspected that he was being bounced into a certain course of action he would be clever enough to work out the rest. He would realise there was no such thing as UUM. That the Museveni government to which he was heavily committed was under no serious threat.

That there was no reason to drop Okello in favour of a more powerful grouping, because that grouping was the figment of someone's imagination – someone who's only motive was to destroy him. And once he had reached that conclusion, exit 'Corrigan Dentwood-Smithe' – in a coffin.

Craig knew that he would have to control the forthcoming meeting, without appearing to do so, and without knowing how reliable his ally was. It would be like trying to make a bridge contract without being able to see your partner's hand.

As far as possible he kept out of Sylvestri's way in the hope that he would simmer down. It was no help that Mouriba did not call till mid-afternoon. He indicated that he was prepared to listen to Sylvestri's proposition and invited Craig and the Italian to dine with him at a nearby restaurant. By then the Italian was in a better frame of mind and as they walked the hundred yards to the rendezvous Craig tentatively proffered some advice.

'Mr Sylvestri, may I suggest that it would be unwise to let Mouriba know that I have told you everything? If he suspects you know of Gaddafi's involvement or where the arms are going, there'll be no question of doing business with him. Worse than that, our lives won't be worth a candle.'

The mafioso sneered at him. 'You think I'm stupid? You think I know nothing about doing business? I'm here because a Libyan customer wants a large consignment of arms. That's all.'

Craig metaphorically tugged his forelock. 'Of course. Good. Thank you, Mr Sylvestri. I just wanted to make sure our stories coincided.'

The man called Mouriba kept them waiting twenty minutes. As they sat at the corner table to which the head waiter had conducted them Sylvestri's impatience mounted by the second. Craig sweated and wondered what the hell was going on. At last the Italian got up to leave. Craig was frantic.

'Please, Mr Sylvestri, just give him another five minutes.'

'No one keeps me waiting. No one.'

'Ah, Corrie, how good to see you again. Signor Sylvestri, I presume. Welcome to Libya.'

The fat Arab-looking man appeared apparently from nowhere. Craig half rose to greet him, then fell back onto his chair with shock. Under a black moustache and swarthy make-up he saw the features of Pierrepoint Adam.

The new arrival shook hands energetically, seated himself and chattered incessantly.

'I'm sorry we could not meet earlier. But this is important business. I had to check with certain . . . colleagues. You understand, I'm sure. But, my dear Corrie, what an unpleasant bruise. You haven't been brawling, I hope.'

Craig fingered the painful swelling above his left eye, well aware of the pleasure his discomfort gave Adam.

'A fall, down some stairs.' Craig grinned and wished he could tell Adam what he thought of him.

The fat man smiled solicitously. 'You must take more care of yourself. We would not want to be deprived of your services. They are very valuable to us.'

Sylvestri cut across the pleasantries.

'Mr Mouriba, can we get down to business?'

The Arab held up a hand. 'Time enough for that. Let us first apply our minds to the serious matter of ordering our food.'

After the head waiter had departed with his notebook and the menus, Mouriba said, 'Now then, Corrie, I hope you realise just what a difficult position you've placed me in. Our negotiations must be highly confidential. That is why we employ you and why we do not expect you to convey details to third parties.'

'Believe me, Ahmed.' Craig noticed a slight twitch of

Adam's right eyebrow as he bestowed the first name upon him. 'I would not have departed from our agreed procedure had I not felt that Mr Sylvestri's proposal should be taken seriously.'

'Very well, then let us hear this proposal.' Mouriba turned to Sylvestri with a faint smile.

'Mr Mouriba, you want four billion dollars' worth of arms and you want them in a hurry. There aren't many people who can handle that kind of business. I can.'

Mouriba frowned. 'You are suggesting we allow you to supply the entire consignment?'

'Yes.'

The Libyan shook his head. 'Out of the question!'

'But . . .' Craig began.

'Such a large quantity of arms being moved by one organisation would attract attention.'

'They wouldn't come from one source, of course.'

'No, Mr Sylvestri, it is impossible. The CIA and other western imperialist agencies have Libya under constant surveillance (which is another reason why you should not have come here). Doubtless, they are also interested in your activities. Any suggestion that you were acting with . . . certain interests in this country would arouse the greatest suspicion and could jeopardise the entire operation.'

A waiter arrived with a large silver dish of kefta. No one spoke until the rice and the balls of spiced lamb had been served. Then Sylvestri explained.

'There would be no problem over my involvement. I would keep a very low profile. Corrie would act as intermediary.'

'Then what brings you here, Signor Sylvestri?' The question was asked with deliberate disdain.

Craig thought, 'Adam's going too far.' He kicked the Englishman under the table, but gained no response.

'I just wanted to check things out for myself.'

225

'Then I must make it clear to you that we are not accustomed to being "checked out" by tradesmen.'

Craig watched as Sylvestri opened and closed his mouth twice and let his fork fall onto the plate. He intervened quickly.

'What Ahmed meant to say . . .'

'What I meant to say was precisely what I did say. It is really very simple. We wish to buy some merchandise. Payment will be in cash, through our agent, Mr Dentwood-Smithe. Our suppliers, likewise, will deal with him. If they don't trust him or are not prepared to accept our terms, then they will not do business with us and Corrie will find us other sources of supply.' Sylvestri struggled to control his temper. 'That may not be quite as easy as you seem to think.'

'I assure you there are several dealers who can meet our requirements. We know. We are experienced in these things. Corrie will back me up, won't you Corrie?'

To Craig the situation seemed to be getting completely out of hand. He said, 'There are certainly other suppliers who would be interested in doing business . . . but Mr Sylvestri does have excellent connections and resources, Ahmed.'

Mouriba shook his head. 'I'm sorry, Corrie, the matter is closed. We do not wish to do business with Signor Sylvestri.'

The Italian could take no more. 'Cut the crap!' he snapped. 'Do you think I can't recognise cheap hustling when I see it? You're just trying to get the price down.'

Mouriba gazed at him as a long-suffering teacher might gaze at the classroom dunce. He shrugged. 'Do I have to express it in words of one syllable, Mr Sylvestri? Please listen carefully.' He spoke with exaggerated slowness, driving home the insult. 'WE DON'T WANT YOU. This project is vitally important. We are determined that it shall succeed. Therefore, we can take no risks.'

226

Craig felt like weeping. He thought, 'Adam's flipped. He's really flipped. The play-acting has gone to his head.'

Now, Sylvestri was on his feet, trembling with rage. 'Don't talk to me like that! Don't you dare talk to me like that! You haven't heard the last of this!'

He strode away from the table, motioning Craig to follow. There was no time for the American to exchange more than the briefest glance with Adam. He glared his anger across the table. Adam returned a smile of supreme self-satisfaction.

Sylvestri stopped to collect his topcoat from the cloak-room counter. As they waited Craig caught a glimpse of Cartwright. He was going into the men's lavatory. Craig muttered something to Sylvestri and followed.

Inside, Cartwright grabbed his arm. He thrust a piece of paper into Craig's hand.

'Call that number, if you get a chance. Adam wants a full report.'

'Tell Adam to take a powder! He has just loused everything up! We had Sylvestri right there and Mr God Almighty Adam blew it!'

Cartwright grinned. 'Ours not to reason why.'

He stepped to the door.

'You'd better get back before our sweet-tempered friend starts worrying about you.'

Craig glowered. Just as Cartwright opened the door he said, 'Hey, how did you know we were in Tripoli, anyway.'

Cartwright winked. 'Flight plan,' he said. 'Every pilot has to file a flight plan.'

Sylvestri did not explode until they were back in his suite. Then, for twenty minutes he shouted and raged, striding up and down, swearing at Craig and blaming by turns him, Mouriba and Gaddafi for treating him like 'scum'.

227

Craig sat very still and listened. Every moment he expected Carlo to be set on him again. He might even expect worse. With the deal off Sylvestri had no more use for him.

When the tirade had subsided he said quietly, 'I'm sorry about the way things have turned out. It might have been better if you'd trusted me in the first place. Perhaps . . . even now . . . I might be able . . .'

Sylvestri struck him hard across the left cheek with the back of his hand.

'I'm not going on my knees to these wogs.'

Craig felt blood running from a cut made by the Italian's heavy signet ring. He thought, 'One day, you bastard. One day.' He said, 'I apologise for getting you mixed up in this. Now that it's over . . .'

'Over!' Sylvestri shouted the word. 'I never said it was over. Listen, this deal means a lot to Gaddafi and his fat arse-licker. Well, I've got a surprise for them.'

He walked towards the bedroom.

'I'm going to get some sleep. You'd better do the same. We leave for Uganda in the morning.'

Chapter Twenty One

During the flight Sylvestri spent most of his time dictating radio messages in rapid Italian and checking the replies. He ignored Craig. The American had been relegated, for the time being, at least, to the status of an item of baggage.

Craig watched and listened, desperate to find out what was going on. He felt as though he was leaping, not from the frying pan into the fire, but in and out of a sizzling row of frying pans. That impression was confirmed when he heard an exchange of messages with Kampala, in English. Sylvestri had a call put through to Mr Samuel Okello to say that he would see him in his office that afternoon. The answer came back that regrettably the minister was out of town but that a car would be sent to the airport to meet Mr Sylvestri and convey him and his party to a rendezvous point.

Craig knew he dared not let Okello get a good look at him. The big African would certainly recognise him. And that would be that. He had a vivid picture of Sylvestri and Okello tossing a coin for the privilege of putting a bullet in him.

There was a government limousine flying the red, black and yellow Ugandan flag and a motorcycle escort waiting on the tarmac at Entebbe.

'You seem to have some clout here,' Craig ventured as they sped through a vivid landscape of dark green banana plantations and orange earth.

'I have contacts.' Sylvestri was giving nothing away.

'I didn't know you were familiar with Uganda.'

'There's a lot you don't know.'

'And a hell of a lot I do,' Craig thought. He said 'Where are we going?'

Sylvestri was silent for a few moments. Craig reckoned he was weighing up how much to tell him. He must have concluded that Corrigan Dentwood-Smithe posed no threat in the middle of the African bush, because he said, 'We're going to meet a man called Okello. He's just another gullible nigger but he's big in Uganda and very close to the president.'

'Why's he important to you?'

Sylvestri lit a cigar. The car slowed for a road check. While other vehicles queued up to be searched a soldier in khaki combat gear, his automatic slung over his shoulder, waved the government limousine through. Craig looked at him and thought that he could not be more than fourteen. Behind him, in the shade of a wall, three decrepit beggars sat, wailing their supplication. The Mercedes spurted forward and the scene was drowned in a wave of dust.

'Gaddafi wants to start another war here – right?'

Craig nodded.

'And Gaddafi is fanatical enough to do it.'

'He'll get his weapons from somewhere. There's no doubt of that. Then – poor little Uganda.'

'It takes two armies to make a war and both armies need equipment.'

'You mean you would sell arms to Museveni?'

Sylvestri shrugged. 'Why not?'

'I can think of one good reason: Museveni doesn't have any money. His government is bankrupt and over its ears in debt to IMF and major banks.'

'There are other ways than cash of paying for merchandise.'

Suddenly, Craig saw the direction Sylvestri's mind was going. He was planning to turn the situation to advantage by warning the government against invasion and offering the means to repulse that invasion. Museveni would have no alternative but to accept. And then he would be well and truly in the mafioso's pocket. For the hundredth time he cursed Adam's over-acting. He cast around for an effective argument.

'That's OK as long as you end up on the winning side. If the invasion succeeds you could be billions down the drain. That's why the arms business has to be strictly COD. Post-dated cheques have a dreadful habit of bouncing.'

Sylvestri stared at him but said nothing. Craig decided to push the argument a stage further.

'Of course, with two evenly matched forces in the field the war could go on for years, swallowing up resources. Taking sides is always a mistake. Once you're committed, it's like pouring whisky down an alcoholic's throat; no end to it. In our business you deliver the goods, you pick up the money, you *turn your back* and you *walk away*.'

The Italian's eyes had narrowed. Craig knew that he had activated the suspicion which was his sixth sense.

Through an exhalation of smoke Sylvestri said, 'You're suddenly very eloquent. What does it matter to you what happens in this one-horse republic?'

'If I'm not involved, what am I doing here?' In the last week Craig had come to understand the White King better. His respect ('fear' would have been a more accurate word) for the man's brutal power had not diminished but he knew that there were times when it was actually safer to stand his ground, rather than cringe and cower. 'Let me go back to England. I can't do anything useful in this "one-horse republic", as you call it.'

Sylvestri stared out of the window at a village of round huts flanked by a *shamba* of sparsely-sown, rickety maize plants.

'You're here because I want you here. I may have a use for you sometime.'

Carlo and the other minder sitting opposite in the limousine's spacious interior understood sufficient of their boss's words to find them amusing. They grinned inanely.

Sylvestri fell silent and Craig was relieved to turn his thoughts away from fictional armies and problematical wars. He had a more pressing problem: how to avoid meeting Okello.

It was about an hour later that he realised, with a shock, that there was something familiar about the road they were travelling. They had turned north at Jinja and had now entered a marshy, sparsely populated region. To the left sunlight glinted on an expanse of water. Outlined against it an immense, lightning-smitten thorn tree stretched black, supplicating branches towards the sky. Craig had seen that dramatic arboreal specimen before. During his visit to Sue Hayward's mission she had brought him out to Lake Kyoga and he had photographed that very tree.

'Where exactly are we going?' he asked.

Sylvestri was working on some papers and using a briefcase across his knees as a table. He glanced up briefly.

'It's a place they call Soroti. They're building a hospital there. Okello regards it as very much his baby. Spends a lot of time there, checking progress.'

Craig thought, 'Sweet Jesus! This gets worse by the minute.' Now it was not only Okello he had to avoid. Any of the mission folk might penetrate his disguise – Sue, her ill-mannered colleague, their assistants. 'Damn! Damn! Damn!'

The car stopped in a swirl of murram dust. The chauffeur held the door open and Craig followed Sylvestri out of the air-conditioned limousine into the parching African heat. Before them the hospital was up to first floor height. A dozen men worked at a desultory pace, on the scaffolding or pushing wheelbarrows to and fro.

Craig saw Okello immediately. Immaculate in a light-weight suit and carrying a flywhisk, he stood speaking earnestly with a small group of officials and two senior construction staff wearing helmets. Craig noted that as soon as the big African saw Sylvestri he broke off his conversation and hurried to greet him.

The Italian waved genially and stepped briskly forward. Craig held back. Then his arm was gripped roughly. Carlo muttered 'Avanti!' and pushed him forward. Craig deliberately stumbled, stuck his foot into a pothole and fell heavily with a cry of pain.

Carlo pulled him roughly to his feet.

Craig grimaced and swore at him. 'Careful, you brute! I've sprained my ankle!' He made a show of trying to set the 'injured' foot to the ground and half stumbling. He limped, clinging to Carlo for support.

'Your friend is hurt.' Okello was standing a dozen yards away, shaking hands with his patron.

Craig called out, 'A slight sprain, I think. It'll probably be all right if I rest it for a bit.' He turned and started hopping back towards the car before anyone could come up with an alternative suggestion.

Behind him he heard Sylvestri call out 'Carlo, stay with him.' Okello said, 'I'll get someone to have a look at his foot.' Then they moved away towards the building site.

In the car Craig put on an act for Carlo's benefit. The thug stared blankly at him, offering no help, as he removed his shoe and sock and gingerly massaged the 'damaged' ankle. Then he lifted it onto the back seat until he was half-sitting, half-lying along it. He closed his eyes. After a few moments there was a rustling sound. Through part-opened lids he saw that Carlo was engrossed in a magazine. Craig lay very still and wondered how much longer his luck could possibly hold.

'Hello, I hear you've hurt your ankle. I'm a doctor. Can I help?'

Craig came to with a start and saw Sue Hayward smiling at him through the open doorway. Instinctively he swung his legs off the seat and retreated as far as possible into the dim interior.

Sue bent her head inside the car. 'No, don't move.' She eased his legs back onto the seat with firm, gentle hands. 'There, I can examine it properly now.'

Expert fingers felt the ankle joint.

'Move your foot, will you? Fine.' The voice was cheerful, reassuring. 'Now your toes. Good. No bones broken. No swelling either. You've just wrenched it badly. It'll mend quickly. Still, we'll strap it up just to be on the safe side.'

She turned away and Craig saw her bend to open a first-aid box and take out a roll of crêpe bandage.

'These are very scarce out here.' There was a hint of reproach in her voice. She began to bind Craig's ankle. 'Mr Okello told me your name but I'm afraid I didn't catch it. Something double-barrelled isn't it?' She looked up at him.

Craig lowered his head. 'Dentwood-Smithe,' he muttered. 'It is a bit of a mouthful. Most people call me Corrie.'

Sue worked efficiently and quickly, though not as quickly as Craig would have liked. He avoided looking at her directly but was aware of her inquisitive glances.

'Are you a colleague of Mr Sylvestri's?'

He mumbled something non-committal.

'You're lucky. He's a wonderful man – so generous. You know, of course, that he's paying for this new hospital. It's something we've been praying for for years. I never really believed that it would happen.'

Sue prattled on with innocent enthusiasm. She was on cloud nine, happier than Craig had ever seen her before. He longed to cut through her naivety – to take her by the shoulders and force her to understand the sordid truth. Seeing this unworldly woman duped by an incubus like Sylvestri was almost too much for him. If it would have done any good he would have revealed his identity there and then, warned her what was happening, urged her to get out of the country before the Italian's parasitic hordes battened on the helpless people she loved so much. It was a stupid notion, of course. Any remote, outside chance that still existed of stopping Sylvestri depended wholly on keeping up the masquerade, doing nothing to arouse suspicion. That being the case Craig found Sue's interest in him disconcerting. She had fastened the bandage with a large safety-pin and was staring at him quite unashamedly.

'You've been here with Mr Sylvestri before, haven't you?'

'No.'

'Strange, I thought I recognised you.' She laughed and bent to close the first-aid box. 'I suppose its seeing so few white faces. After a while all Europeans look alike. Now, keep your weight off that ankle as much as possible for a couple of days. It should be as right as rain by then. Well,' she grinned up at him. 'Can't stay chatting. I've got to phone through an order for some supplies. Cheerio. Nice to have met you.'

Craig watched her walk briskly in the direction of the old hospital.

Phone! The mission had a telephone! He remembered it now – an old heavy black thing in the general office, by the main door. Was there any chance, any way? Craig looked at Carlo. The magazine lay limp across his knee, open at a picture of two naked women doing something complicated with a plastic broom handle. Carlo's head drooped. He snapped it up again, fighting sleep.

Stationary under an equatorial sun, the car was like a miniature sauna, the air inside like dry steam. The open

235

door admitted no cooling breeze – just red dust and flies. Craig lay still – and sweated – and waited.

The magazine slipped to the floor. Carlo grunted but did not move. Slowly, noiselessly Craig slid along the shiny leather. He eased himself through the open doorway and winced as his bare foot touched a hot rock. He reached into the car for his shoe and put it on. He rolled his trouser leg down over the bandage and stood up.

He looked round. To his left the new building and two African workmen slumped against a wall. Close to that, and partly hidden by the near end of the limousine, the site office. Craig had seen Okello and Sylvestri go in there fifteen minutes earlier. With any luck they were too busy to be looking out of the window. The old mission station was to his right, fifty yards away. Between him and the white-painted building with a red cross over the door were three mud huts where the mission's African staff lived.

Limping for the benefit of anyone who might see him, Craig made his way round the front of the car, passed between two of the huts and reached a side door of the hospital. The few patients sitting in the inner courtyard paid no attention to him. There were so many white men coming and going these days that another one was of no interest. But any moment Sue or her objectionable young sidekick might emerge from a door. Then there would be questions, and chatter, and wasted minutes. Craig was already on borrowed time.

He reached the office and put his ear to the door. Nothing. Cautiously he opened it. The room was empty. And there was the telephone on a trestle table against the far wall. Craig ran the few paces and grabbed up the receiver.

Craig dialled the operator and waited. 'Come on! Come on!' The monotonous tone trilled on, un-urgent, unheeded.

Through the window Craig could see the site office across a hundred yards of builders' material and machinery. A door opened. Craig swore. A man came out. Not Sylvestri. The man wore shorts and a pink shirt. He closed the door and shouted at the two slumbering Ugandans who rose to their feet in a languid, African way.

'Sweet Jesus! Come on!' Craig shouted into the mouthpiece.

'Number please.' A woman's voice – bored.

Craig explained slowly, that he wanted a call to Nairobi. He read the number Carter had given him. The voice said it would transfer him to the international operator. Back came the call tone.

Seconds seemed like minutes. At last Craig was snapping the Nairobi number impatiently at another minion of the telephone company. He heard the call signal again, fainter now.

'Hello!' Adam managed to make the single word sound confident, authoritative.

'Adam? Calvin.'

'Where are you?'

'Soroti. It's in Central Uganda . . .'

'I know where it is. Sylvestri's there?'

'Yeah, and Okello. Thanks to your Oscar-winning performance the Italian wants to do a deal with the government.'

'That's a non-starter, old boy.' Adam was at his most infuriatingly calm and superior.

'Well you persuade him!'

'My dear Calvin, that's why we have you here.'

'Well, you can damn well figure a way of getting me out of here.'

'No need to be overly dramatic. You just deliver Sylvestri to us here, in Nairobi. Our man is at the Pan Afric Hotel, as arranged.'

'And how the hell . . .'

Another voice cut in.

'Calvin Craig? It *is* you!' Sue Hayward stood in the

237

doorway, looking like an avenging angel.

Craig dropped the receiver on its rest and stared back. With anyone else he would have bluffed. But the lies and stratagems which normally came so readily to his lips cowered and cringed before the gaze of this transparently honest woman.

'Yes, it's me. I guess you recognised my voice.'

'You forgot your cut glass accent.' She advanced a couple of paces, not taking her eyes off him. 'So, what brings you back to Uganda? Nothing good, I'm sure.'

Craig opened his mouth to reply but Sue immediately held up her hand.

'No, don't tell me. I wouldn't believe you, whatever you said.'

Craig leaned against the table. 'I can't blame you for that. But, look, Sue, I've got to explain something to you that you *must* believe.'

'Explain it to Sam Okello. He's *longing* to meet you, as you can imagine.' Sue turned towards the door. 'I'll tell him you're here.'

He crossed the room in three long strides and grabbed her arm. 'Sue! You can't! You mustn't! This is vitally important. Not for me. For you, your people here, this country.'

'Since when did you care anything for this country?' She shook herself free and walked out into the hospital compound.

Craig followed. 'Look, give me a Bible to swear on – anything to convince you I'm telling the truth!'

Sue stopped. She turned to face him. 'You can only swear on something if you hold it sacred. And I don't think there's anything you hold sacred. You swindled this poverty-stricken country out of . . . of, I don't know how much. Those sort of figures don't mean anything to me. Did you stop to think – for just one moment – what that money means to people like that?'

She threw open the door of one of the hospital's two wards. Recumbent forms were crammed into every available space, some on beds, others on mattresses or the bare floor in the spaces between. A few patients turned emaciated faces towards the sudden disturbance but most lay listless in their pain, mere shadows of humanity, whose contact with the world of the living was a fragile thing.

Craig returned her gaze. 'OK. I deserved that. And I guess there's no way you'll ever change your opinion of me. But you must realise that the men Okello's gotten mixed up with now are a million times worse . . .'

He was talking to Sue's back again. She was making quick, short strides across the sparsely-grassed dust of the compound, her open white coat flapping behind her.

'For Chrissake, Sue,' he shouted after her, 'we're talking about the Mafia!'

If she replied, Craig did not hear her, for, at that moment there was a loud roar from somewhere very close. They turned in the direction of the sound and saw a military helicopter rise into the air from beyond the new hospital site.

'Okello?' Craig stood beside Sue and watched the craft whirl away southwards.

She nodded.

'I guess your denunciation will have to wait.'

'Well, don't think that I shall relent.' She glared at him. 'To think that I was taken in by you! Oh, I wish Mike wasn't out on clinic.'

Craig grabbed her by the shoulders. 'Will you just shut up and listen? I don't have time to debate high moral issues. Sylvestri . . .'

'Hey you! What you doing?' It was Carlo, coming into the compound at a run. He strode up to Craig, glowering. 'You try to give me the slip?'

'I came over here to use the toilet. You were fast asleep.'

'You're not supposed to go anywhere without me. Come on. We gotta drive to the city. Mr Sylvestri's gone by helicopter.'

He turned to walk back to the car.

Sue Hayward called after him. 'Just a minute. There's something you should know.'

Carlo stopped and treated Sue to what he probably thought was a smile.

Sue went up to him and pointed at Craig. 'You must be very careful of this man. He's an impostor, a crook. He's an American and his real name is Calvin Craig.'

Chapter Twenty-two

The Italian was not intellectually equipped for responding creatively to the unexpected. He glanced, puzzled, from one to the other. He asked Sue to repeat what she had said. Then he pulled out the gun which served him as a makeshift answer to all difficult problems.

For several seconds, the three of them stood motionless, like a group posed for some Victorian photographer. Carlo was sweating with the unexpected effort of initiative. Sue's face registered stunned disbelief. Craig went at high speed through his mental filing cabinet and found nothing relevant to the present crisis.

'Back to the car!' Carlo motioned with the pistol.

Sue turned. 'Well, if you'll excuse . . .'

'You, too, signora!'

She stooped and faced the gunman. 'Don't be absurd. I have work to do . . . patients. I can't possibly leave.'

Her fear was a lubricant to the simple mechanism of Carlo's mind. He grinned, more sure of himself now. 'You do what I say, girlie. We go to see Mr Sylvestri. He will decide whether we let you live or not.'

Sue looked at Craig. 'This is ridiculous. Tell him to let me go. He's not going to use that thing, anyway.'

Craig spoke quietly, trying to calm the situation. 'Don't count on it. He's killed before and he'll kill again – without hesitation. Best do what he says.'

Carlo marched them back to where the limousine was parked, it's driver lounging against the bonnet. At the sight of Dr Hayward being held at gunpoint the chauffeur's eyes became white-rimmed saucers in his black face. A few words from Carlo sent him hurrying back to his seat and the engine sprang immediately to life. Carlo shepherded his captives towards the open back door.

Craig could see that Sue was more angry than afraid but he was not prepared for what she did next. She entered the car first. Craig stooped to follow and saw her push open the far door and leap out. Carlo shouted something and pulled Craig aside. He fired through the car's passenger section. Craig saw his chance and grabbed it. He slammed the door on the Italian's arm and threw all his weight against it.

Carlo bellowed his pain. There were two more shots then the pistol clattered through the part-open doorway and fell to the ground at Craig's feet. Carlo groped with his free hand and caught hold of Craig's shirt, forcing him back. Craig felt the door slipping from his grasp. That was the point at which the chauffeur panicked. He let the clutch in with a screech and the limousine reared forward.

The two men sprawled on the ground. Craig got to his knees, blinded by swirling dust. Then he heard Sue shout out, 'Quickly!'

She was running beside the car as it swung round the front of the new building.

'Come on!'

She wrenched the rear door open and scrambled inside.

Craig got to his feet, ran forward and stumbled over Carlo, who was on his hands and knees scrabbling in the dust for his pistol. The Italian grabbed at him as he regained his stride. Craig swung an arm wildly, connected with Carlo's head. He heard a muttered curse and felt the other man's grip released.

Choking and gasping, Craig sprinted after the limousine. He drew alongside. Sue grasped his arm. He tripped, felt his knees scrape the road. Then he was half-clambering, half-pulled inside.

As the vehicle bumped and lurched over the rough road its two passengers sprawled, panting on the floor.

Sue slipped off the white coat, seated herself primly in a corner and brushed the dust from her skirt.

'We'd better stop the car. I must go back.'

Craig stayed on the floor. He rolled up his torn trousers and dabbed a handkerchief at his bleeding knees.

'Go back? With an armed psychopath on the loose? Don't be stupid!'

'Don't speak to me like that!'

'Talk sense, then. I know you feel a responsibility to everyone at the hospital. But you'll be no use to them dead. They'll manage without you for a few hours. When we get to Kampala you can go straight to Okello and he'll send you back with an armed escort.'

She stared out of the window, expressionless. 'Just who is that man back there?'

'You wouldn't believe me if I told you.'

'Try me.'

'A little while ago I wanted to explain and you wouldn't let me. Then it was important. Now it doesn't matter. If anything, you're better off not knowing.'

Sue faced him angrily. 'I've been lied to, exploited, and shot at. I don't know why all this is happening. I've just saved your life. And you refuse to tell me what it's all about.'

Craig eased himself into the other corner of the seat and sank back wearily, eyes closed. Suddenly everything seemed so futile and he was glad that it was over. It was over because he had exhausted his stock of schemes and stratagems. He was in a corner and someone would deliver the *coup de grâce*. It did not matter whether it was Okello, Sylvestri or Adam.

'Well, say something.' Sue's voice cut in on his thoughts.

He gazed at her frankly – more in sorrow than in anger. 'OK, here it is, straight between the eyes. That thug is called Carlo. He works for Paolo Sylvestri.'

'I know that.'

'But what you don't know is that Sylvestri is one of the world's biggest Mafia leaders. As soon as he can, Carlo is going to pass on to his boss the information you so obligingly gave him about me. When that happens I'm as good as dead. That won't bother you greatly but there's more at stake. Your friend Okello will be manipulated by unscrupulous men and this country will fall back into the cesspit it's been trying to crawl out of.'

Sue slumped forward, head in hands. 'I don't understand what you're saying. Explain! Make me see it!'

Craig gave her a simplified version of Sylvestri's plans and Adam's scheme to frustrate them. Sue listened in silence. When he had finished she sat back with something between a sob and a groan.

'It's horrible, horrible!' There were tears in her eyes. 'You're all trying to fight evil with evil. It'll never work. Can't you see that? That's all the politicians and business-men have been doing here for years – ever since independence. And look at the results – mass murders, reprisals, burned villages, piles of unburied bodies, once-productive land reverting to wilderness, ruined businesses and a ruined land.'

'That's the way of the world, Sue.'

'Only for cynics like you. I believe in something better.'

'God and suchlike?'

'Yes, God. I believe he cares and he can change things.'

Craig sighed and stared out at the flat landscape bordering Lake Kyoga which was passing sedately because the car had now slowed to a more normal pace. 'Well, you'd know more about that. God and I haven't been on speaking terms in a long time.'

'Perhaps it's about time you re-established contact. It's never too late.'

Craig shrugged. 'It would take a miracle to get us out of the mess we're in now.'

Sue smiled a wan smile. 'God specialises in miracles.' She closed her eyes and her brow was ridged in a frown. 'You please yourself but I'm going to pray.'

Craig watched her for a few moments, the little body clamped in religious fervour, lips moving in silent, earnest supplication. Then he stretched out his long legs, eased himself into a more comfortable position on the supple leather and allowed his eyelids to droop. He was at the end of his resources and he could not remember ever having felt so tired.

Whether he had dozed for a few seconds or much longer Craig didn't know but he was aware of a sudden surge of speed and the chauffeur babbling excitedly.

Sue leaned forward to slide open the internal glass partition. She questioned the driver crisply in his own language. His replies were voluble and high-pitched.

'Well, what is it?' Craig asked.

'He says we're being followed.'

They both turned to stare out of the rear window but could see nothing through the billowing wake of dust.

Craig shrugged. 'He's just panicking. They're an excitable race.'

'You'd be pretty jumpy if you'd lived in this country over the last few years. Nowhere is safe. Not the city, not the villages; and not the roads – especially not the roads.' She was kneeling on the seat and straining her eyes for any sign of movement on the murram track behind. 'There *is* something,' she said. 'Look, there – a Land Rover.'

Craig followed the direction of her pointing finger. On a bend in the road about half a mile back he saw a flash of white and a plume of dust against a banana plantation.

'Army? Police?' he queried.

Sue turned from the window, worried. 'No. I'd recognise that vehicle anywhere, even at a distance. It's one of the mission transports.'

'Does that mean what I think it means?'

'I reckon it must. No one on the staff drives at such a speed. Its an old van, kept going by a mixture of prayer and Mike's mechanical skill. It's very precious. Only four of us are allowed to drive it and we treat it very carefully. Whoever is driving it now is throwing it around like a dodgem car.'

'If it's Carlo he'll catch up with us pretty fast. This plush model is made for dignity and comfort not safari work.'

'It's only three or four miles to the highway. We should outstrip it easily on tarmac. The Land Rover has an absolute top of seventy.'

'If we get to the tarmac. The way this guy's driving we could be in the ditch any second.'

Sue spoke a few calming words to the chauffeur. They made no obvious impression. He continued to submit the car's suspension to the ultimate test. The big Mercedes swayed, bumped, skidded and swayed over the corrugated surface.

Then Carlo started firing. Craig did not hear the shots but he heard the metallic ricochet of a bullet glancing off the roof. He looked through the rear window and saw with alarm that Carlo had closed the gap to a hundred and fifty yards. He was still drawing nearer and was firing wildly.

'Do you know if this thing's bullet-proofed?' he asked Sue.

In answer to his question the window behind them shattered, showering them in glass fragments.

'For God's sake get down!' he shouted.

They crouched on the floor. Craig carefully picked some slivers of glass from Sue's hair. He looked at her anxiously. Once again her eyes were closed and her lips moving – not in terror, but prayer. He directed a few words of his own heavenwards. There was nothing else to do.

Minutes passed. Uncomfortable, frightening minutes. There were no more shots. Craig reckoned that Carlo was confident now of catching up with the limousine. What he would do then Craig could all too easily imagine.

'How far to the tarmac, now?' he asked.

Sue gazed at the road ahead.

'We're almost there. Half a mile, perhaps . . . no more.'

Craig smiled. 'Well, could be there is someone up there after all.'

On a sudden impulse, Sue grasped his hand. 'You'd better believe it,' she said, in a very passable American accent.

Suddenly they were rolling on the floor as the big Mercedes braked hard.

Sue was the first to pick herself up and stare out of the window.

'Military road block.'

Craig looked at the three soldiers in camouflage battle drill with slung automatic rifles who were blocking the road.

Behind them there was another squeal of brakes as the Land Rover pulled up fifty yards behind.

'Christ, this is it,' Craig muttered.

Sue got up and opened the door.

'I'll go and talk to him.'

'Sue! No!' He tried to grab her arm but she was already outside.

'He can't do anything here; not in front of the military.'

Craig watched through the shattered back window as Sue walked towards the Land Rover with purposeful strides. Carlo jumped down, brandishing his gun and shouting excitedly. Surely he had seen the soldiers. If he had he showed no sign. Craig heard the Italian shout out, 'Stop. Stand there.' He saw Sue ignore the order and carry on walking. He saw Carlo point the gun. He called out, 'Sue! For God's sake, do as he says!'

She never heard him. There were three shots. Sue sank to her knees. Then she fell forward and lay motionless.

Craig jumped out of the car but one of the soldiers, with sergeant's stripes on his arm, shouted something and held up an arm. The three men were running past, rifles at the ready. Carlo turned to face them, gun in hand. The sergeant would afterwards claim that he pointed it. There was a long volley. Carlo spun, like something suspended on a string, then collapsed as though the string had been cut. Two soldiers ran forward to examine the sprawled figures. They gestured that both were dead.

Craig stared at what had been Sue Hayward, stunned, immobile, one hand on the car door as though fused to it. He watched with disgust the breeze rippling her skirt and the flies already congregating around the blood which oozed through her white shirt. Loathing possessed him. Loathing for Carlo who had pointed the gun. Loathing for Sylvestri who had pointed Carlo. Loathing for himself and Adam and ISIF and everyone who had pointed Sylvestri.

Suddenly, he was aware that the sergeant was talking to him, ordering him to turn around and stand against the car, arms and legs outstretched. The African frisked him and the driver then told him to wait while he gave orders to his subordinates. They carried the bodies to the Land Rover and laid them in the back. They did it matter-of-factly, used to death. What were two fatalities against the slaughter of hundreds of thousands? One of the soldiers climbed into the driving seat, turned the vehicle round and headed back along the dirt road.

'What is it all about?' The sergeant stood squarely in front of Craig covering nervousness with authority. Craig guessed that he was out of his depth dealing with Europeans who killed each other, especially when one of them was travelling in a ministerial car.

Craig needed time to gather his wits. 'Where are you taking the bodies?' he asked.

'To Dr Hayward's mission station. It is the best place. They have the facilities there.'

'You knew Dr Hayward?'

'Everyone around here knew her. She will be very much missed. She was a friend of yours?'

'Er . . . yes . . . a very dear friend.'

'Your name please?'

Craig gave his name as Dentwood-Smithe and said he was in Uganda on important and urgent business with Mr Samuel Okello. He stressed the word 'urgent'.

The sergeant was determined to carry out his duty thoroughly. 'Who was the other man?' he asked.

'I'm afraid I don't know his full name. I called him Carlo. A very violent man. An Italian. He went berserk at the mission station.' Craig improvised. It was second nature to him. 'I believe he made advances to Dr Hayward, which she rejected. He was very angry.'

The sergeant turned his attention to the chauffeur and questioned him for several minutes in his own tongue. When he was satisfied that the man had no more to tell him, he said, 'I must take you both back to headquarters. This is a very bad business.'

Craig frowned. 'You have your duty to do, of course, but it is vitally important that I get back to Kampala. The minister is expecting me. Wouldn't it be possible for me to give my statement to someone there?'

The sergeant wrestled with the unfamiliar situation for several seconds before reaching a decision. He held a hurried conference with his subordinate, after which the man set off, alone and dejected, along the highway – making an official report to headquarters, Craig guessed. Then he motioned the others back into the car and climbed in himself, beside the driver. 'I will see that you reach Kampala safely,' he said.

The drive to the capital took two hours. They were the most depressing two hours Craig had ever spent. A hundred and twenty solitary, brooding minutes. Minutes he should have devoted to planning his next moves. Minutes crowded with the sickening reality of Susan Hayward's death. He had few memories of her but they were all vivid, intense. His mind insisted on re-running them like favourite gramophone records. Susan crying over a dying child; Susan naively believing all his lies; Susan angry with frustration because there weren't enough drugs or bandages or hypodermics; Susan who believed in miracles, till the supply of miracles ran out; Susan gunned down while he did nothing to save her.

It was many years since Craig had felt guilt.

The impromptu architecture of corrugated iron, old beer crates, mud, sticks and strips of plastic sheeting told Craig that he had reached the edge of the city. Despite the chauffeur's irritated blasts on the horn, little attempt was made to clear a path for the government car. Wide-eyed, naked and semi-naked children stared up at him. The little crowd at a roadside market were only briefly diverted from the trestle tables sparsely covered with bananas, maize, scrawny chickens and second-hand clothes. Cyclists, men in shorts and torn vests, women with large baskets on their heads, moved languidly out of the way. Mangy dogs and goats had to be shooed.

Craig forced himself to think constructively. The first thing to do was find Sylvestri. Carlo had had no chance to contact his boss since the helicopter had left, so the Italian had no way of knowing the latest turn events had taken. Craig had to convince Sylvestri with his version – brazen it out with an old man who would be angry and suspicious. Finding Sylvestri, Craig thought, would not be a problem. There was only one hotel where accommodation was permanently reserved for government guests. That bit was easy enough. Getting the mafioso out of the country as soon as possible and avoiding a meeting with Okello – that would be, to say the least, problematical.

The car slowed to a standstill outside tall iron gates. With a shock Craig recognised the entrance to the government buildings. He saw the sergeant lower his window to talk to the security guard.

Craig slid open the internal partition. 'What are we doing here?'

The sergeant half turned. 'To see Mr Okello, of course. We must report this tragic event to him – personally.'

Chapter Twenty-Three

Craig showed no panic. He even forced a smile. 'I don't think the minister would be very pleased if I arrived in his office in this state.' He indicated his torn trousers and dust-stained face. 'I must go back to my hotel for a bath and a change of clothes.'

The soldier shook his head. 'It will not matter. Mr Okello will want to know everything without delay. Events at the hospital are very important to him.'

'Well, of course. You must go in and make your report straight away.' He hesitated. 'And, perhaps, you're right. Perhaps I should come and help you break the bad news. He will be very distressed – very angry. He is very unpredictable when he's angry – as, perhaps, you know.' Craig read doubt in the African's face and pressed home his advantage. 'I assumed you would make your report to army headquarters and that Mr Okello would summon us later to give him eye-witness accounts. But probably you're right to go straight to the minister and tell him personally about the brutal murder of his friend.'

The sergeant pushed his beret back and drew a hand across his forehead. He made a decision. 'I will take you to your hotel and telephone from there for instructions. Where are you staying?'

'Nile Mansions Hotel.'

The soldier gave instructions to the driver, and the car pulled out into the city traffic.

At the hotel Craig strolled casually over to reception while his young escort found a phone booth. He asked for

Sylvestri's room number, earnestly hoping that his guess was right.

A tall, haughty Ugandan looked him over disapprovingly. Europeans were not supposed to arrive in tatters. 'Mr Sylvestri is in the presidential suite. I will tell him you are here. What is your name, please?' The last word was almost an after thought.

He spent a few seconds on the phone and then announced that Mr Sylvestri would receive Mr Dentwood-Smithe. He did not offer to have anyone carry the visitor's bag.

On his way up in the lift Craig decided that frightened, angry bluster would be Dentwood-Smithe's reaction to the present situation. When he entered the suite Sylvestri gave him the perfect cue.

'What the hell have you been doing?' The Italian, clad in silk dressing-gown, a glass of scotch in his hand, stared at the dishevelled figure in the doorway.

Craig advanced into the room with quick nervous steps. 'For God's sake, give me a drink!'

Sylvestri nodded and the minder poured out a measure from a bottle of Teachers.

Craig dropped into a chair and downed the spirit at a gulp. 'We've got to get out of here!' The words came in a half-strangled cry.

Sylvestri stood over him, frowning. 'What are you talking about? Where's Carlo?'

'Carlo's dead – shot by President Museveni's army!'

For the first time Craig saw the mobster shaken. His mouth sagged open. His whole body drooped. But the loss of control was only momentary. Sylvestri lunged forward, grabbed Craig by the hair and hoisted him to his feet. 'What do you mean, "shot"? Carlo's my nephew. He's a good boy.'

Craig responded with an anger that was not feigned. 'Your "good boy" was a bloody, gun-crazy psychopath. This afternoon he killed a woman in cold blood. A missionary doctor. A personal friend of Samuel Okello.'

'You're lying,' Sylvestri shouted. 'Carlo never killed anyone without my orders.'

Craig turned his back on the trembling little Italian and poured himself another drink.

'After you left Soroti, Carlo made a pass at Dr Hayward, the woman in charge of the hospital. She slapped his face. He got angry and started waving a gun about. I got her into the car for her own safety. Then he actually started shooting. The driver took off like a scalded cat. Carlo chased after us in another vehicle. When he caught up the woman got out to talk to him. And he just shot her. He was berserk, crazy. He'd have killed me and the driver if the troops hadn't shown up. Carlo tried to take them on, too. That was a mistake – his last mistake.'

Sylvestri glared angrily. 'I don't believe all this! You're lying!'

'For God's sake, Sylvestri, what the hell does it matter what you believe! The fact is your homicidal sidekick has murdered a Ugandan resident. That makes you *persona* very *non grata*. And that goes for me and laughing boy here. Do you know what they do in country's like this to foreigners suspected of serious crime? They lock them up and throw away the key.'

'We can't leave now. The deal is going very well. I have too much at stake.'

'Have you ever seen the inside of an African prison? Nor have I, but it's not hard to imagine. You can stick around if you want to. I'm taking the first flight out.'

Sylvestri bellowed something in Italian, and Craig found himself grabbed in a choking neck-lock by the mafioso's number two thug. Half pushed, half lifted, he was hustled into an adjoining room and dropped onto the bed. He heard the key turn in the lock as he lay gulping air into his lungs. Thankfully he yielded to the soft mattress and stared up at a corner of the ceiling where brown termite tracks fanned out like veins. 'Must keep a clear head. Must think. Must . . .'

He was wakened by angry voices in the next room, and immediately went over to the door.

'. . . five witnesses, as well as your English associate, who seems to have gone to ground. There's no possibility of a mistake.'

Craig recognised Samuel Okello's normally soft tones, now tightened up an octave by outrage and fury.

'It's a frame-up! Can't you see that?' Sylvestri was also on the edge of hysteria. 'Someone's trying to screw up our deal. Someone who doesn't want to see this country make a strong recovery!'

Okello was not listening. 'There will be diplomatic protests from London and perhaps a backlash among the Teso – Dr Hayward was very popular. The president will want an explanation from me. *My* credibility will be on the line! My position at stake!'

'Your position! What about mine? I've got a lot of money tied up in this country, and don't you forget it!'

'If you kept your own men under control neither of us would be in this mess.'

There was a silence on the other side of the door, then Sylvestri spoke – quieter, trying to defuse the situation.

'OK, let's not get excited. If we think calmly and clearly we can sort this thing out.'

'*We* can sort it out?' Okello was not to be pacified. '*I* have got to sort it out. The only thing you can do is get out of the country.'

'That's crazy. We've a lot of business to . . .'

'Can't you see? I can't protect you. You've got to get out of here today, now! When things have settled, then we can meet and resume our negotiations.'

'You're being short-sighted! You don't have time. Within weeks Uganda will be invaded. For Chrissake, can't you see that, you black . . . baboon!'

255

Craig could feel electricity in the silence that followed. When Okello spoke again it was in a tone of frigid dignity.

'Signor Sylvestri, I can keep the police away from here for an hour, perhaps two. If you are still here then, they will take you for interrogation. You will find their methods primitive – but, of course, you would expect nothing better from baboons. If they wish to implicate you in this crime they will come to me for corroboration. Do you imagine that I would be in any position to spring to your defence? There is an official car outside. Use it.'

A door slammed.

Before the African's time limit expired his unwanted guests were airborne. Sylvestri had wasted precious minutes raging in noisy, slanderous Italian before accepting the inevitable. Okello's limousine had rushed them to Entebbe. An officious passport control officer had made a great show of finding a discrepancy in their papers until the appropriate number of banknotes had changed hands. When they reached the Italian's plane there was no sign of the pilot. The co-pilot was sent to prise him out of a local bar. When he appeared Sylvestri squandered another five minutes in character assassination of the man and all his ancestors back to the Fall. But at long last the small craft screamed into the African night.

The mobster sat in furious silence working his way steadily through a bottle of Laphroaig Highland Malt. From the chair opposite Craig watched and knew precisely what the Italian was thinking. His whole elaborate scheme for a transfer of operations to Uganda was in ruins, loused up by one of his own subordinates. He was angry at being thwarted. He was desperate for some way out. Ready to grab at any lifeline.

Craig gazed at him, expressionless. He thought, 'Gotcha!'

Sylvestri looked up. Scowling. Half-sober. Dangerous. 'I should have left you behind. This whole goddam mess is your fault.'

Craig risked truculence. 'If you'd done things my way we'd have the deal sewn up by now.'

The White King was not about to own up to any mistake.

'I'm surrounded by idiots. First you, then Carlo. You screwed up!' He was shouting now. 'You screwed everything up. I told you if you screwed up you were a dead man. Enjoy the ride. As soon as we get back . . .'

Craig interrupted – quiet, cautious, probing. 'How's killing me going to help? I'm the only one who can save this deal.'

'You screwed up. All the bullshit with Gaddafi and his arse-licking sidekick.' Sylvestri was ranting but Craig knew that underneath the bluster doubt and hope were locked in combat. The man wanted to believe he had an escape but that meant trusting the Englishman in front of him.

Craig said 'You rubbed Mouriba up the wrong way. You should have let me handle him.'

'You telling me how to do business? You're nothing! I can buy you a thousand times over!'

'The UUM trust me to buy their arms and the UUM is set to take over Uganda. I don't know what other things you have going in Uganda but if you're in on this deal the new regime's going to be pretty grateful to you. Okello and Museveni are yesterday's men. You don't need them.'

Sylvestri was listening, now. 'But that fat Arab in Tripoli . . .'

'Mouriba is a greedy, conceited politician. As I said before, the man who does the hard dealing is General Foncet. He's tough. He's a mercenary. He understands war. Amin and Gaddafi trust him. If you persuade him you can deliver the weapons he wants, he'll go over Mouriba's head.'

'Where is this Foncet?'

'Right now he's in Nairobi.'

Sylvestri scowled. His unblinking eyes fixed themselves on Craig's face. The American returned the stare, without flinching.

'I still don't know I can trust you.' Sylvestri screwed the cap back on the whisky bottle and sat back in his armchair.

'For God's sake, Sylvestri, my life is on the line, as you take great delight in pointing out. Don't you think I'm going to do everything I can to get you a deal.'

'You may be just buying time.'

'A few hours? That's all it'll take. Look, we go to Nairobi. You meet the Belgian. You convince him. He puts a call through to Tripoli. You shake hands. And we all sleep more easily in our beds.'

'You can reach this Foncet character by radio phone?'

Craig looked at his watch. 'At this time of night? I don't know. He's probably out enjoying himself somewhere. He's a work hard, play hard type.'

'Try!' Sylvestri handed him a handset and held another to his own ear.

Craig took out his diary, found the number Adam had given him and punched it. 'Dear God, don't let Adam come on the line with any of his wisecracks,' he thought.

'Hello?' Sara's voice.

'Hello. My name is Corrigan Dentwood-Smithe. It's very important that I have a word with General Foncet.'

'Well, I don't know . . .'

'It's very urgent. Please tell him I have a client with me.'

There was a long pause, then a muffled conversation at the other end of the line. Then Sara came back on.

'The General's in bed, right now and doesn't want to be disturbed.' She filled the sentence with suggestive overtones.

'It will only take a minute.'

There was a rattling sound, then a man's voice with a heavy French accent. 'Foncet.'

'Guy, how nice to hear you. This is Corrie.'

'Corrie, you son of a bitch! You'd better have a good reason for interrupting.'

'Well, think of the pleasure of starting again, you old goat!'

Foncet laughed. 'Well, what can I do for you, my friend?'

'If you can give my client and me an hour tomorrow, I think we can conclude that little bit of business we've been discussing.'

'I thought it had run into problems.'

'A mere technical hitch.'

'I'm glad to hear it. I was beginning to worry.'

'No need. I assure you.'

'*Bon*. Then, let us say midday. You know where to find me.'

'Excellent, Guy. See you then.'

'*D'accord. A bientôt, mon ami.*'

'*Au revoir*, Guy. Oh and, *bon appetit*.'

Sylvestri laid down his handset. Silently he scrutinised the man sitting opposite. Then he sent orders to the pilot for a change of course.

Craig had met Jules Lagrange, the man playing the part of Foncet, at the Manor. A rugged, thickset, ex-Paris Sureté sergeant, he made a very convincing hard-bitten mercenary. He was standing at the bar of the Pan Afric hotel with a Pernod in one hand and a black woman in the other. As Craig and Sylvestri approached, he whispered something to his companion and slapped her bottom. She made a brief, involuntary grimace, as she walked away.

After introductions and ordering drinks, Foncet led the way to a corner table. There were few other people in the

259

bar but one of them was a solitary drinker shielded from view by an airmail copy of the London *Times*. Never had Craig found Adam's proximity so reassuring. He was also immensely relieved to be back in a play of which he knew the script. The improvisations of the last few days had put years on him.

The soldier took charge of the conversation.

'Monsieur Sylvestri, I'll be frank with you. I have dealt with Corrie before – very satisfactorily – but you I only know by reputation.'

'It's a pretty impressive reputation, don't you think?' The White King clearly resented being on appro, a rôle with which he was unfamiliar.

Foncet shrugged 'In drugs, prostitution, gambling, political assassination, *bien sûr*. But I am involved in the very serious business of war. I need *matériel* – considerable quantities, top quality, in perfect working order. I must have a good supply of spares and one hundred per cent reliable delivery dates.'

Craig chipped in. 'Mr Sylvestri has international connections and vast, readily accessible, funds. That is why I approached him on your behalf. Frankly, Guy, I don't think there's anyone else who can get things moving fast enough for your purposes.'

Sylvestri nodded. 'I tried to persuade your Mr Mouriba of that but he didn't want to listen.'

Foncet pouted. 'Mouriba is a fat fool. He suffers from *folie de grandeur* – like many politicians. They want other people to fight their wars for them, yet they expect to make the terms. I have twenty thousand men under arms. They look to *me* for food, clothes, equipment – not Mouriba.'

'When do you plan to launch your offensive?'

'That is a piece of information I keep locked up in here.' The Belgian tapped his forehead. 'All you need to know is that I require everything to be ready – delivered to ports and airfields in Libya and Syria – in six months.'

'I'm sure we can meet that deadline.' Sylvestri took out a small, leather cigar case and offered it to Foncet.

The general held up a hand and smiled. 'It is necessary to resist *one* vice, just in case there is someone up there, *hein*.' He raised his eyes. 'One day I may need a bargaining counter.' The grin stretched wider over his ample features. Then, suddenly, it disappeared. 'There is, however, some equipment I want even sooner than six months. I need to train my men in night fighting, using the latest surveillance aids. For this, I shall require, *within one month*, ten thousand British IWs fitted with image intensifiers.'

Craig frowned. 'One month, Guy? That's pushing it. We could come up with Gewehr 3A3s in that time.'

'No,' Foncet shook his head emphatically, 'the rate of fire of the German gun is too slow. I must have IWs.'

To show that he had done his homework Sylvestri suggested, 'What about the American AR18?'

For several minutes they discussed the technical merits and availability of various assault rifles. Eventually Craig and Sylvestri agreed that they could supply the British weapons in six weeks.

Foncet checked his diary. 'October 28th. Good. This is how we'll arrange delivery. The consignment will be put aboard a Panamanian vessel, the *Trico Galaxy* with lading bills for Banghazi.'

Craig said, 'You get her to Marseilles by the 23rd and I'll see that she's loaded.'

'Not Marseilles, Genoa,' Sylvestri intervened. 'I have my own cargo handling arrangements there.'

Craig shrugged and said 'OK. Genoa. And the consignment is to be delivered to Banghazi? What about payment?'

Foncet made a clicking noise with his tongue 'Not so fast, *mon ami*. From my point of view this is a trial shipment. You will both be aboard the *Galaxy* when she sets sail. Off the coast of Libya I will join you. My men and I will check the cargo. When I am satisfied I will pay you in cash. Then we will drink a bottle of champagne together and I will confirm the rest of the deal.'

'Just a minute!' Sylvestri smelt something fishy. 'I'd prefer it if you just came to Genoa and concluded the deal there.'

Foncet laughed. 'I have good reasons for not wanting to set foot in Europe. For the same reasons I prefer not even to venture inside Italian territorial waters.'

'And just how safe are we going to be on a ship in the middle of the Med, surrounded by your men?'

'I suggested we do our business aboard the ship because it's neutral territory. You can, of course, bring along as many of your own men as you think necessary for your safety. *Naturellement*, if you prefer, we can meet in Banghazi.'

Sylvestri was still not convinced. 'How do we get away afterwards?'

'The *Galaxy* has a helicopter pad. You can fly to Genoa, Rome, Naples – *n'importe où*.'

The three men spent another twenty minutes discussing details. When the meeting broke up each participant was, for different reasons, pleased with the way it had gone.

In Nairobi Craig finally broke free of Sylvestri's clutches. They agreed to return to Europe separately and to meet again in London as soon as Craig had located a supply of rifles. The Italian took off the same afternoon. Craig checked into the Norfolk Hotel, dropped, fully clothed, onto his bed and slept for hours. Not a deep sleep. A dream-invaded sleep in which he saw, over and over again, the face of Susan Hayward, eyes fast closed in death – or was it prayer? Either way it was an accusation.

The telephone woke him at last. It was Sara, summoning him to dinner.

When he walked into the restaurant an hour later Adam and Sara were already at the table. The Englishman was obviously in ebullient mood.

'Ah, Calvin, there you are. Sit down, sit down. I've taken the liberty of ordering champagne. I don't normally permit myself to celebrate before everything's wrapped up but this is an exception. We really are doing remarkably well.'

Craig spread his long legs under the table. 'Is that the royal "we"?'

Adam laughed as he filled the glasses. 'Teamwork, Calvin, teamwork. A good plan and a co-ordinated effort always bring results. Let's drink a toast – to success.'

He raised his glass and Sara dutifully followed suit. Craig did not respond. The wine looked like aerated urine, as unpalatable as Adam's self-satisfied triumphalism.

'It was a godawful plan and a godawful team,' he muttered.

'Oh come now, Calvin. We've manoeuvred Sylvestri into walking straight into our trap. That was the objective all along. And you've played your part superbly. Some of us were not sure about you,' he glanced briefly at Sara, 'but I never doubted that you would pull it off. And you have. Well done!'

'For God's sake, Adam! This isn't some game on the playing fields of Eton. And things only worked out because something happened you couldn't possibly have foreseen.'

Adam was not to be deflated. 'Ah, yes, Sylvestri's man running amok with a gun. I agree, that really verged on the miraculous. Things certainly were coming a trifle unhinged at that point. It just goes to show that if you're on the side of the angels miracles sometimes happen. Yes, yes, I'm a great believer in miracles.'

They were the words Sue had used. On Adam's lips they sounded blasphemous.

Craig got slowly to his feet. Slowly he lifted his glass from the table, gazed at it for a moment, then dashed its contents in Adam's face. As he turned to walk unhurriedly away he said, 'I quit.'

Chapter Twenty-four

Only, of course, he did not, could not. The conflict with Sylvestri was personal. That was why, at 2.00 a.m. on the morning of 27 October, he was leaning against the rail of a cargo ship and watching the lights of Crotone sparkle along the horizon.

The *Trico Galaxy* had been three and a half days at sea. She had chugged and rattled her way south from Genoa, skirting Sardinia and coming onto a S.E. heading, to pass through the Malta Channel, as though making course for Banghazi. But after nightfall on the 26th, while her passengers had been at dinner, the ship had turned through ninety degrees and was now heading for the coast, not of Libya, but Calabria.

It was a clear, chill night and Craig was thankful for the heavy topcoat he had brought with him. A couple of hours and it would all be over – or, at least, his part in it would be over. What then? A new country? Another new identity? Enforced retirement, obviously. He could not continue a highly profitable profession with the risk of bumping into Adam's organisation round every corner. Craig gazed up into star-cluttered infinity. Perhaps that was no bad thing. He had had enough excitement over the past few months to last him a very long time. A year or two to contemplate the deeper issues, confront the big questions? Arguably every life should contain space enough for that. Susan Hayward would certainly have endorsed such a proposition.

Sue. No new start for her. Unless, of course, her view of ultimate reality had been right all along. In which case perhaps she was looking down at him now. Would she be understanding? Would she be able to forgive what he had done to her, to her father, to the thousands of Africans who relied on her?

Craig shuddered and turned away from the rail. He walked briskly across the freighter's undulating deck, swinging his arms to encourage the circulation. To the eastward the sea was black and empty. By dawn Sylvestri and his cronies would be on their way to an Italian jail.

If there was no last minute foul-up. Everything had gone well, so far. Too well. The arms Adam had borrowed from the Ministry of Defence ('Pledging my very life, old boy. It's a hanging, drawing and quartering job if anything goes wrong') had been shipped from Liverpool by Juventus Ltd., docketed as a consignment of assorted computer games being sold to a Greek hotel chain. In Genoa they had been transhipped to the *Trico Galaxy* with no questions asked, because Sylvestri controlled the stevedores' union and the authorities did not dare to interfere. The mafioso himself had come aboard just before the ship sailed with a posse of eight 'assistants'. He had spent most of the short voyage grumbling about the accommodation, the food and the arrangements generally but he did not, apparently, suspect a trap. Craig had feared that Sylvestri would comment on the size of the crew, half of whom were, in fact, Italian police. Presumably he knew nothing about the running of a ship. Presumably, also, he had not noticed a similarity between one of the vessel's officers and the fat Libyan who had so angered him in Tripoli. Craig was furious that Adam had insisted on taking personal command of the operation. However, the ISIF chief did keep largely out of sight and never came in to meals with the other officers and passengers.

The engine noise changed. Craig gazed down over the starboard rail and saw the luminescent bow wave narrow as the ship lost way. Then came the sound of a motor and the rattle of anchor chain. *Galaxy* came to rest upon the gently heaving surface of the Ionian Sea.

'Where the devil is he?'

Craig had not heard Sylvestri come up behind him. He turned. The older man looked out of place and very uncomfortable. His light raincoat was tight-belted, his hands thrust deep into its pockets. A trilby was pulled firmly down to his ears.

'He won't be long,' Craig said.

'I've just come from the radio room. No message yet.'

'It'll only take him a few minutes. We're about five miles off Banghazi.' Craig pointed across the port bow to where the lights of Crotone were now showing up more clearly.

'Well, the sooner I'm off this foul-smelling lump of rust the better.' He took his hands out of his pockets, cupped them to his mouth and blew into them. 'I can't make out why its so cold. It doesn't feel like the African coast.'

'It can be quite chilly, even in the southern Med.'

'Not in my experience. I've never . . .'

They both heard the distant drone of a helicopter.

Foncet took a long time examining the cargo. Craig and Sylvestri stood in the hold and watched as the Belgian selected a dozen cases at random, had them pulled out and opened by a couple of burly sailors, then carefully checked the contents. That done, he made a count, ticking off all the items on a bill of lading. His performance was thorough, convincing. It made Sylvestri impatient to be out of the cavernous hold and back in the warmth of the saloon, tying up the deal. That was good. The mark should always be more eager to do business than the con man. But Craig was worried that valuable time was passing. At first light someone was sure to realise that the sun was in the wrong place, and that the *Galaxy* was not anchored off the barren coast of Libya.

At last Foncet stuffed the sheaf of papers into a pocket of his combat jacket and smiled. 'Well, Monsieur Sylvestri, everything looks in order. I congratulate you and I am happy at the prospect of doing more business with you. Now, I think we deserve a drink.'

They all clattered up the companionway and Craig mentally crossed his fingers. If the Belgian did not overdo the *bonhomie* they were only minutes away from clapping the handcuffs on Sylvestri. The arrest was to be made as soon as the mafioso received Foncet's money.

As Craig emerged on deck he saw a small knot of sailors standing by the port rail shouting and gesticulating. He ran across. Some fifty yards off, a large motor boat was approaching. A powerful arc-lamp in her bows was trained on the *Galaxy*'s superstructure. A loud hailer crackled into life.

'*Trico Galaxy*, this is Italian Customs. We wish to come aboard to examine your papers.' The order was delivered in Italian but Craig understood it only too well.

'Damn and blast! Bloody fools!' Adam's *sotto voce* curse came from the knot of men at the rail. 'For God's sake someone answer him quick, before Sylvestri . . .'

It was too late. The mafioso had turned from the saloon doorway and was crossing the deck. 'What's going on? Who are those men?' He marched to the side and shouted, 'Who are you?' The words were English. Sylvestri was still not sure he had heard right.

Craig took his arm. 'Just some officious Libyan harbour officials.'

The amplified reply from the boat drowned his voice. 'Italian Customs from Crotone. Throw a line. We're coming aboard!'

Then, everything happened at the speed of light. Sylvestri shouting and swearing. His bodyguard forming a circle round him. Shots fired. Someone grabbing Craig's arm and twisting it behind his back. More shouted orders and Craig being forced along the deck towards the stern. Deck lights were switched on. A burst of automatic fire, a crash of glass and semi-darkness returned. Not before Craig saw the helicopter and realised he was being pushed towards it.

The engine whined into life. The rotor blades began to turn. He saw someone helping Sylvestri aboard. Others scrambled in. The mafioso's face appeared in the doorway. He pointed at Craig. 'Bring him,' he shouted above the roar. Craig was half-pushed, half-dragged into the machine, already lifting off the deck. One of Sylvestri's men tried to follow him, missed his hold and fell back with a grunt.

The chopper swung upwards and sideways. Momentarily it hung fifty feet above the *Galaxy*. Craig looked down at the crowd of men on her deck. He saw flashes of light. Something whined past him. A row of holes appeared in the metal frame close to his head.

'Christ! They're firing!'

'Move it! Move it!' Sylvestri shouting hysterically at the pilot.

With elaborate slowness the machine turned, climbed. Another bullet rattled against the fuselage.

Beside Craig the door was still open. He looked down. Sickeningly far below, the sea glistened faintly. Craig groaned, leaned sideways and fell into the void.

The impact and the sudden cold of the water drove all the breath from his body. He sank, limbs flailing, involuntarily gulping brine. He fought for the surface but his sodden overcoat wrapped him like sheet lead, bearing him down, down. Lungs bursting, he tore at buttons. He couldn't wriggle free. His body was turning, struggling in inky blackness. He no longer knew where the surface was.

Then, suddenly, he was gasping air. Everything was still black. He paddled furiously to keep afloat. He took deep breaths and coughed out sea water.

A blinding flash of light tore the night and was instantly gone. It was followed by an explosion that seemed to shake both sky and sea. Then things were splashing into the water around him. He looked up just as a piece of painted, twisted metal hurtled towards him. It struck the back of his head. Craig entered a new kind of darkness.

TAKE THREE

'*C'est double plaisir de tromper le trompeur.*'
La Fontaine

('It is doubly pleasant to deceive the deceiver.')

Chapter Twenty-five

Craig knew he was dead when, through a swirling mist, he saw the face of Amy Sullivan.

'Welcome home, Mr Hartley,' the face said, then went into ectoplasmic spasm and dissolved back into the haze.

The face emerged again. But this time it was Adam's sardonic smile that hovered in the ether.

The next time Craig opened his eyes everything was clear. He saw in crisp-edged reality the green velvet drapes framing the view of the bay, and the muted but glowing colours of the Degas sketch on the wall beside the window. He turned his head and there were the pair of Venetian giltwood mirrors flanking the door to the bathroom. He sat up in the bed. Yes, everything was in place – all the precisely-arranged, familiar objects. He was in his own bedroom, in his own house on Long Island. He was even wearing his own pyjamas.

Craig swung his legs out of bed and stood up. He felt a bit unsteady but otherwise none the worse for wear. He was certainly fit enough to find out what the hell was going on. He grabbed a dressing gown and went out onto the landing. Leaning over the balustrade, he heard the sound of a vacuum cleaner below. He descended the stairs, pushed open the study door.

The next moment he had to steady himself against the jamb. Someone who looked remarkably like Amy Sullivan was vigorously cleaning the room and humming to herself, just as Amy had on hundreds of other mornings during the five years she had worked for him. Only, of course, it could not be Amy. She turned round from the far corner, saw him and her hand flew to her breast.

'My goodness, Mr Hartley, what do you think you're doing out of bed?'

It *was* Amy Sullivan. It *really* was her.

Craig groped his way to the chesterfield and fell into it.

Amy switched off the machine and stood before him, hands on hips, a cross between Florence Nightingale and Benito Mussolini. 'Now you just walk yourself straight back up to bed. The doctor was most insistent. Said you weren't to stir from your bed till he gave the say so.'

'Doctor?'

'Yes. *Doctor*. The one who brought you from the nursing home. Doctor Adam. You don't remember him?'

She sat down beside him, took his hand in both of hers and spoke softly, as though to a sick child. 'Well he did say you might be a bit mixed-up about things. And no wonder, after all you've been through.'

Craig was trying to dam the flow of commiserative chatter. Trying to concentrate. Trying to make a picture with only two or three pieces of the jig-saw. 'If Amy . . . But then, how . . .' No use; he needed more facts.

'And just what have I been through, Amy?'

She sat back and regarded him with adoring eyes, as though he had been a plaster image of the Blessed Virgin. 'These things are secret aren't they? Wild horses wouldn't drive me to pry. All I know is what that man from your department said who called a few weeks back. "Important work for national security," he said, "Answerable directly to the White House." And Dr Adam told me you'd almost laid down your life for your country. And I'm just so proud to know you, Mr Hartley. You can be sure your secret is safe with me. But my, was I worried when they brought you home in that ambulance, all pale and unconscious. The man – the one from your department – said you'd been away some time on a dangerous assignment but, well, it sure was a shock to see you like that. Why I . . .'

Craig dived into the rapid current of her prose. 'When did they bring me home, Amy?'

'Why three days since, Mr Hartley.'

'And the doctor's been to see me every day?'

'Twice a day. Only sometimes it's not him, but a pretty young nurse.'

'And what time do you expect them today?'

'Well it's usually around ten – ten in the morning and four in the afternoon. That's when they come for your injections.'

The Tompion long-case clock by the door registered 9.35. Craig got up. 'Then I'll go and change. I must look my best for Dr Adam.'

By the time Adam and Sara arrived at ten past the hour Craig had worked some of it out for himself – or thought he had. And yet, surely, they couldn't . . .

Amy showed them into the study. Of course, they looked the part; Adam in pinstripes with a battered brown bag, Sara crisp and demure in hospital white with a starched cap perched on hair drawn back into a tidy bun.

Craig stared at them across the wide, leather-covered expanse of his partners' desk.

'Sit down,' he ordered, 'and give me some answers. Answers, not bullshit.'

From deep in a leather armchair Adam said, 'Well, first I must congratulate . . .'

'I said no bullshit!'

Craig's mind was still struggling with the unbelievable. 'Just how much of it was a set-up?'

Adam flicked imaginary dust from an immaculate trouser leg. 'Just about all of it.'

'That guy with the moustache, the threats, the upstairs room with the junkie?'

'Phoney as hell, old boy.'

Adam was hugely pleased with himself. Craig hated adding to his self-satisfaction but he had to know.

'But all that . . . it could have made me drop everything.'

'We believed you had too much at stake. Even so, we had to calculate very carefully – enough violence to convince you but not enough to scare you off.'

'Well you got it wrong. I knew there was something that stank about that mafia set up.'

Sara scoffed. 'Oh, really? Isn't that just being wise after the event?'

Craig ignored her. He sat silently for several seconds, brooding over the implications.

'So there was never any mob interest in my activities? I was never in any danger from Sylvestri – till you threw me to the lions?'

Adam shook his head. 'He'd heard the name of Calvin Craig, of course. Because he was operating in Uganda and was in cahoots with Okello, he couldn't fail to. It was the Ugandan connection that drew our attention to you. The FBI had had their suspicions about you for some time. You were too clever to give them a firm lead but they had a file. Add to that the wizardry of modern computer technology and Sara's programming genius and we soon knew more about you than your own mother.'

Craig scowled. 'Am I supposed to applaud?'

Adam ignored the interruption. He was the Ancient Mariner incarnate. Nothing would have stopped him telling his story. 'So we could either net a sprat or use it to catch a particular vicious shark.'

'I was just live bait, then – expendable?'

Sara scoffed, 'You can't complain about using people. It's your whole way of life.'

'But, unlike you, I don't regard people's lives as expendable.'

Adam was momentarily jolted onto the defensive. 'Nor do we, I assure you.'

276

'Hafid?'

Adam laughed. 'Hafid is alive and well and living in Paris.'

'But . . . I saw . . .'

'What we intended you to see. Or, more accurately, what we intended you to *think* you'd seen. In fact, Hafid co-operated fully. But then, as you know, he'll do anything for money.'

'And the account of Louise Traille's death – that was bogus, too?'

Adam shook his head. 'Ah, sadly not. She really was the victim of a hit-and-run driver. If it's any consolation, the police did catch the lout responsible. It was poor Louise's accident that actually showed me how we could draw the noose tighter round you.'

'But you couldn't know I'd read about it.'

'We'd have brought it to your notice one way or another. In fact, you almost caught us on the hop, rushing straight off to your office. We had to wheel Hafid on stage very quickly for his little act.'

Craig got up and poured himself a drink, deliberately not offering anything to the others. He stood sipping the whisky slowly, staring at his guests, trying to catalogue his emotions rationally.

Sara smiled at him. It seemed to be a genuine smile. If so it was the first time she had looked at him without metaphorically holding her nose. 'Don't feel too badly, Calvin. You helped rid the world of something unutterably vile.'

He carried his glass over to the french windows and watched dead leaves twitched across the lawn by an autumn breeze. They were banking up against the laurel hedge.

Sylvestri. Carlo. Louise. All whisked away. By what? 'Unseeing fate'? 'God'? Or were those just convenient euphemisms for the bloody stupid tricks men played on

277

each other. And Sue. Anger churned inside him as the vivid image of a body sprawled in the African dust filled his mind for the thousandth time. He only half heard Adam's continuing paean of self-praise.

'Of course, concocting that story of Amy's death, that was the master stroke. That was what really convinced you that your life was in danger. But, you know, you helped us with that. You'd created such an intriguing alias as 'Mr Hartley the enigmatic – something-to-do-with-national-security-public-servant' that it was easy to enlist your friends' support. We didn't have to convince them that you were engaged in something secret and dangerous. We gave them a story to tell if someone called 'impersonating Mr Hartley' and appealed to their patriotism. It worked like a charm.'

Craig spun round, rage twisting his face, shouting the first words that came into his head.

'You sadistic son of a bitch. You don't give a damn what happens to other people as long as your plans work out. You get the praise. Other poor bastards take the risks. Some end up dead.'

Adam missed the point.

'I admit you had a close shave.' He crossed and uncrossed his legs. 'That was very unfortunate, dear chap, but you must see that by then we had no choice. Those over-zealous bunglers of Italian customs men had blundered in and ruined everything. We couldn't let Sylvestri get away. We'd never have had the chance for another crack at him. Months of planning would have been wasted.'

'What you mean is that you'd have lost face.'

Adam bridled. 'Don't trivialise matters by reducing them to personalities!'

That was the point at which Craig snapped. 'Trivialise?' He strode round the desk and towered over the English-man. 'You play around with people. You get me beaten

278

up. Imprisoned and damn near killed! Then, when I've played along with your game, you callously try to shoot me out of the sky! Who's being trivial?'

Adam was unruffled. 'You were a dead man the moment Sylvestri dragged you into that chopper. What do you think he'd have done with you? My guess is that, somewhere over southern Italy, he'd have shoved you out. Let you fall ten or fifteen thousand feet without a chute. The *carabinieri* would have scraped you off someone's backyard, an unknown, unrecognisable chunk of jelly. As it is, you live to tell the tale.'

'No thanks to you!'

Now it was Sara who stood up. She stared into Craig's eyes. 'You won't like hearing this, Calvin, but you owe your life to Adam. He organised a search for you. Within seconds he had boats out scouring the wreckage.'

Adam nodded. 'I thought I saw you make a jump for it. I hoped I wasn't wrong. They dragged you out of the water just in time. You were half-drowned and badly concussed. You still might not have survived without some pretty dedicated nursing – from Sara among others.'

For some moments the three of them stared at each other in silence. Then Craig said, 'Well, at least it's over. You've got what you wanted: Okello's finished. Sylvestri's dead.'

Adam eased himself out of the chair. 'Oh, I don't know. Things are seldom as tidy as that. Okello? He'll survive. His sort always do. As for Sylvestri, well, yes, I suppose things really did turn out for the best.' He motioned to Sara and they both moved towards the door.

Adam opened the door. He turned back. 'We were on pretty shaky ground, you know – trapping Sylvestri into a phoney arms deal. My advisers reckon that his lawyers would have driven a coach and horses through our case. So, all in all, I suppose everything turned out for the best. Well, goodbye Calvin – and . . . thanks.'

Sara hung back. She held out her hand. 'You've been

through a hell of a lot, Calvin. If it means anything, I respect you for it.'

Craig shook her hand firmly. He managed a faint smile. 'You're not walking out on me are you? There's a little matter of a debt of honour you owe.'

The old, petulant frown returned. Sara snatched her hand away. 'You mean b . . .'

'Oh don't worry Sara.' He held the door open for her. 'You're quite safe from me. You see . . . there's someone else.'

DEEP SIX
Clive Cussler

COUNTDOWN TO CATASTROPHE

For the President of the United States, the crisis point is approaching fast. With his new Soviet initiative entering its most crucial phase, he suddenly finds himself faced with a pollution disaster of potentially cataclysmic proportions. And then – incredibly – he vanishes into thin air, leaving his country poised on the brink of chaos.

It's left to troubleshooter extraordinaire Dirk Pitt to hotwire the connections between these two shattering events. From the icy Alaskan waters to a Korean shipbreaker's yard, from a Caribbean shipwreck to a blazing inferno in the Mississippi Delta, he tracks down a conspiracy so fiendish and sophisticated that even the superpowers are helpless in its grip!

0 7221 2754 5
ADVENTURE THRILLER

A THIEF OF TIME
Tony Hillerman

Joe Leaphorn is looking for an anthropologist who has mysteriously disappeared. Jim Chee discovers the corpses of two men, caught despoiling an ancient burial ground. Their investigations converge on the lost canyon in the barren brush of the Sacred Mountains, haunted by ghosts of the ancient Anasazi and of a more recent, violent past . . .

'In *A Thief of Time* Tony Hillerman does what only the very best writers can do: he gives us a compelling story, richly detailed, about people that matter to us, in lucid prose and, at the same time, he makes a kind of magic'
Robert B Parker

'Fine inchmeal detection, a mystic landscape . . .'
Observer

'Hillerman rattles the bones thunderously across a brilliant landscape of secrets, resurrections and Indian signs. One of his very best' *Sunday Times*

'Enthralling – a fine crime story, so carefully constructed . . . Hillerman is a gifted writer'
Campbell Armstrong, author of *Jig*

0 7474 0329 5
CRIME

A DANGEROUS AGE

Martin Sylvester

"THE SECOND BULLET SMACKED THE GRANITE
WALL EIGHTEEN INCHES FROM MY LEFT EAR"

Wine merchant William Warner looks settled for life. He
has a thriving trade, a full-bodied wife and a frisky mistress
to keep him happy. Maybe he's reached that dangerous
age when a man craves a bit of action, but he needs hired
killers like he needs a hole in the head . . .

A little knowledge is a dangerous thing and someone
thinks Warner knows too much. He's stumbled on
something very nasty indeed. Murder, conspiracy and the
cool but lethal plots of Whitehall combine to form a
knockout cocktail of thrills and spills with a magnum of
suspense as Warner breaks into his first case . . .

0 7474 0029 6
CRIME

All Sphere Books are available at your bookshop or newsagent, or can be ordered from the following address: Sphere Books, Cash Sales Department, P.O. Box 11, Falmouth, Cornwall TR10 9EN.

Please send cheque or postal order (no currency), and allow 60p for postage and packing for the first book plus 25p for the second book and 15p for each additional book ordered up to a maximum charge of £1.90 in U.K.

B.F.P.O. customers please allow 60p for the first book, 25p for the second book plus 15p per copy for the next 7 books, thereafter 9p per book.

Overseas customers, including Eire, please allow £1.25 for postage and packing for the first book, 75p for the second book and 28p for each subsequent title ordered.